He couldn't have recognized her!

Susan barely recognized herself in this disguise. She kept her eyes glued to Lucas Andrew's tall form, following him from the dim underground subway into the glaring sunlight. She had no idea where she was. The streets no longer had names, just numbers, and the neighborhood was shabby.

The sidewalks were crowded with both street people and the obviously affluent, so she was able to keep him in sight without following too closely. He moved easily through the crowd, dressed in his handsome, custom-tailored suit.

Suddenly he turned and looked over his shoulder. All rational thought vanished when their eyes met. She felt like a deer caught in the headlights of an oncoming car. And, as much as she wanted to deny it, she also felt that by-now-familiar attraction.

Love at first sight was certainly more than a myth.

ABOUT THE AUTHOR

Saranne Dawson is a voracious reader and has an avid interest in current events, which, she says, stems from "living in the middle of nowhere" in central Pennsylvania. With a master's degree in public administration, she works as a human-services administrator. In her spare time, Saranne sews, bikes, plays tennis, gardens and tends three "hopelessly obnoxious and pampered cats." She also visits her children in New York on a regular basis.

Books by Saranne Dawson

HARLEQUIN AMERICAN ROMANCE

180—INTIMATE STRANGERS
222—SUMMER'S WITNESS
364—A TALENT FOR LOVE
448—BEWITCHED

SARANNE DAWSON

DECEPTION AND DESIRE

Harlequin Books

TORONTO • NEW YORK • LONDON
AMSTERDAM • PARIS • SYDNEY • HAMBURG
STOCKHOLM • ATHENS • TOKYO • MILAN
MADRID • WARSAW • BUDAPEST • AUCKLAND

Published March 1993

ISBN 0-373-16480-7

DECEPTION AND DESIRE

Printed in U.S.A.

Chapter One

"Dammit, Teddy, get down here! I've got an overheated car from sitting on the George Washington Bridge for an hour, and a trunk full of luggage. And I'm parked at a fire hydrant."

"I can't come down, Peggy Sue. I'll explain when you get up here."

"What am I supposed to do with my car?"

"The perennial New York question. Double-park it, like everyone else. The meter maidens frown upon fire hydrants, but they're okay on double-parking."

"You'd better have a *very* good excuse, brother dear!"

Susan Trent, who did *not* like to be called Peggy Sue, even if she did bear the unfortunate appellation Margaret Susan, stomped back to her car. She managed—or so she hoped—to double-park in such a way that the legal parkers could maneuver past her. Then she got out, locked the car and went back through her brother's outer door to press the buzzer again. This time, the only response she got was an answering buzz from the inner doors. She pulled them open and strode through the tiny lobby, then jabbed viciously at the elevator button.

"Welcome to New York," she muttered. If her car wasn't bashed in by the time she saw it again, her luggage would probably be gone.

"I *want* to be here," she reminded herself as the elevator crept upward with some alarming groans. "I *love* New York."

But thus far, New York did not seem to be reciprocating.

The door to Teddy's apartment stood ajar, and she pushed it open, ready to resume her harangue. But instead, she stopped in her tracks and stared at her brother, her anger canceled by the sight in front of her.

"What happened to you?"

Teddy gave her that charming smile that had been devastating women for years and might have destroyed her sisterly anger even without the assistance of casts on one arm and the opposite leg.

"Sorry to defuse that righteous anger, old girl," he grinned. "It was a skiing accident."

"A skiing accident? But you don't ski."

"Obviously. However, I didn't want to tell the gorgeous Amanda that."

"You mean Amanda the bra model?"

"She only started out that way. Now she models sportswear."

"Teddy," she said in exasperation, "do you think you could fill in the picture just a bit?"

"She had an assignment up at Killington—that's in Vermont—and she invited me up for some skiing after her work was finished. Naturally, since I'm so suave and sophisticated, she just assumed I could ski. So there I was, facing the expert slope and forced to either admit that I'd never been on skis before or wing it."

He crooked the elbow of his good arm and flapped it. "So I winged it."

Susan sank into a chair. "And where is dear Amanda now?"

"In the Caribbean, modeling swimwear. But she calls every day."

"And then goes off for a swim with some gorgeous beach bum," Susan finished wickedly.

"Who probably can't swim," he added, not about to let his sister get the better of him in their never-ending battle of wits.

She dissolved into laughter, then sobered quickly. "But how can you work?"

"Uh, well, I was planning to discuss that with you. See, I thought that maybe since you don't have a job yet, you could take over some of my work for a while, just until I get the casts off."

"Teddy, I'm a psychologist, not a comedian—though I'll admit that a lot of people think psychologists are a joke."

"I didn't mean *that* work. I meant my bill-paying job." He wriggled his thick, dark eyebrows. "Private investigator."

"What?" She got up. "I think I need a drink before I hear any more of this."

"In the kitchen, left-hand cabinet above the sink. I'll have a Stoli and tonic."

"Are you sure you're okay? You're not on painkillers or anything?"

"No, Mother, I'm suffering in silence. Bring the Chinese take-out menu, too, and we'll dine in style—if the health department hasn't closed them down again."

She brought the drinks, and he proposed a toast. "To my big sister, the shrink. Joyce Brothers and Dr. Ruth—move over."

"I think they're safe for a while," Susan observed dryly. "Now tell me how you became an overnight private eye. I thought you needed a license for that sort of thing."

"You do, but I'm working for a friend, and he has the license."

"Well, I suppose if he'd hire a comedian, he'd hire a psychologist with a brand-new degree. Teddy, get real! I've never even held a gun, and I don't own a trench coat—although I have aspirations to own a Burberry."

"This isn't that kind of work. He's been inundated lately with women who want to have their prospective mates checked out, and that's what he turns over to me. It pays pretty well."

"Are you serious? Women actually hire a private eye to investigate their future husbands?"

He nodded. "Believe me, it's gotten to be a growth business for Greg."

"What ever happened to the notion of actually getting to *know* each other before you decide to get married?"

"Gone the way of the dinosaurs, m'dear. These are busy people. See, the thing is that it didn't used to matter so much. Women were usually pretty glad to grab what they could get and hope for the best. But now they've got good jobs, and assets they want to protect. And if they marry some dud and then split with him—which is statistically pretty likely—they could stand to lose some of those assets."

She grinned. "Now that you've put it that way, I think I like the idea."

"Great! You can start tomorrow."

"Wait a minute! I meant that I like the idea of checking out men before you marry them. I didn't mean that *I* want to do it."

"Let me get *very* serious for a minute. If you'd care to go into that medium-sized closet I use as an office, you will find my medical bills, and you will see that they've made a considerable dent in my net worth."

"In other words, if I don't help bring in some bucks soon, we'll be sleeping in the subway."

"*Now* you get it. I think there might be a law against tossing an invalid out onto the streets, but I wouldn't want to count on it."

"'Come to New York,' he said. 'I'll take care of you until you get a job. That's what brothers are for.'"

"Well, this is how I'm going to take care of you, Peggy Sue."

"Knock off the 'Peggy Sue' routine, Teddy, or you'll be wearing another cast."

"Where's your compassion? I thought people in your profession were supposed to be oozing that."

"Mine oozed out sometime during the hour I spent on the George Washington Bridge. Or maybe I'm just becoming a New Yorker fast. Besides, it's difficult to feel compassion for a brother who pretends he can ski to impress a bra model."

"Ah, well, after a good night's sleep, you'll be fine. You can begin your surveillance tomorrow."

"Surveillance? Teddy, I have interviews to set up with those agencies I contacted."

But the idea was beginning to intrigue her just a bit. Hadn't she come here to put some excitement into her life? Wasn't that part of the dream that had kept her going through the years of drudgery in grad school?

"What would I have to do?" she asked, against her better judgment, as she conjured up an image of herself lurking in the shadows, the collar of her nonexistent Burberry turned up, and a matching hat pulled low over her face. V. I. Warshawski, meet M. S. Trent!

Teddy reached for some papers on the table beside him. "Well, first of all, you can go up to Connecticut and check out this guy's antiques shop."

Antiques shop? The image began to fade. "Maybe you'd better start at the beginning. And I can't be running all over New England while I'm looking for a real job here."

"This part of Connecticut isn't really New England," Teddy said. "Well, it is and it isn't. It's more of a suburb of New York. It's only an hour away."

"Oh." Geography had never been one of her strong points.

Teddy looked at the papers he held. "Our clients usually want only the kind of stuff I can pretty much get through a computer or by making some phone calls—things they could get themselves if they had the time and knowledge. But this one wants a little more.

"Her name's Natalie Kroft. She owns a couple of boutiques and she is one very intense lady. She wants to know *everything* about this guy. I just got this case today, so I haven't had time to run any of the usual checks on him yet. But he's an antiques dealer who has a home in Connecticut and an apartment here in Manhattan. But his shop's in Connecticut. His name's Lucas Andrews."

"Nice name," Susan commented.

"Sounds pretty phony to me," said Teddy, peering at the papers.

"Oh, I don't know. Some people are more imaginative when it comes to naming their kids. Not every boy ends up with a name like Teddy Trent. I think you're just jealous."

Teddy snorted derisively. "I'm not jealous of this guy, believe me! Natalie Kroft bears more than a passing resemblance to the Glenn Close character in *Fatal Attraction*."

"Really? This is getting interesting. So you think he might have a wife and kids up in Connecticut? Does he look like Michael Douglas?" She could see that there was a photo attached to the papers, and she was a big Michael Douglas fan.

Teddy studied the photo. "No. But he doesn't look like an antiques dealer, either. See for yourself."

She got up and took the photo from him, then sat down to study it. Teddy was right. Lucas Andrews bore no resemblance to Michael Douglas, and he certainly didn't fit the stereotype of an antiques dealer, either.

The photo was a casual snapshot, taken on a city street. It might even have been taken without his knowledge. Lucas Andrews was a hunk, the rugged type that appealed to almost all women. He had thick, slightly wavy brown hair with a hint of red in it, and a nice, neat mustache. She peered closer. He might even have a cleft chin, but she couldn't be sure. And he looked tall, with a build that suggested natural athleticism, rather than regular workouts at a health club. He was also wearing a Burberry over his suit; the distinctive plaid lining showed a bit along one side.

Susan felt a pang of envy as she stared at the photo. For her, men had become something to be viewed from afar, for these past three years, anyway. She'd been far too busy with grad school and a job even to date, let alone get involved with someone. And now she'd be too busy establishing herself in her career. That depressing thought was enough to make her understand what could drive some women to hire a private investigator. She was thirty now, and it would be another couple of years before she could even begin to consider getting serious about anyone. By then, maybe even *she* could get desperate.

"I'm glad you find him so interesting," Teddy stated dryly, breaking into her thoughts as she continued to stare at the photo. "But that guy can't have both oars in the water if he's planning to marry *her*. She'll eat him alive."

Susan focused on the photo again. Somehow, Lucas Andrews didn't exactly look digestible. What he looked, she thought suddenly, was *dangerous*—the kind of man who wore an invisible sign that read Don't Mess with Me. Not the swaggering macho type, but rather the kind of man those types were trying to be.

"Please don't drool all over the picture. She might want it back."

"Teddy, how can I follow him? That sort of thing takes training. He'll spot me in a minute." She continued to stare at Lucas Andrews. *Did* he look dangerous, or was it just her overactive imagination? How could an antiques dealer be dangerous?

"Not when he isn't expecting to be followed. And women can get away with it easier, too. Besides, you can wear disguises, and you've got acting talent."

"Right! The star performer of the Oakwood Community Theater," she scoffed, stealing yet another glance at the photo. He wasn't dangerous; he was just your standard gorgeous hunk. Of course, *she* wasn't affected by such things. Looks didn't matter. What mattered was kindness and intelligence and a sense of humour. He was probably mean and stupid and totally wrapped up in himself.

RIDGEFIELD, CONNECTICUT, looked like a movie set. As she drove past a group of beautiful big old homes and a quintessentially New England tall-steepled church, Susan kept expecting to see a film crew at any moment. The impression held even as she entered the downtown, where well-kept stores had planters or window boxes filled with a profusion of flowers.

Teddy had been wrong. It had taken her over two hours to get here. The first hour had been spent just getting out of the city, spinning about on layers of ramps where stripped carcasses of cars had her praying that her Subaru wouldn't break down.

New York was scary. She wouldn't have admitted that to anyone, of course, but it was. She'd been in Chicago a number of times, but New York was different. It seemed alive—not just the hordes of people, but the city itself. She still felt that tingling awareness, that sense of imminent danger.

But up here, all was peace and quiet and affluent shoppers and expensive cars. She had just begun to relax when she spotted the street where Lucas Andrews's shop was located. She turned onto it, then cruised along slowly, watching the signs. The street seemed to be filled with antiques shops: Den of Antiquity, Something Old ... Yesteryear. She wrinkled her nose in distaste at all the cuteness.

She didn't know the name of his shop, but she had the address. The only problem was that she hadn't yet seen a number amid all the signs. Would the man in that picture give his business a name like that?

Then she spotted it—a rather large double storefront with several bowed and paned windows. Over it was a handsome black sign that matched the shutters, with gold lettering announcing Lucas Andrews—Antiques and Collectibles. She felt vindicated.

She had to drive another half block before she could find a parking space, and as she started back toward the shop, her nervousness grew. Her hands even felt clammy. She was irrationally certain that he would spot her for what she was immediately.

Maybe he wouldn't even be here. His fiancée had told Teddy that he spent a lot of time in the city. She began to hope that this would be one of those times. Her interest in Lucas Andrews was decreasing in direct proportion to his closeness.

She paused to peer through the windows. What was she doing here? Why had she let Teddy talk her into this? She was a psychologist, not a private eye.

Finally she drew in a breath, squared her shoulders and marched into the shop, willing herself into the role of prospective customer, albeit a rather shabby one. Still, she could be one of those ultrarich who were beyond caring about their appearances, couldn't she?

The distinctive aroma of fine furniture polish greeted her as delicate chimes announced her presence. The shop surprised her; she hadn't been able to see much of it through the windows. Both her mother and her aunt liked antiques, and they had occasionally dragged her along on their excursions, so this was not her first experience with antiques shops. But Lucas Andrews's shop was unlike any of those they'd taken her to. Those shops had been cluttered, musty places that to her had looked like someone's ill-kept attic. And they'd been crammed full of things that Susan had privately called "junque."

By contrast, Andrews's shop was neat and spacious, and the gleam of fine old wood was everywhere. Even someone with her nearly nonexistent knowledge of antiques could tell that this was not "junque." Her fear of confronting the owner temporarily forgotten in her curiosity about prices, Susan bent to check the discreet tag on something she thought was called a secretary.

She drew in her breath sharply, blinked and stared again, carefully counting the zeros this time. Seventy-five thousand dollars! Surely there was some mistake! She backed off to stare at it. It *was* lovely; there was no doubt about that. But seventy-five thousand dollars' worth of loveliness? Back home, people often paid less than that for their houses!

"May I help you? Or are you just browsing?"

Susan jumped at the sound of the woman's voice, then felt relief wash over her—mixed with just a bit of regret. She smiled at the attractive gray-haired woman and glanced quickly around to see if Andrews might be lurking somewhere in a corner. But they appeared to be alone.

"I'm just browsing," she said with another smile. "Actually, I'm on a scouting expedition. My mother loves antiques, and she's coming to visit me soon, so I thought I'd look around. Someone told me that Ridgefield would be a good place to come."

How easily she lied! But who knew? Maybe she and Teddy *could* persuade their parents to visit sometime.

The woman nodded. "Yes, it is. What are your mother's interests?"

"Well, she collects pressed glass, and she likes Shaker furniture."

"We don't carry glass, and we rarely have any Shaker items, but I can give you the names of some shops in the area you might want to visit."

The woman seemed friendly, so Susan turned on the smile again. "That would be really nice. If everything else here is as expensive as that piece, I'm afraid your shop's out of her price range. Are you Mrs. Andrews?''

"Oh, no. Lucas isn't married. I just take care of the shop for him when he's in the city, and help out when he's busy."

"Does he have a shop there, too?"

The woman shook her head. "No. Lucas has clients who ask him to find specific items for them—private customers, or interior designers—so he spends quite a bit of time at the wholesalers."

Lucas Andrews sounded like a class act. But she still couldn't see him as an antiques dealer.

The woman went to write down the names of some shops, and Susan examined other items, then came to a halt in one corner, where two handsome wood-and-glass cabinets held a collection of objects.

"This is scrimshaw, isn't it?" she asked when the woman returned.

She nodded. "Lucas has them here because he likes them. He's been collecting for years. Some are quite old, but others are new. There are two scrimshanders on Nantucket whose work he carries."

Susan bent to examine them more closely. She guessed from the prices and the yellowed appearance of the ivory which were the antique pieces, and the woman confirmed that.

"As you may know, they were originally carved at sea by whalers, from the teeth of whales. But today scrimshanders use deer antlers and elk horns and sometimes just animal bones. The best of them, like the two we carry, make their own dyes, the old way."

Susan saw that the three pieces she liked best were marked NFS: Not for Sale. There were two ornately decorated combs and a small box, and it was clear that they were quite old. The woman confirmed that they were part of Andrews's private collection.

"He said he became interested in scrimshaw when he was in the navy and spent a lot of time at sea himself."

It occurred to Susan that she'd finally heard something about Lucas Andrews that she could believe. She had no trouble at all envisioning him as a sailor, although the boat she envisioned him on was more along the lines of a sailboat than a U.S. Navy ship. Still, it was oddly comforting to be able to categorize him at least to that extent.

"This looks like a good location," she remarked to the woman. "Is the business doing well?"

"Quite well. Mostly, I think, because of Lucas's eye, and his contacts all over the world. He's able to find just about anything a client could want... often even before they know they want it," she finished with a smile.

At that moment, an obviously affluent older couple came in, and the woman excused herself, then greeted them by name and began to discuss a pretty little table that they'd apparently looked at before.

Susan debated staying for a while, hoping to gain some more information. The saleswoman hadn't seemed suspicious at all. But then she decided not to push her luck. It wasn't likely at this point that the woman would mention her to Andrews, but that could happen if she became too inquisitive. Besides, she'd gained *some* information: He wasn't married, he'd been in the navy, and he had a thriving business. Teddy should be pleased with her work.

She waved goodbye to the woman and left the shop well pleased with herself. As she returned to her car, she mused that investigative work wasn't really all that different from clinical psychology. In both professions, one had to elicit information without appearing to be prying and risking putting the client on the defensive.

Her next stop was the town hall. Teddy had asked her to find out if Andrews owned his home, and had instructed her about searching records. Nevertheless, she was forced to enlist the aid of an elderly clerk to find her way to the information.

She left the town hall with yet another piece of information. Lucas Andrews had bought his home not quite eighteen months ago, and there was no mortgage. The price he'd paid had shocked her. She doubted that there was a house in her whole hometown worth that much, but a brief check of other home costs suggested that it was about the average here.

Well, she thought as she paused on the sidewalk and considered her next move, at least they could assure their client that Andrews certainly wasn't marrying her for her money.

She had gotten a map of the town, with the intention of going to have a look at his home, but she became side-tracked as she stood there looking at the rows of shops. So instead she began to stroll along, casually browsing in shop windows.

It wasn't a particularly wise thing to do, she quickly discovered after she had gone into a few shops. She'd spent most of the past three years living in jeans, and seeing the offerings in these shops only made her all too aware of her meager wardrobe, and the cost of improving it.

Then she stopped in front of yet another antiques shop. Through the open door, she could see a woman seated in a bentwood rocker, knitting. It occurred to her that in a town this size, dealers were likely to know each other. She might be able to gain still more information about Lucas Andrews from one of his competitors. Pleased with the idea, she walked in. There was no one else in the shop.

After admiring a lovely Tiffany lamp, Susan told the woman that this was her first visit to Ridgefield, saying that it had been recommended to her by someone she'd met recently at a party.

"He has a shop here, too," she said. "I think his name was Lucas."

"Oh, you must mean Lucas Andrews. Yes, his shop's not far from here. I can give you directions, if you like."

"Good." Susan grinned. "Maybe, if I'm lucky, he'll be there."

The woman laughed. "He *is* attractive, isn't he? And he's single, too."

"Yes, but not for long, from what I was told."

"Really?" The woman appeared to be very surprised. "I didn't know Lucas was involved with anyone."

"I believe she lives in New York."

"In the city, you mean? Well, I know that he spends a lot of time there, but…" She shrugged, clearly still having her doubts about this bit of news. "You'll like his shop," the woman continued. "It's certainly the finest here. Lucas carries only the best."

Susan heard no jealousy in her voice, and she wondered about that. "Has he been here long?"

"A little over a year now. We were all pleased to have him join us."

"Really?" It was Susan's turn to be surprised. "I would have thought you wouldn't want the competition."

"No, the antiques business is different from others in that respect. In order to draw good crowds, you need a number of shops in one location."

Susan then recalled that when she'd gone antiquing with her mother and aunt, they had indeed sought out places where there were a number of shops. But she was still curious about the woman's surprise over Andrews's engage-

ment, and she was about to try to find out just how well
she knew him when the telephone rang.

Susan decided to heed her earlier advice to herself and
leave instead of continuing the conversation. If this woman
did in fact know Andrews well, word might get back to him
that someone was asking questions. It was becoming apparent to her that reining in her curiosity was just as important as eliciting information in an innocent manner.

She returned to her car and studied the town map. After a few wrong turns on the narrow, winding roads, she
found his street. It ended in a wide cul-de-sac, and his
home was at the very end, with a stretch of woods beyond.

She couldn't see much of the house, since it was set back
at the end of a long driveway and a thick screen of evergreens bordered the road. But she could see that it was a
fairly large two-story affair with cream shutters and nicely
weathered cedar shakes. The overall effect of the neighborhood was one of quiet, pastoral affluence.

She turned around in the circle and headed back to New
York. It was, she thought, not a bad start to her temporary career as a private eye.

"ANDREWS WASN'T in the navy."

Teddy greeted her with that bit of news two days later,
when Susan returned from a job interview.

"So maybe he was in the Swiss navy," she replied in a
definitely half-hearted attempt at humor. Lucas Andrews
and their client, Natalie Kroft, were not exactly upper-
most in her mind at the moment.

"Why didn't I think of that? Or maybe the Tibetan
Navy?" Teddy stopped and peered at her closely. "My infallible instincts tell me that the interview didn't go well."

Susan nodded with a sigh. "They said they needed
someone with more clinical experience. I think I might

have made a serious miscalculation. It's certainly true that there are far more opportunities here, but I'm starting to realize that there's also a lot more competition.''

"It's only your first interview," Teddy pointed out.

She nodded again, having spent the trip back to the apartment telling herself just that. But she was beginning to feel like a very small frog—maybe even a tadpole—in a very large puddle. Conquering New York was going to be a lot more difficult than she had thought.

Her gaze fell on the papers strewn across Teddy's desk, which included that picture of Lucas Andrews. Once again she felt that little spark of interest. "Are you sure he wasn't in the navy?" She frowned.

"Well, the Pentagon says he wasn't. And who am I to quibble with them?"

She rolled her eyes. "Perish the thought! We all know they're infallible. But it doesn't make sense that he would lie about a service record. He's not a politician, after all."

"And there's something else that doesn't make sense. The man's credit history goes back only two years."

"So?"

"So, he's thirty-seven years old. By my calculations, that leaves about fifteen years unaccounted for. What was he doing all that time? Stuffing his money in a mattress?"

"Lots of people don't believe in buying on credit," she persisted, wishing she were one of them.

"Not people with his bucks. They always have credit cards. They just pay on time, that's all. And he went straight from nothing to heavy-duty lines of credit."

"Have you talked to your client about it?"

"No, she's out of town on a buying trip. But I *did* talk to Greg, and he agrees that something smells here. The redoubtable Ms. Kroft has given us carte blanche to dig into this guy, so we're going to do some major excavating.''

"'Redoubtable'? Have you started reading dictionaries? I know you're bored, but—"

"Just part of my never-ending effort at self-improvement," he stated smugly.

"To impress a bra model?" she inquired archly.

"I'm beginning to be sorry I ever told you about her."

"But you did, and you even did so braggingly."

Teddy muttered something unintelligible, then turned back to his notes. "This guy bothers me. For once, I think the lady is right to want him checked out."

Susan picked up the photo and thought again about that sense of danger she'd felt. An overreaction, or a premonition? She was very eager now to get a look at the man himself.

SUSAN WATCHED the rain drip off the edges of her umbrella and wondered why all those detective novels never talked about the unpleasant business of standing around waiting for something to happen. If this were a novel instead of real life, Lucas Andrews would have appeared just as she had taken up her position across the street from his apartment building.

Get *with* it, Andrews, she muttered to herself. You're supposed to *go* somewhere, so I can follow you. Instead, you're probably up there making mad, passionate love to dear Natalie, while I'm standing down here getting soaked. She cursed silently, wishing she hadn't been gifted with such a vivid imagination. It made her feel like a voyeur, and she was already feeling like one in any event.

Then she recalled that Teddy had said their client was out of town. That made her feel somewhat better. Of course, he might have someone else up there; there sure couldn't be any dearth of candidates.

She pushed back the wet sleeve of her rain slicker and saw that it was 9:30. She'd wait another half hour, and that was it. If Andrews was the respectable businessman he purported to be, he should certainly be out there hustling by ten. She stood there stoically, whiling away the time by mentally composing the cover letters to go with her résumé for two jobs she'd seen advertised.

Two people emerged from his building: a man and a woman. But they immediately raised umbrellas and angled them against the wind-driven rain, effectively hiding their faces from her. She was certain, however, that the man wasn't Andrews: he was too short and too heavy. But she was beginning to see the disadvantages of the spot she'd chosen for her surveillance. Anyone coming out would do just what they had done, and she probably wouldn't be able to get a look at their faces.

She scanned the street, trying to decide what to do. If she moved, she'd be more exposed . . . and more obvious. The spot she'd chosen was another apartment building, just across the street from his, with a nice canopy that half protected her from the rain, and no doorman to question her presence. His building had a canopy, as well, but it also had a doorman, which made it difficult for her to stand there for any length of time without arousing curiosity.

Still, hadn't Teddy said that a woman was far less likely to be questioned about loitering than a man? If his doorman *did* approach her, she could always claim that she lived in a nearby building and was simply taking advantage of the protection offered by the canopy while she waited for a friend.

She glanced at her watch again. Nine forty-two. Where was he? Teddy had called his shop in Connecticut and had been told that he was in the city. Was it possible that he'd left before she got here?

She moved out from beneath the canopy into the full force of the wind and rain, then decided to walk down to the far corner and approach his building from that direction. She would just have to hope that the doorman hadn't noticed her standing over here in her bright yellow slicker. She wasn't exactly dressed to be unobtrusive, she realized belatedly. But the slicker was all she had.

She was about thirty feet from the entrance to Andrews's building when the outer door opened and a man appeared, pausing briefly in the doorway to talk with the doorman. He was tall and wide-shouldered and had wavy reddish-brown hair. She was certain it was Lucas Andrews even before he turned her way.

For one brief moment, Susan was paralyzed. She was sure he was going to demand to know why she was following him, even though she hadn't yet begun to do so. She urged herself forward, trying to ignore her pounding pulse.

He glanced her way only briefly as he stopped beneath the canopy to open a big black umbrella. Her steps faltered, and her breath caught in her throat until he turned away again. He looked even better in person than he had in the photo, and she felt now what that picture hadn't quite conveyed: an indefinable but very real aura of totally undiluted masculinity. It was something felt, rather than seen . . . and she definitely felt it.

By now she had reached the shelter of the canopy, and he glanced her way again. He had deep-set dark eyes, and when they met hers briefly, she felt her face grow warm. The scene felt absurdly intimate to her, heavy with a sensuality that was totally irrational under the circumstances. How long had it been since she'd reacted like that to a man? She wasn't sure she *ever* had. Was it only her secret knowledge of him and her general nervousness about being discovered?

The whole episode lasted no more than a few seconds, but even that was long enough for her to feel a rush of heat that left her entire body tingling with heightened awareness.

He began to walk in the direction she, too, had been traveling. She let him get ahead of her by twenty or thirty feet, still irrationally expecting him to turn at any moment and ask why she was following him. But instead he merely picked up his pace and then disappeared into a subway entrance. She hurried after him.

The evening before, she'd pored over a subway map, trying to familiarize herself with that underground maze. As Teddy had pointed out, it could be difficult to follow someone if you didn't know where you were or where you were likely to be going. And after having taken a cab to and from her interview, she'd decided that she'd better learn to deal with the subway. She could have fed herself for several days on the cab fare.

When she reached the upper platform, she saw him descending the stairs to the downtown tracks. The platform at the bottom was nearly empty, and she slowed her pace, not wanting him to notice her again, even though there was no reason to think it would make him suspicious. Just as she was beginning to think that it might be interesting to initiate a conversation with him, a rush of hot, fetid air announced the imminent arrival of a train.

It screeched to a halt just as she came up alongside him on the platform. He started toward the opening door, then saw her and stepped aside to let her enter first. Their eyes met again, and this time she looked away quickly, murmuring her thanks as she moved past him. Once again there was that jolting awareness, that sense of intimacy.

The car was about half-full. She quickly took a seat next to a young woman in jeans and a pea-green poncho. He sat down across from her. When the train lurched forward, she reached into her bag for her subway map to see where they were going. She had unfolded it and was studying it intently before she realized her mistake. If Andrews or anyone else should ask where she was going, she would have to come up with something, and it wasn't likely to be *his* destination. She began to refold it quickly, but she was too late. The young woman beside her asked if she needed help.

No, dammit! she shouted silently. How is it that I managed to sit beside the one helpful person in this whole city? Don't you know what New Yorkers are supposed to be like?

Fortunately, she had had time to study the line, so she told her too-helpful seatmate that she wanted to go to the South Street Seaport. She *did* want to go there, but certainly not at this moment.

She had kept her voice low, hoping Andrews wouldn't hear her above the clatter of the train.

Unfortunately, the woman had a voice that could have been heard across the width of Manhattan. "South Street Seaport? Oh, that's way down. I'll let you know when we're near it."

"Thanks," Susan said with a false smile, at the same time risking a glance at Lucas Andrews to see if he was paying attention to them.

Their eyes met again, and once more she looked away first. She was sure he must have heard, and she cursed herself for her blunder. It didn't seem likely that he would be getting off there, too, although if there was such a thing as beginner's luck in the private-eye business, he would.

But Lucas Andrews was still sitting there, reading the *Times,* when her seatmate announced the exit in a tone far clearer than the PA system. Susan got up and walked past him to the doors, swaying a bit as the train braked. It *did* cross her mind that with little effort on her part she could sway right into his lap, but she quickly dismissed that notion as being perhaps just a bit too extreme. Instead, she simply got off the train, avoiding those eyes she was sure were following her.

She stood on the platform, staring after the departing train balefully. So much for her belief that the private-eye business was a snap. But it wasn't her fault if New Yorkers refused to live up to their bad reputation.

When she reached the street, she wandered about aimlessly, assuming she'd bump into South Street Seaport sooner or later. It couldn't be far away. Teddy had told her that the Fulton Fish Market was close by, and every breath she drew suggested she was about to walk into it. Finally she saw some ships' masts rising above the buildings.

Teddy had said that the South Street Seaport was a "yuppie paradise," and it didn't take her long to confirm that. Instead of wandering through shops she couldn't afford, she chose to stroll along the outdoor walkways. The rain had now tapered off into a fine mist that lent a certain authenticity to the nautical scene.

When she reached the top level, she paused at the railing to stare out at the murky grayness of the East River. To either side of her, the city's bridges rose above the water. The grand structure to her left was the Fifty-ninth Street Bridge of Simon and Garfunkel fame, and off to the right she could see the concrete arches of the even more famous Brooklyn Bridge. She remembered from her study of the map that the two in between were the Williamsburg and the Manhattan, but couldn't recall which was which.

So here you are in the big time, she told herself, even if your hold on it is a bit tenuous at the moment, and even if you did screw up your first mission as a private eye.

She chuckled to herself, wondering what her professors and classmates would think if they knew about her temporary "career." They probably wouldn't be all that surprised. It had been made clear to her more than once that she didn't always show the proper degree of seriousness for her chosen profession. She trusted her instincts too much, and she tended to use unconventional therapies. But she had gotten results, so they'd been forced, however grudgingly, to give her her degree.

And the truth was that she was enjoying following Lucas Andrews...perhaps *too* much. The very attractive man was adding definite spice to a life that had been mired in studies for too long. She reviewed her encounter with him, shivering slightly at the memory of those times their eyes had met. She still couldn't quite dispel that sense of danger.

Would he remember her? She didn't consider herself to be particularly memorable: average height, average figure, dark brown hair worn in a loosely curled shoulder-length style. At least a zillion women looked like that.

But of course there *was* that accursed turned-up nose of hers. People often thought it was "cute," and she supposed it would be—on a five-year-old. And there were also her overly large gray-green eyes. Those two features had been largely responsible for her reconsidering her childhood dream of becoming an actress. Great dramatic roles were not given to women who looked like the nice girl next door or someone's cute kid sister. Lately she'd even begun to worry that her appearance could prove a hindrance to getting a job.

She sighed softly, deciding that Lucas Andrews just might remember her. She looked down at her bright yellow slicker. It was so bright that if he remembered her at all he would probably associate her with that and not re-call much else about her.

Only one thing was certain: She would have no trouble at all remembering Lucas Andrews.

Chapter Two

Lucas Andrews had a subconscious awareness of his surroundings that in anyone else would have been truly uncanny. But for him it was nothing more than a simple matter of survival. And it was that subliminal sense that drew his attention to her.

He hadn't noticed her on the platform, where a small group had gathered for the trip downtown. When he got on the train, his gaze roved discriminately over his fellow passengers out of the force of long habit. Then he turned to reading the *Times.*

But something began to nag at him, a mental shove that disrupted his reading. His reaction to this betrayed no outward alarm, even though for the first time in a long while he felt keenly the absence of the slim automatic he'd carried for so many years, tucked into the back of his waistband or occasionally in a shoulder holster.

He turned a page and refolded the paper, taking that opportunity to study his fellow passengers again. His casual sweep of the car revealed nothing, but he trusted those instincts. So, when the train made its next stop, he used the temporary confusion to study the other passengers more carefully.

Two things betrayed her, even though each of them alone would have been sufficient: her nervousness and that upturned nose. He continued to watch her as the train pulled out again, his task made much easier by the fact that she was assiduously avoiding even glancing in his direction.

It was the pretty woman in the yellow slicker from the day before. He was certain of it, even though the image presented to him this day was very different.

She appeared to be a middle-aged, slightly overweight tourist, as evidenced by her unfashionable and inexpensive clothes and her equally unstylish haircut—or wig, rather, since her dark brown hair was now a mousy shade threaded with gray. She betrayed her nervousness by plucking at her pants, straightening her blouse and making periodic movements to open her cheap plastic purse. He noticed that she was wearing low-heeled, inexpensive shoes, as well.

The only item that didn't fit the image was a pair of large, smoky sunglasses with expensive-looking frames—worn, no doubt, because she knew her nose and her big, green-flecked eyes were her most outstanding features. She probably hadn't thought of that soft, sensuous mouth as being worthy of note, since she'd made no attempt to disguise it, other than wearing an unattractive orange-red lipstick.

Lucas let his gaze drift back to his newspaper, but still caught a movement in his peripheral vision that told him she had at last glanced his way. He tried to dismiss his thoughts as paranoia, something he knew he had to guard against. But there was no doubt in his mind that it was the same woman. Had she reappeared without any attempt at disguise, he would probably have thought nothing of it, but the disguise required some serious consideration.

After a few moments, he looked up again. This time he caught her staring boldly at him. Somewhat to his surprise, she held his gaze for a moment before once again lowering her head to inspect her pants for some nonexistent lint. He ran his gaze over her body, thinking that she'd done a good job of hiding the curves he was certain had been beneath that slicker yesterday.

She'd also done a professional job with her makeup, creating shadows that hinted at middle-aged skin. To the casual observer, she would have presented just the impression she sought. All these observations, while interesting, distracted him only temporarily from the real question: Why was she following him?

Lucas actually shook his head slightly in bemusement. What the hell was going on here? This was the second time in a month that a woman had displayed an unnatural interest in him. Was it possible that his past was coming back to haunt him? It seemed unlikely, but he couldn't afford to dismiss the possibility. Still, why would they send amateurs? That made no sense at all.

HE *COULDN'T* have recognized her; she'd barely recognized herself after she'd gotten into this disguise. But rational thought had vanished the moment their eyes had met. She'd felt like a deer caught suddenly in the headlights of an oncoming car.

One part of her wanted to deny the attraction, but another part accepted it and wanted to analyze it. Recent research suggested that "love at first sight" was more than just a myth. For certain people, said the researchers, a powerful mutual attraction happened instantaneously. Pheromones, those chemicals whose sexual effects upon human beings were still little understood, were believed to be the cause.

Well, that's all fine and good, said the practical side of her. But she didn't know that it *was* mutual, and besides, it could just as easily be the result of too many years of denying herself the pleasure of male companionship while she'd buried herself in her studies. Still, if that was all it was, New York was full of attractive men. There were even one or two others on this very subway car, including the man who sat next to Lucas Andrews.

Maybe it was the aura of mystery that surrounded him now that Teddy had dug up some contradictory information. Or maybe it was the essence of danger that continued to cling to him, despite her efforts to rationalize it away.

The train stopped at several other stations, and Susan began to worry that she wouldn't be able to get off where he did without attracting his attention. There weren't that many passengers left.

Still, as Teddy had pointed out repeatedly, he had no reason to believe anyone would be following him. She knew that, but she'd still practiced a look of innocence combined with total disbelief in case he did confront her. It would be easier to convince him without the sunglasses, because that nose of hers, and her big, thick-lashed eyes, virtually screamed innocence. But she'd had to wear the glasses, since they disguised her most distinctive features.

Lucas Andrews got up as the train began to slow to a stop. He glanced her way again, but she avoided direct eye contact. By the time they had come to a full stop, he was standing just inside the doors. She waited for two women to get between them, then lingered a moment longer as several people got on. By the time she got off, he was well ahead of her and starting up the stairs.

She kept her eyes glued to his tall form, clad this day in a handsome tan summer suit that spoke clearly of custom tailoring. When she emerged into the sunlight, she had no idea where she was, other than that it was lower Manhattan. The streets had names instead of numbers, and the neighborhood was rather shabby. But the sidewalks were crowded with everything from street people to the obviously affluent, and she was able to keep him in sight easily without following him too closely.

He stopped at an intersection and turned casually in her direction. She felt a moment of alarm that was quickly stilled; his movements had seemed perfectly natural. Still, she felt exposed enough to stop and feign interest in a shop window.

The leather goods on display were surprisingly handsome, given the appearance of the neighborhood, and she was surprised too at how low the prices were. There was a great burgundy leather bag that caught her attention, and she was straining to see the price when she remembered that she wasn't here to shop.

When she turned quickly back to the street, he was crossing the intersection. She hurried to cross herself before the light changed, and just barely made it. All that darned padding was slowing her down.

The street into which he had turned wasn't as busy, and she had to slow her pace, dawdling along but not allowing herself to get too interested in the shops again. It would be rather embarrassing, to say the least, to have to tell Teddy that she'd found a great purse but lost Lucas Andrews again.

Half a block farther on, he suddenly turned into a building. He didn't look in her direction again, but she still proceeded cautiously. With no idea where the door led, she couldn't risk going too quickly behind him. When she judged that enough time had passed, she walked up to the spot where he had disappeared.

The only sign on the door was a street address, and it was clear that it led to the upper floors of the building. She peered through the glass and saw a tiny lobby with an elevator at the far end and a signboard on one wall. He was nowhere to be seen, so she pushed open the door and hurried over to the sign.

Two antiques wholesalers were listed, together with the warning that they were closed to the public. It didn't matter. Obviously he was just conducting business. She went back outside, feeling faintly foolish and very much relieved. What had she been expecting? A sign announcing the headquarters of the Mafia, perhaps?

Teddy had begun to voice the opinion that Lucas Andrews might be engaged in illegal activities, or that he at least had a criminal past. But she was still inclined to give him the benefit of the doubt, although she knew that her reasons for doing so wouldn't withstand close scrutiny. Now she felt vindicated.

She returned to the shop where she'd seen the bag and bought it, ignoring the fact that her credit card was approaching its limits. Then she decided to treat herself to a cab ride back uptown, at Natalie Kroft's expense, of course. The padding was beginning to slip a bit, probably from all that jostling in the subway. It was a good thing the ride hadn't been any longer, or she might *really* have attracted his attention.

"IT DOESN'T prove anything," Teddy insisted. "So maybe the guy *does* have a legitimate business. So do a lot of criminal types. Mobsters are into vending machines and trash hauling and all sorts of businesses."

"Why do you persist in believing he's a criminal?"

"Just a feeling. Why would he lie about being in the navy? And why doesn't he have a long credit history, like any normal guy with his bucks? I talked to Greg, and he agrees. There's something going on here. I also talked to our charming client, and she wants us to check him out some more. In fact, her very words were 'Money isn't important. I want to know everything about him.'"

"So why doesn't she just *ask* him?" Susan grumbled. "What kind of relationship could they have?"

"A strange one, I'll admit that. She said they've only known each other for a couple of months." He paused. "I've been thinking that maybe we should find some way for you to get to meet him and pump him for some information."

Susan remained silent. She'd been thinking the same thing herself, but perhaps for different reasons. She was convinced that if she could meet Lucas Andrews she would know if he was for real. And maybe she could get rid of this absurd attraction to him.

She paced around the small living room, then suddenly stopped. "I think I know how to do it! Let me get that bag of costumes again."

She went to the closet in Teddy's office and dragged out the big box. Teddy occasionally used an assistant in his comedy routines. His most recent partner had taken a summer job on a cruise ship, leaving behind an assortment of costumes, wigs and other items. Susan had costumed herself as the middle-aged tourist from this collection, but now she was seeking something very different.

She pulled out a slim-fitting shirtwaist-style dress in an orange so bright it almost hurt her eyes. It was a great stroke of luck that Teddy's assistant wore her size. Next, she dug out a tawny, sun-streaked wig, shook it out and considered it. Then she dug some more, recalling that she'd seen what looked like a contact lens case. She returned to Teddy, carrying these items.

"This will do just fine, but I'm going to need a really devastating perfume."

"What are you going to do? Seduce the guy? I admire your dedication to your job, but as your brother, I have to frown on such things."

"I'm going to seduce him, all right, but not physically. You could call it a mental seduction. Do you know what scrimshaw is?"

NEARLY HALF AN HOUR after she started applying makeup, Susan stepped back from the mirror and put on the glasses she'd found in the costume box. The frames were oversized wire-rims, and the lenses were slightly smoky clear glass.

Not bad, she thought. It was just the effect she wanted: bold, brash and sexy. About as far from her true nature as it was possible for her to get.

The tawny wig was a wild mass of curls that tumbled over her shoulders. She put on the dress, grateful for the bold colors that were in fashion just now, since they tended to distract the eye. Then, just to add to the distraction, she left the two bottom buttons undone, providing a peek of tanned thigh. After experimenting with the top buttons, she settled for leaving just one of them undone. Then she put on every bracelet she owned, and a pair of huge braided silver hoop earrings from the costume box, and slid her feet into high-heeled sandals she'd bought last summer but hadn't worn before. Walking in them was going to be a chore for feet that had grown far too accustomed to sneakers.

Finally she dabbed on the boldest, sexiest perfume she'd been able to find at Bloomingdale's. The saleswoman had given her a sample tube when Susan had hesitated, saying that she just wasn't sure it was *her*. If ever there was a perfume that *wasn't* her, this was it.

She went down the hall to Teddy's office. He had his back to her as he worked at his computer, tapping away with one hand while his injured leg rested awkwardly on a low stool. She cleared her throat loudly, and he turned around.

"Who are you?" he asked with feigned suspicion.

She pirouetted in the doorway, not making too good a job of it in the high heels. "So, Teddy?"

"I wouldn't know you if you walked up to me on the street," he said admiringly, then paused for just a beat. "Except for the nose, of course. And speaking of noses, are you sure you're not planning to seduce Andrews? He's likely to leap on you the minute he gets a whiff of that perfume."

She wrinkled her upturned nose. "Thanks a lot. There's nothing I can do about my nose, except to draw attention away from it. And I doubt that it matters, in any event. As for his leaping on me, well..." She gave him a deliberately sexy smile and let her words trail off.

Teddy groaned loudly, then asked if she was sure she didn't want some fake press credentials. "Greg could get them for you."

She shook her head. "I'm free-lance, remember?"

"But shouldn't you have studied up on scrimshaw first?"

"No. I'm going to him because someone recommended him, and I'm hoping he can suggest some books. It's called flattering the good old male ego."

"I think I'm actually beginning to feel sorry for Andrews. Not only does he have Natalie the Intense to contend with, now he's got *you*."

"Something tells me that Lucas Andrews can hold his own," she replied, checking her bag to be sure she had a notepad and the small cassette recorder she'd borrowed from Teddy.

SUSAN'S CONFIDENCE in her ability to deceive Lucas Andrews and pry information out of him began to ebb as she drove into Ridgefield. For seven years she'd performed regularly before hundreds in her hometown community theatre, but this was different—a performance for one, with no dress rehearsals and no set script. She'd been known to ad-lib on a few memorable occasions, but she'd never given a totally extemporaneous performance. But she *was* a psychologist, wasn't she, despite her difficulties in finding a job in that profession? And if a psychologist couldn't get someone to talk about himself, who could?

She found a parking place about a block from the shop. As she walked toward the shop, she spotted a dark green Mercedes parked out front. It was Andrews's car. She'd seen it listed, together with his license number, on Teddy's information sheet. Her upwardly mobile brother, whose own car was a five-year-old Honda, had pronounced it "not quite top-of-the-line, but not the cheap one, either."

The shot of self-confidence she'd given herself began to wear off once more. What if this man really was a criminal? What if he saw through her disguise or her questions?

Don't start getting paranoid, she told herself sternly. This isn't some stupid melodrama. He's an antique dealer, period. And for all they knew, maybe he *had* served in the navy. Maybe there was even a perfectly logical reason for his lack of a credit history.

Still, when she pushed open the door to the shop, setting off the tinkling chimes, Susan was struggling hard against an urge to turn around and run all the way back to New York.

LUCAS GLANCED automatically toward the door when the bells chimed. The woman who entered was an unlikely customer for an antiques shop. She looked like a thousand other stylishly dressed, overly made-up young women with hair styled carefully to total disarray. Not that the young didn't buy antiques, although few of them could afford what he offered. But those who did buy them were usually preppy types, not would-be models for *Elle*.

He smiled briefly at her, then turned back to his customer, a wealthy widow who bought regularly from him for her home here and her Fifth Avenue duplex. He knew she would end up buying the secretary. He'd had her in mind when he'd found it.

The other woman moved out of his line of vision, but something about her continued to worry at him as he resumed his discussion with his customer.

"Well, Lucas, you've done it again—found something for me that I didn't even know I wanted. This will be perfect for that corner."

With the sale completed and a delivery time arranged, Lucas walked over to where the other woman was bent over, examining his scrimshaw collection.

"Can I help you with something?" he inquired politely.

She jumped, obviously startled—much more so, he thought, than the situation warranted. And then he knew why. When she turned to face him, the first thing he saw was that by-now-familiar upturned nose.

SUSAN'S HEART leapt into her throat. She'd been so busy rehearsing her approach that she'd failed to hear him come up behind her. And when she turned to face him, her heart seemed to be stuck there in her throat, pulsating wildly. For a few seconds, she simply stared at him blankly, having all but forgotten her purpose in coming here as she felt that treacherous heat steal through her.

Up close, Lucas Andrews's dark eyes were even more compelling. Something gleamed briefly in them. Was it recognition? Amusement?

No doubt it was amusement. He could probably see the effect he was having on her and believed it to be solely the result of his attractiveness. She was darned sure she wasn't the first woman to be attracted to him. He probably had an ego to match the prices in his shop.

She smiled pleasantly. "Are you Mr. Andrews?"

He nodded, and a smile curved his neat mustache, which, like his hair, was flecked with red.

She hurried on, putting out her hand. "My name is Susan Todd, Mr. Andrews. I'm a free-lance journalist, and I'm planning to do an article on scrimshaw. I've been told that it's becoming quite popular. Someone recommended you to me, and I was hoping you might have a few minutes to talk with me."

The final part of her carefully prepared opening came out with a distinctly breathy quality as he folded his hand around hers. It was a surprisingly hard and callused hand, more appropriate for a construction worker than a businessman.

Did he hold her hand just a second too long? Or was that only her imagination? They disengaged, and she kept the professional smile on her face with difficulty. His touch and his closeness unnerved her. She even wobbled slightly in the unaccustomed high heels, but surely not enough for him to notice. She took a small step away from him to cover it.

"If you can wait just a minute, I'll be glad to help you," he said, and she thought that his voice, at least, suited his profession. It was deep and smooth, with no trace of a regional accent.

He went to a small walnut-fronted counter in one corner and began to write something. Coming closer, Susan saw a check lying on the glass top. The woman must have bought the secretary. She already knew its price from her previous visit, but she walked over to the secretary anyway, bent to examine the tag, then drew in a deliberately audible breath. She just couldn't resist hamming it up a bit, now that he seemed to be buying her act.

"Wow! She came in and bought it—just like that?"

He chuckled. It was a very pleasant and wholly masculine sound that sent little ripples of pleasure through her. "Not quite. She was in before to look at it, and she's a regular customer."

Susan cast an exaggerated frowning glance at the secretary. "What makes it worth that much—whatever it is?"

"It's called a secretary. The style is Hepplewhite, and it's one of the finest I've ever seen. Like any fine antique, it's worth whatever the market will bear at any given time."

His tone was indulgent. As well it should be, she thought, given the bucks he'd just raked in.

"You mean that a year from now it might not be worth this much?"

"In the case of that piece, that's unlikely. But it often depends on how many are on the market and how badly someone wants it. Some pieces *do* fluctuate in value over time, but pieces like that are classics."

"I guess it's pretty obvious that I don't know much about antiques," she said with a self-deprecatory smile and a shrug that was meant to flatter his superior knowledge.

He smiled. "Well, I'm not going to criticize you for it, since you obviously *do* have an interest in scrimshaw, which happens to be a personal interest of mine, as well."

Such mannered conversation, she thought. They both sounded as if they were in a drawing room comedy. But was the underlying falseness she sensed hers alone, or his, as well? She reminded herself not to underestimate this man.

"You mean you don't care about any of this?" she asked, sweeping her many-braceleted arm around the shop.

"No, I didn't mean that. I like most of the things here. But this is a business, and sometimes you sell pieces you don't really like because they're what customers want."

"What's your favorite thing here, besides the scrimshaw?"

"That," he replied, indicating the secretary behind her.

"Then it must be hard to part with it."

"No. I can't afford to keep everything I like." He gestured to a doorway that led to the back of the shop.

"My office is in the back. Why don't we go there, and I'll see if I can answer your questions. Would you like some coffee or tea?"

"Coffee would be fine, thanks—black."

She followed him through the doorway, suddenly and unaccountably too much aware of the fact that they were alone. What was she expecting—that he was going to pull a gun out of his desk and blow her away after demanding to know why she'd been following him? She had to swallow a nervous giggle at that thought, but her conviction was growing that beneath that layer of sophistication and civility was a very different, and possibly dangerous, man.

His small office was almost unbearably neat. There were no piles of papers, no scattering of pens, no personal items of any kind. And no photo of his fiancée, either. She was reminded of that other dealer's surprise at his engagement.

The only item of interest was what appeared to be an antique letter opener with an elaborately carved jade handle. She picked it up to examine it more closely just as he returned with their coffee. The blade was thin, but surprisingly strong. It was also rapier-sharp.

"Be careful," he cautioned. "It's actually a dagger."

She put it down quickly, not really certain what to say to a man who kept a dagger in plain sight on his desk. The knowledge of their isolation brought another surge of uneasiness. He picked up the dagger, and she had to force herself to remain seated.

"It's Chinese, probably about a hundred and fifty years old. These were often carried as personal weapons because they're quite easy to conceal. Properly used, they're also quite deadly."

And you know just how to use it, she thought. Fortunately, she was able to prevent herself from saying it aloud.

To cover her fear, she quickly got out her recorder and notepad. She explained that she hadn't yet done any research and was hoping that he could direct her to some good sources. He nodded and gave her the names of several, then added that she should try to visit the museum on Nantucket, which had the best display he'd seen, and a number of modern scrimshanders, as well.

She asked what she hoped were intelligent questions, and he answered them expansively, showing no inclination to hurry her along. Her uneasiness began to dissipate.

He remained completely businesslike, even when she shifted her position in her chair, deliberately exposing more thigh. When their eyes met, she could read nothing in his but polite interest. It didn't feel right to her. How many men would avoid even a mild flirtation under the circumstances?

And she still could not shake that near-certainty that this man could be deadly. She searched her mind for anyone else she'd met over the years who projected that aura, but could think of no one. Finally she put it down to Teddy's suspicions regarding Andrews.

Just as she was trying to think of a way to segue into more personal conversation, the phone rang, and he excused himself to answer it. She started to rise, thinking he might want privacy, but he waved her back to her seat.

As soon as he had identified his caller, Andrews switched into what sounded like flawless French. Her own college French was rusty from lack of use, but she was able to pick out enough to be reasonably certain that he was merely talking business. The conversation was brief, and after he hung up, she smiled brightly.

"Have you spent much time in France? It sounds as though your French is very good."

"I go to Europe regularly on business, but this was a dealer in the city. My French is better than his English."

"It seems to me," she said, in another blatant attempt at flattery, "that this must be a very complex business. I mean, you must have to know so much about so many different things. How did you learn all this?"

"First of all, it isn't as complicated as you're probably thinking. Most dealers, myself included, specialize to some extent. And we often consult each other when something comes up that we don't know much about.

"As to how I learned the business, I started at an early age. My mother was a dealer. Back when I was growing up, rural areas like mine were an antiques dealer's paradise. Families tended to live in the same houses for generations, and things just collected in attics until finally there was no one left who wanted old furnishings and they had to be cleared out. People would hold auctions, and often neither the heirs nor the auctioneer would know the value of the items.

"Now, of course, it's very different. There aren't many real bargains left. That's certainly true here in New England, at any rate."

"So you're from this area?"

He shook his head, and his dark eyes once again gleamed with amusement. "No, I'm from the Midwest, just as you are."

She froze, certain that he was about to expose her charade.

"Your accent," he said, after a very long pause that seemed calculated to maximize her discomfort.

"Oh," she said, relieved but chagrined. "I thought I'd gotten rid of the worst of it."

He chuckled. "It isn't that noticeable. I just happen to be good with accents. How long have you been here?"

"Just a short time. I'm staying with my brother in the city until I can get myself situated."

"Do you like it?"

"I love it, but if I'm going to stay, I'll have to find a job soon."

The moment the words left her mouth, she realized her mistake. She couldn't believe she had let herself slip like that. She hurried to clarify her statement. "I mean, I can't survive in New York as a free-lance writer."

She became angry with herself for having let him turn the tables on her like this. The way things were going, he'd learn more about *her* than she'd ever discover about *him*. She was trying to decide if she could salvage anything of this discussion when the chimes at the shop's door sounded. The expression "saved by the bell" took on a whole new meaning. She hastily put away her things and stood up.

"I won't keep you any longer. You've been very helpful."

He stood, too, and glanced at his watch. "That's probably Anne, my assistant. It's lunchtime. Would you..."

He stopped as footsteps approached the doorway. Susan had barely registered his final words. His assistant! He was almost certainly talking about the woman she'd met on her last visit here. Fear made her rigid, and she turned awkwardly as he greeted the woman and introduced them.

If Anne recognized her, she gave no indication. Susan began to relax. She now felt even more certain that Andrews couldn't have seen through her disguise. After all, if this woman with whom she'd carried on a conversation didn't recognize her, why should he?

Anne returned to the front of the shop, and Lucas Andrews turned to her once more. It was then that she realized what he must have been about to say. Fortunately, that gave her a second or two to decide before he completed the invitation.

"Would you like to join me for lunch before you return to the city?"

Having rapidly weighed the advantages against the disadvantages, Susan accepted for no better reason than that she was unwilling to end this encounter.

"Are we walking?" she asked as they left the shop. "My car is down there about a block."

"Mine's here. We'll take it. The restaurant is on the other side of town." He opened the passenger door of the Mercedes.

Susan slid past him and into the leather seat, belatedly wondering if she was doing something she'd come to regret. But regret was far from her mind as he, too, got into the car, filling it with his presence.

Let's be honest about this, she told herself. This guy turns you on. Maybe it's just because there hasn't been anyone for a long time, or maybe it's just because of the sticky web of deceit you're so busy weaving. But, whatever the cause, it's a new experience. And wasn't that why she'd come to New York?

"This is a pretty town," she commented. She wished she could come up with something better, but his closeness was doing unpleasant things to her brain, and very pleasant things to every other part of her. She glanced at his hand on the gearshift and remembered its pleasing roughness. If he hadn't responded, she would undoubtedly have drifted off into some very erotic fantasies.

"Yes, I like it. It's both large enough to afford privacy and small enough to get to know people. And there are also enough other antiques shops to draw customers to the area."

She was back in control again, having pushed her incipient fantasies aside. "It also looks like a nice place to raise a family. Are you married?"

He glanced at her briefly before turning his attention to his driving, and she saw that familiar sparkle in his eyes. Did he find her all that amusing, or was he always like this?

"No, I've never been married. But you're right. It would be a good place to raise kids."

She felt irritated with him on behalf of his fiancée. What was his game? Was he denying any relationship so that he could try to seduce her?

Well, she couldn't exactly blame him, could she? She'd been sending out all sorts of signals. But she was going to be truly disappointed in him if he tried to get her back to his house after lunch . . . never mind the fact that she'd be tempted to go. Human behavior, Susan had learned early in her studies, was only occasionally rational.

The restaurant was a French bistro, housed in a rambling old Victorian on the edge of a residential neighborhood. The hostess greeted him warmly by name, then led them out onto a glass-enclosed porch. Along the way, he paused to greet several people, who seemed to cast curious glances at her. It took her a few minutes to realize that her disguise probably made her an unlikely companion for Mr. Savile Row. She'd actually forgotten that she wasn't quite herself this day.

As soon as they'd ordered, he began to ask her questions about herself. How had she happened to come to New York? Had she sold any articles? What did her brother do? Where was she living in Manhattan?

But none of it felt like an interrogation. Rather, he seemed genuinely interested, and the questions appeared to arise quite naturally. She responded with a mixture of truth and lies before she quite realized how much information she was giving him. And even then she didn't really feel threatened, because she was convinced that she had succeeded in deceiving him. Nevertheless, she belatedly became aware of the fact that once again he had managed to shift the conversation away from himself.

Their food arrived, and talk gave way to eating for a time. Susan began to consider just what it was about him that had made her open up so easily, if not exactly honestly. Part of it, she decided, was his voice. It was low and pleasant and almost hypnotic—the kind of voice that invited confidences.

The other thing she noticed was his tendency to make and hold eye contact, almost—but not quite—too often and too long. Eye contact was an interesting thing, and something every budding therapist struggled with. How much was too much, risking making the client uncomfortable? Lucas Andrews seemed to have an innate talent for bringing one to the brink of discomfort and then backing off.

She also did not fail to notice that he had as yet made no attempt to flirt with her. So much for Teddy's prediction. But it also robbed him of an excuse for not mentioning his fiancée. She became determined to get this discussion back on the right track—off her and onto *him*.

"You mentioned that you've been here only a few years. Were you in business somewhere else before that?"

"I worked for a large import-export firm that deals in antiques worldwide."

That didn't exactly sound like a description of the U.S. Navy. "Oh. Then you must have done a lot of traveling. I envy you. I've never been out of the country, except to Canada a few times."

He nodded. "The travel finally got to me. That's why I decided to go into business myself."

"Well, I can see why you've never been married. It would have been difficult to have a wife and family when you were traveling all the time."

He merely nodded, failing once again to mention his plans to marry now. Instead, he asked her about her seafood quiche. She pronounced it excellent, but refused to let him sidetrack her this time.

"Did you study antiques in college? I don't even know if that's possible."

"I was a business major, with a minor in history."

"Where did you go?"

"Michigan. How about you?"

"Indiana. I grew up there."

A small silence followed, during which they both returned to their eating. Susan tried to think of ways to gain more information, but she wasn't sure what else she could find out without arousing his suspicions. It was strange, she reflected, how he could seem to invite confidences while at the same time withholding them himself.

Lucas let the silence between them grow while he continued to try to guess her purpose. He suspected that at least some of what she'd told him about herself was the truth, but he was equally sure that some of it was lies. What was her game? He still couldn't believe that anyone from his past would be sending an amateur to check up on him, but in the world he'd lived in, anything was possible.

He smiled to himself, thinking that if they had been responsible for sending both women, they'd certainly chosen better this time. Underneath that disguise, she was indeed very appealing. And he knew that she found him very attractive, as well. He was sure it was real, and not part of her act, because he could see that she was struggling against it.

The other woman had been blatant in her attempts to seduce him, but Susan Todd, or whatever her name was, was succeeding without even trying. He didn't dare respond, of course, but he wanted to.

She began to talk again, having apparently given up, for the time being, her attempts to pry information from him. Instead, she settled on the safe subject of New York—what she liked and what she didn't.

"New York *can* be overwhelming," he agreed. "There's no other city quite like it in the world. I have a place in Manhattan, a co-op I own jointly with an old friend who travels a lot. I'm generally in the city a day or two every week, just long enough to make me want to come back here."

"That must be nice." She sighed. "I've been thinking about maybe looking for a job in the suburbs instead, but I hate to give up my dream of living in the city."

"Sometimes dreams can turn to dust," he replied, surprising himself with the confession. "Traveling the world was *my* dream, but it lost its attraction after a while."

"But at least you had it for a time. I just keep being afraid that I'll have to go home again, and that feels like a death sentence."

"But surely there are more opportunities here for a writer than there are back in Indiana?"

She actually stared at him blankly for a moment, but then she nodded quickly. "Yes, you're right, of course."

Lucas did not fail to notice her brief confusion. She was apparently having trouble mixing her lies with the truth. He wondered what her real profession was. It was possible that she was an actress, although somehow he doubted that.

He considered the possibility of seducing her. The idea certainly had its appeal, for more than one reason. But he decided he'd be disappointed if he succeeded. He wanted to continue to believe that she was somehow an innocent caught up in something she didn't understand. It was a very strange thought for someone like him, to whom cynicism had long ago become a way of life.

They finished their lunch over casual conversation, doing their best to ignore the subtle tension that hummed like a muted electrical current between them. Lucas found himself wanting to tell her that he'd seen through her disguise from the beginning, in the hope that they could put that behind them and move on to honesty, something that had been in short supply in his life.

Unknown to him, Susan wanted that, too. She wanted to strip off the ridiculous wig and the makeup and tell him that she'd gotten into this by accident and wanted out. What was a guy like him doing with a woman like Natalie Kroft, anyway?

Instead, they continued to talk about everything and nothing. They left the restaurant a short time later, and she commented on the perfection of the day. It was, in fact, one of those glorious June days when Nature deigned to give the world her very best.

He heaved a sigh. "I'd like to be at home gardening myself." He gave her an almost apologetic look. "I've recently gotten interested in it, and I think I'm becoming a fanatic. I've never really had a hobby before."

More than anything he'd said before, this had the flavor of the real man. His tone hadn't really changed, but she was still sure she heard a poignancy there, a suggestion that he was trying to remake his life.

"I like gardening, too," she replied, since a response seemed called for. "But I won't be able to do that in the city."

"Maybe that's another reason you should be job hunting out here in the suburbs," he suggested as he opened the car door for her.

"Yes. I suppose there must be a lot of jobs for psy— writers up here, as well."

She had been sliding into the seat as she spoke, and she froze as she caught herself. Maybe he hadn't heard her. He was closing the door at the time. A thin sheen of nervous perspiration crawled over her as she waited for him to get in.

But Lucas *had* heard. When he had an interest in someone, he didn't miss anything about them, not the slightest change in tone or the smallest slip of the tongue. And he was *very* interested in Susan Todd.

Had she started to say "psychologist"? As he walked around the car, he tried to think of other possibilities. Psychiatrist? Scientist? The last seemed unlikely. She would have been more specific than that. Psychiatrist seemed unlikely, as well; he didn't think she could be old enough to have graduated from medical school and completed a residency.

He glanced at her as he got into the car. She was very nervous, almost ready to bolt from the car. Once more he was tempted to demand the truth from her. He knew she'd be vulnerable now; fear made people do dumb things.

Susan tried to meet his gaze with equanimity as her heart pounded noisily in her chest. Then, when he said something, she finally began to relax again. Obviously he hadn't heard her slip of the tongue.

A short time later, she was on her way back to the city, both relieved and disappointed. He'd given her his business card and told her to call if she needed any more information, but there had been no suggestion that he wanted to see her again.

She wondered if it might have been different if she'd been herself.

Chapter Three

"Don't give me 'nice,'" Teddy scoffed. "This guy's as phony as your journalism credentials. What's the name of the 'import-export' firm? La Cosa Nostra?"

"I didn't ask him," Susan admitted. "I couldn't push too much."

She'd spent the trip back from Connecticut thinking about Lucas Andrews, and the farther she'd gotten from him, the more doubts she'd had herself. It was amazing how well she could think when those darned pheromones weren't zapping her. But she still couldn't quite accept Teddy's judgment that he was some sort of criminal.

"Look, those guys aren't all no-neck types who say 'dese,' 'dem' and 'dose.' They need respectable-looking guys, too. And the more I think about it, the more I realize that a business like his could make a good front for drug running. He probably imports that overpriced furniture with cocaine stuffed in false drawers."

"I don't believe that. Teddy, the man knows his business."

"So what? It's part of the act." He regarded her solemnly. "Have you got a thing for Andrews, Peggy Sue?"

"No, of course not," she protested, knowing it was useless.

"Well, you'd better forget about it. Even if he *is* legitimate, which I doubt very much, he's got a fiancée."

"I think it's strange that he didn't mention her."

Teddy snorted. "Get real! He was probably planning to put the make on you."

"Then why didn't he?" she asked angrily.

Teddy shrugged. "Maybe he had a last-minute attack of conscience."

"From the way you're talking about him, I wouldn't think you'd believe he *has* a conscience."

Teddy looked at the notes he'd taken. "Well, I'd better get busy on this before I end up with a hit man for a brother-in-law."

"What are you planning to do?"

"Check out the information you got. I'll start by calling the University of Michigan to see if he really did go there. If he did, then I can contact the alumni office to see if they have anything on him. He might be telling the truth about that, since he also told Natalie that he grew up in Michigan. It's a start, anyway."

OVER THE NEXT FEW DAYS, Susan's time was divided between studying the help-wanted ads and roaming about the city. She sent off more résumés, though with decreasing hopes. Every ad seemed to ask for more experience than she had. She was beginning to think that her four years of work with Children and Youth Services counted for nothing at all, although she hadn't yet reached the point where she thought of her degree as being useless, as well.

In the meantime, she staved off her despondency over the job situation by visiting museums and galleries, riding out to the Statue of Liberty and eating a hot dog on the observation deck of the World Trade Center while gazing in awe at the panoramic view.

But Lucas Andrews was never far from her mind for very long. How much of her fascination with him was real and how much the result of the mystery surrounding the man, she couldn't have said. But he certainly intrigued her. Without telling Teddy, she got the address of Natalie Kroft's boutique on the Upper East Side and decided to have a look at their client. Her curiosity about Lucas Andrews had broadened to encompass his fiancée, as well.

She had no idea if Natalie would actually be there, since she also owned another boutique, in SoHo, but the moment she saw the woman step out of the rear of the shop, Susan knew it had to be her. She was several inches taller than Susan, with jet-black hair that was styled in one of those severe cuts that must require weekly trips to a hairdresser. She wore a lime-green skirt that stopped just short of indecency, and a formfitting lime-and-raspberry top that was shirred to exaggerate her almost nonexistent breasts.

Susan made a pretense of examining the clothes, most of which were the kinds of things she saw in magazines, but almost never on real live women, Natalie Kroft and her customers excepted. She was half-afraid she'd be asked to leave, since she was so underdressed.

A salesclerk with raspberry eye shadow that matched her tube dress came over and asked if she could help. Susan jumped, because she'd been covertly watching Natalie.

"Uh, yes. Could I try these?" She grabbed a pair of bell-bottom pants in an orange sherbet shade. Surely they wouldn't fit.

Natalie Kroft's dark eyes snapped to her as Susan went past, carrying the pants. Teddy was right; she could actually feel the waves of nervous energy emanating from the woman.

What on earth could a man like Lucas Andrews see in her? It wasn't as though she were any great beauty, although Susan had to admit that she'd done the best she could with what she had. But how could any man want to live with such a bundle of raw nerves?

Unfortunately, the pants fit perfectly and looked really good on her. Her tastes had always run to quiet, neutral colors; perhaps it was time to change that. The dress she'd worn for her meeting with Lucas Andrews had made her rethink her wardrobe.

The saleswoman appeared just as Susan was admiring herself in front of the dressing room mirror. "They're perfect for you," she pronounced. "And I have just the top for them, too."

Susan was still frowning at the price tag when the woman returned with a brightly flowered short-sleeved jacket. She obligingly tried it on, as well, wondering why people let salesclerks bully them into buying things.

"Perfect," the woman repeated. "All you need is a T-shirt under it."

"I have one," Susan said quickly, before she could have that pushed at her, too.

She left the shop with her unplanned purchases while Natalie was busy working on another customer who clearly had more money to spend than she did. Natalie's voice was a low purr that grated on Susan's nerves and made her think that it could probably rise to a feline shriek at the slightest provocation.

She returned to the West Side and stopped at a supermarket to buy some groceries, then transferred her new clothes to those bags and got rid of the electric-blue bag from the boutique. She didn't want Teddy to know that she'd been engaged in some unauthorized snooping.

"Ready to hear about Luke the hunk?" Teddy asked the moment she put her head in the doorway of his office. "You'd better sit down."

"I can take it standing up," she replied, ignoring that sinking feeling that shouldn't have been there in the first place.

"Okay, but I can't catch you if you faint dead away. He was born in a town called Thomasville, not far from Ann Arbor. It's a little place, and the police chief remembered the family. 'Poor as church mice' is how he described them. Father—an alcoholic who never held a job for more than a few months. Mother—a weak, dependent sort who was abused and refused to press charges. The father died in a drunk-driving accident. The chief thought that Andrews was about ten at the time, and he had a younger sister.

"According to the chief, things didn't improve after the father's death. They were on welfare, and Andrews's mother just took off with some guy who was passing through. The authorities stepped in, of course, and Andrews spent the rest of his childhood in a series of foster homes. A relative in Pennsylvania took his sister. The chief said she was an older woman and couldn't take care of two children.

"It seems that Andrews was a good student, though, and a star football player. He went to the University of Michigan on a football scholarship. University records show that he graduated with a business degree, and he even made runner-up all-American. And that's that. No alumni information on him. He didn't keep in touch.

"Now here's the *really* juicy part. The chief said that a couple of years after Andrews graduated from college, some 'government men' came to town asking questions about him. They didn't come to the police, though, which

the chief thought was kind of strange. No one they talked
to seemed to know what branch of government they were
with, even though they apparently showed some ID.''

By this time, Susan had sat down. She was both stunned
and sad. In Teddy's brief words, she saw far too much of
Lucas Andrews's childhood, thanks to her own work with
Children and Youth Services.

She thought about the tale he'd told her about learning
his love of antiques from his mother, whom he'd said was
a dealer. How very credible he'd seemed. Well, he wouldn't
be the first person from that type of background who'd
fabricated the kind of life he'd *wanted* to lead. Even his
career as an antiques dealer made a sad sort of sense, she
thought. He was borrowing other people's histories, in a
way, rooting himself in others' pasts.

"How did you find out all this?" she asked finally.

"Greg has an uncle who's in the investigative business
in Chicago—a big outfit. That's how Greg got his start. It
turned out that one of his uncle's people was working on
something that took him to Ann Arbor, so he just piggy-
backed this onto his case."

Susan sat there, thinking about Lucas Andrews's life.
The odds had been against his making it. But he *had* made
it. He'd not only finished high school, but college as well.
And that told her that Lucas Andrews, whatever the rest
of his story might be, was a remarkable man.

"Yeah, it's pretty sad," Teddy agreed, seeing the expression on her face. "And the guy sure deserves some
credit. But what about these 'government' guys? Why
would they be investigating him?"

"It could have been for a security clearance, Teddy.
Remember how they came around about Jack Snyder
when he went to work for the Defense Department?"

"Yeah, you're right. But they sure wouldn't have been doing a security clearance if he was working in the antiques business—which is what he told you. Greg's running an FBI check on him, by the way." Teddy's voice softened. "Look, I know you're hung up on this guy. But, dammit, he's lied to his fiancée, and he lied to you. Why would he lie about his background if he just worked for the Pentagon or something?"

"I am *not* hung up on him, Teddy. And anyway, even if he did something illegal in the past, that doesn't mean he's doing it now."

"True, but it sure would explain his lack of a credit history, wouldn't it? You don't need credit if you're in jail."

"If he was in jail, then where could he have gotten all that money? He certainly didn't inherit it."

"A very good point," Teddy agreed. "Doesn't that suggest to you that maybe he's *still* involved in something illegal?"

She ignored the question. Was it only her pride that was hurt? She was so sure of her instincts when it came to people, and although those instincts had told her that Lucas Andrews wasn't your ordinary antiques dealer, they *weren't* saying that he was a criminal.

The phone rang while she was putting away the groceries she'd bought, and she heard Teddy pick it up in his office. When she had finished, she went back there, braced to hear even worse about Lucas Andrews.

"Well, he's clean," Teddy said with a frown. "I guess that's good news, but it sure doesn't solve the mystery."

"You mean he has no criminal record?" she asked hopefully.

"Right. But that doesn't mean he *isn't* a criminal. It just means that he hasn't gotten caught. Greg thinks we should

try to get into his house. He's got to have something there
that ties into his past.''

She stared at him, aghast. ''You mean *break in?*''

''Yeah, unless you want to go up there and play the
temptress.''

''Teddy, that's illegal!''

''We're not going to steal anything, just look around.''

''What's this 'we' business? You're not in any condition to do any burglarizing.''

''I was hoping you'd notice that. Actually, what Greg
and I had in mind is sending you up there to check out the
place, then sending one of his guys if it looks feasible. You
could get away with nosing around a lot easier than a guy
could. Maybe you could be the Avon lady or something.''

''He doesn't exactly look like a potential Avon customer,'' she replied as she thought about it. Illegal or not,
it *was* tempting. Teddy was right—it was probably the only
way they were going to learn anything more.

''I can tell you what to look for in the way of burglar
alarms. Then, if he doesn't seem to have one, Greg will
send someone up when we know he's in the city.''

''Teddy, Mother and Dad would not be happy to know
that you're enticing me into a life of crime.''

LUCAS PUT DOWN THE PHONE, then, after a few seconds,
picked it up again to call his travel agent. When he'd completed the arrangements, he pushed his chair away from
the desk and sat there, staring out at the woods beside the
house.

He'd planned to go to Europe next month on a buying
trip in any event, so it wouldn't be a waste even if he didn't
turn up anything. His contact here felt much as he did—
that it was highly unlikely that anyone could be after him.

Still, both of them heard the silent "but" after the disclaimer. It *was* possible.

He'd struck out in his attempt to learn anything about Susan Todd; obviously she'd been using a false name. He'd wasted the better part of an evening calling all the Todds in the Manhattan directory, but hadn't turned up any men with sisters named Susan. And the theatrical union had no comedian named Todd listed among their members.

Given enough time, he could track her down, but she wasn't really his problem. If he had a problem, it was somewhere in Europe. Lucas continued to sit there as his mind began to review the past fourteen years, seeking a likely candidate. The problem was that it could be *any* of them; no one stood out as being the most likely prospect. Or it could be someone he didn't even know, but who knew him.

Since he'd turned his back on his previous life, Lucas had not permitted himself to think about it. He was determined to put the past behind him. Or was he only kidding himself? Hadn't he felt a surge of adrenaline just from that phone conversation?

He thought about a very wise old man in Geneva, one of the people he'd be visiting, who'd shaken his head sadly when Lucas had told him he was quitting.

"It's not possible, Lucas. No one quits. It's an addiction, just like a needle in your veins."

And they wanted him back in the game, too; his contact had made that clear. Lucas knew he'd been good. The very fact that he had survived for fourteen years proved that. And that was what the old man had *really* meant. No one quit, because they didn't live that long. They just kept on until they made a fatal mistake.

Cold sweat prickled his skin. It was dangerous for him to go back, even if it was just to seek information. The danger wasn't really physical, although that possibility always existed; the danger to him was that he might want to stay.

To push those thoughts away, he conjured up an image of Susan Todd. Not the phony journalist or the middle-aged tourist, but the real woman, the one in the yellow slicker. Somehow, she looked like a Susan. Maybe she'd used her real first name.

She was a pretty woman—not truly beautiful, but then he'd always thought that beauty was a vastly overrated commodity, given its impermanence. But there was more to her than that, he thought. She had spirit; probably that was how she'd gotten mixed up in this. And she had a quality to her that made people want to talk to her, that made them think she wouldn't judge them. If she *was* a psychologist, she was probably a good one.

Well, it did no good to dwell on her. He doubted that she knew the truth about him now, but if she ever found out, she'd judge him, all right. And he couldn't blame her for that.

SUSAN STOPPED in the middle of the cul-de-sac as soon as she saw the car parked in Lucas Andrews's driveway. He was supposed to be in Europe. Could his assistant at the shop have lied?

Then it dawned on her that they'd never considered the possibility of a housekeeper. Of course he'd have one!

She sat there a moment longer, considering this new situation and how she could use it to her advantage. Then she drove boldly into his driveway and parked behind the other car.

As she walked unhurriedly up to the front door, she scanned the front of the house, seeking evidence of an alarm system. With the housekeeper here, she could scarcely start prowling around outside. But if her ruse didn't work, she could always come back. It wasn't likely that the woman would come every day, especially with him in Europe.

She saw no evidence of a security system, but she couldn't be sure. By now she was determined to get into the house. She would pretend to be an old friend of Lucas Andrews's who had just happened to drop by. Then, if she could convince the woman to let her use the phone, or maybe the bathroom...

A tall, gray-haired woman answered the door very quickly, and it was immediately apparent to Susan that she was distracted or disturbed about something. She put on a bright smile.

"Hello. I hope I have the right house. Is this the home of Lucas Andrews?"

The woman nodded eagerly, drawing Susan into the foyer even as she spoke. "I'm so glad you've come so quickly. Come in, come in. I'll just show you where everything is, and then I'll be off."

Susan stepped into the house, her mind racing to guess what was going on and who this woman thought she was. A replacement? Surely that was too much to hope for.

The woman must have seen the confused look on her face. "Oh, you won't have to start today. Mr. Andrews is in Europe and won't be back for a week or more. And he's no trouble at all, a joy to work for, believe me. I've never met a man who was so neat."

Susan's brain processed this information and reached the inescapable conclusion that the gods had indeed smiled upon her this day. The woman had clearly mistaken her for a substitute housekeeper. How fortunate that she'd dressed in jeans and an old T-shirt, expecting to be skulking about the woods.

Did she dare hope that she could pull this off? What if the *real* substitute showed up in the meantime? It took her all of two seconds to decide to take that chance.

The housekeeper hustled her past the handsomely furnished living room and down a hallway to the kitchen, already explaining her duties. Susan asked no questions, since she was as eager as the woman to get it over with before someone else could show up to claim the position.

The housekeeper paused for a breath, then rushed on. "I'm so glad they could send someone over this morning. They weren't sure they could, and I have to leave today. My daughter's up in Vermont, and she just had a miscarriage."

"In that case, I'm glad I can help out," Susan said, pushing down her guilt at taking advantage of the situation. "Do you know how long you'll be gone?"

The woman shook her head sadly. "She has a three-year-old and a six-year-old, and her husband walked out on her a month ago. Not that he was much good when he *was* there."

"I'm so sorry," Susan said sincerely, now really awash in guilt. "But don't worry about a thing. I'm sure I can handle it until you get back."

"That's wonderful! I felt real bad about leaving Mr. Andrews like this, when he's been so good to me."

She gathered up her purse and ushered Susan to the front door. "They probably told you that I come two days a week—Mondays and Thursdays. Be sure to water the plants and bring in the mail. You can leave it in his study. It's just in there." She pointed toward a closed door.

Then she stopped as she reached for the doorknob. "Oh, dear, I nearly forgot to tell you about the alarm system."

She opened a closet door and pointed to a panel, then hurriedly explained how it worked. "You'd better write down the code."

Susan obligingly pulled out a notepad and pen.

"All the windows and doors are covered, even the upstairs windows. Just shut it off while you're here, then reset it when you leave. Be sure not to forget, because it's tied in automatically to the police station."

Susan listened to everything she said, thinking that without this extraordinary piece of luck they would never have gotten in. Teddy had told her that if she saw signs of an alarm system she should check to see if there was a way to get in through an upstairs window. He claimed that people didn't usually have them alarmed, which made her wonder why Lucas Andrews *did*.

They left the house, and the housekeeper handed her the keys, with yet another expression of gratitude. Susan got into her car and sat there for a moment, staring incredulously at the keys. She wanted to go back in there now, but she feared that the real substitute would show up at any moment.

The housekeeper backed out of the driveway, then stopped and got out to hurry toward Susan, who hadn't yet moved. Susan froze, certain that she'd been discovered or was about to be asked some question she wouldn't be able to answer.

"I almost forgot! Mr. Andrews asked me to check his garden and water it if it doesn't rain. The hose is in a cart out back. Do you mind?"

She certainly didn't. The housekeeper left, and Susan backed slowly out of the driveway, still nearly unable to believe her luck. Then she drove through the maze of streets until she reached a main road and found a pay phone.

"Guess what I have!" she exclaimed the moment Teddy answered.

He groaned dramatically. "A cop reading you your rights."

"Guess again."

"It's a nice town. The jail can't be that bad. If the bail is under a hundred, I'll get you out."

"I have the key to Lucas Andrews's house!"

There was a brief silence on the line. "Right! He left it under the doormat, with a note telling you to make yourself at home."

"That would have been stealing, Teddy," she said righteously. "I didn't steal it. But it *does* come with one small requirement." She told him what had happened. Her guilt at deceiving that poor woman must have crept into her voice.

"Cut it out!" Teddy ordered. "I can hear that guilt. The first rule of the private-eye business is that you don't look gift horses in the mouth—or any other part of their anatomy. Guilt is a luxury we can't afford. Our client is pushing hard."

She finally hung up, smiling to herself again as she let Teddy convince her. Then she took out the keys and dangled them before her eyes. "Lucas Andrews, your secrets are about to be revealed. And I might even clean your house for you to salve my conscience."

"TEDDY, I can't find *anything*. It's like he has no past." Susan sat at the handsome antique mahogany desk in Lucas Andrews's study.

"What about a safe?"

"Well, there *could* be one. There's a closet here in his study, and it could be in there. But the door's locked, and I can't find a key."

"How good is the lock?"

"How would I know? A lock's a lock—and it's locked."

"Go look at it now. Does it have a button on the knob, or just a keyhole?"

She didn't have to get up to check. "A keyhole."

"Dead bolt," Teddy pronounced. "Greg has a set of lock picks, but it takes some skill to use them. He'll have to send someone."

Susan hung up and stared at the closet door. Was Lucas Andrews's past in there? It was the only possibility.

In the four hours she'd been in his house, she'd gone through every closet, every cabinet and drawer. She'd even checked the attic and basement. Then, when she'd gone out to get his mail, which had yielded nothing of interest, she'd noticed something she hadn't seen before, and her hopes had soared.

There was a second story to the attached double garage, and when she'd first seen the house, she'd assumed that it was just part of the upstairs. But, looking at it from the driveway, with the house plan in mind, she'd realized that it must be separate. In short order she'd found the outside entrance, nearly hidden on the side of the house behind some shrubbery. She'd gone back inside to get a key she'd found, and discovered that it fit.

But all was for naught. It turned out to be a small apartment, probably for a live-in housekeeper. It was still furnished, but obviously hadn't been lived in for some time. She'd even had to rearrange the dust to cover her tracks on the stairs.

So Lucas Andrews continued to elude her, even though she now knew that he favored British tailors, Italian shoe-makers, classic films, jazz and science fiction. And he also seemed to subscribe to every newsmagazine in existence, including some foreign ones. He played squash, ran, and seemed to be considering taking up golf, because there was a new set of clubs in the garage. Also in the garage was every tool known to man, all of them relatively new and as neatly arranged as everything else in the rest of the house. She wondered how anyone could run a house without a junk drawer or closet somewhere, but Lucas Andrews seemed to manage that.

Interesting as all this was, he continued to elude her. There was not one single item from his past, nothing that even hinted at a past life. No photographs, no mementos—not even from college, where he'd been a football star.

She finally got up and went outside to check his garden. It hadn't rained for the past few days in the city. The plants here were still healthy, but the earth was dry, so she rolled the hose cart over to the garden and began to water it, still thinking about her unwitting "employer." The man seemed to have reinvented himself.

Much as she hated to admit it, she knew that Teddy's speculations were probably accurate—Lucas Andrews must be a criminal of some sort. Why else would he go to such lengths to destroy his past? Or to hide it? There was still the matter of that locked closet.

The phone began to ring just as she reentered the house, and she hurried to his study, where his answering machine was just coming on. When the beep sounded, she heard a woman's apologetic voice.

"Mr. Andrews, this is Helen from HomeClean. I'm sorry to say that we've been unable to find a substitute for Mary. If anyone becomes available, we'll let you know."

Susan waited until the woman had hung up, then erased the message and reset the machine. It looked as though she could play housekeeper for a while longer.

GREG HIMSELF accompanied her on her next trip to Connecticut. He was an impatient passenger in her car, since she'd convinced him that his red Porsche might attract the unwelcome attention of the neighbors. Even in this neighborhood, housekeepers did not drive Porsches.

Greg was a ruggedly handsome blond six-footer—almost a young Robert Redford. Teddy had told her pointedly that he was single, and in their brief acquaintance he'd made it fairly obvious that he found her attractive.

Susan wasn't interested. There was nothing wrong with him, other than his impatience with her cautious driving, but she had room in her thoughts now for only two things: getting a job and solving the mystery of Lucas Andrews. And she didn't appear to be making any headway with either one.

Once they'd reached the house it took Greg an amazingly brief time to open the closet door, but he muttered a curse even as she leaned forward to peek over his shoulder.

"That's a damned good safe," Greg grumbled. "Short of blowing it apart, we'll never get in." He glared at it as though he had just that in mind, and she looked at him in fear. He chuckled as he closed the door.

"Don't worry. I'm not going to go *that* far. But the fact that he'd have a safe this good only tells me that he's got something serious to hide. This isn't the usual kind of safe people have in their homes, believe me."

"There *are* two locked drawers," she said. "But they're both small. One in the desk and one in the nightstand upstairs."

It took Greg even less time to open them, and what they found were two identical guns, one in each drawer. Greg picked up another object that lay beside the one in the nightstand.

"Do you know what this is?" he asked.

She shook her head, and he explained that it was a silencer.

"First of all, they're illegal, and secondly, there's only one reason to have them—to be able to kill someone quietly."

Susan stared at the guns and the silencer and wished she hadn't told him about the locked drawers.

"And even without the silencer, this isn't the kind of gun people keep around for protection. This is the weapon of a professional."

He *isn't* a killer, she wanted to shout. But the words stuck in her throat. The Lucas Andrews with the warm brown eyes and the soft chuckle was fading fast, replaced by a cold-eyed professional killer.

LUCAS RELEASED his seat belt as the Concorde arced its way over the North Atlantic. Never had he been so glad to be going home. Normally, he left Europe with some regrets, but not this time. Instead, he felt as though he'd just barely escaped a return to his past life-style.

He'd found a beautiful refectory table in Hungary, a magnificent armoire in Czechoslovakia, and several items in Lithuania. He was vaguely troubled over buying them from people who clearly didn't want to part with them, but given the economies of those countries, people needed cash more than they needed their past.

He'd learned nothing to suggest that anyone from *his* past was after him. As one of his old contacts had said, "You're history, Lucas. Your name comes up from time to time, and a lot of people would be happy to see you again, but no one's after you. There's too much current trouble to think about the past."

The man was wrong, though. *Someone* was after him. He thought about Susan again. He was glad that she wasn't mixed up in anything related to his past, but what *was* her game?

He thought about just letting it go. Maybe she wouldn't show up again. But he found he didn't want that. He *wanted* to see her again, and not just because he wanted to solve a mystery, even though that was the excuse he gave to himself. By the time the Concorde touched its droopy nose to the tarmac at JFK, he'd outlined a plan to find her.

LUCAS FROWNED at the Subaru in his driveway. Mary must have gotten a new car. This wasn't one of her regular days, but perhaps she'd changed them while he was gone. She wouldn't be expecting him back this soon.

He pulled into the garage, then saw the mailman and went back out to pick up his mail. He let himself into the house through the front door, calling out to Mary before going on to his study. There was no response, but he assumed that she must be upstairs somewhere.

He hit the play button on his machine, then began to sort through his mail as the messages played. The first message was from a neighbor, inviting him to a cookout, and the second was from a dealer in town, extending an invitation to one of her regular cocktail parties. Lucas smiled. Both of them probably had friends they wanted to introduce to him. The available women far outnumbered the available men in this community.

The third message was from the domestic service, and it had played before he'd paid much attention. He rewound it and played it again.

"Mr. Andrews, this is Helen from HomeClean again. We still haven't been able to find a replacement for Mary, but we expect to have someone available next week. Please call when you return from Europe."

Lucas was frowning before the message had finished. If Mary wasn't here, then whose car was in his driveway? And why had the woman said she'd called before, when there was no earlier message on the machine?

He reacted from long years of experience. First, he went to the desk, unlocked the drawer and picked up his gun. Then he moved quietly to the doorway of the study and listened.

He decided to check the upstairs first. If the intruder had been downstairs when he'd arrived, he would most likely have escaped through the back door already. Gun in hand, Lucas crept quietly up the carpeted stairs. A quick but thorough check of rooms and closets revealed nothing, so he went back downstairs and began to search the rest of the first floor. But that sixth sense he'd depended on for so many years was telling him now that the house was empty. Furthermore, as far as he could tell at this point, nothing was missing.

The final room he entered was the kitchen. Two things caught his attention immediately. A woman's purse lay on the counter, and water was running somewhere. He quickly realized that the sound was coming from the outdoor faucet and went back into the dining room to look through the glass doors that led to the terrace.

She was standing with her back to him as she watered his garden. Even from this distance and at an oblique angle, he knew it was her, although for just a moment he was half-certain he must be hallucinating. Lucas was not a man given to flights of fancy, but his normally firm grip on reality began to slip a bit. How could she possibly be here? Only hours ago he'd admitted to himself that he wanted to see her again—and here she was! It was almost enough to make him believe in genies in bottles, or fairy godmothers!

Oblivious to his presence, she continued to water his garden. She was wearing loose-fitting khaki shorts that revealed slim, strong legs, and a bright green T-shirt that hinted at curves. Her soft brown curls gleamed in the bright sunshine as a breeze toyed with them. Lucas was struck by the thought that she looked as though she were right where she belonged, even if that happened to be in *his* garden.

Knowing that he should be hauling himself back to reality, Lucas nevertheless stayed at the edges of this surreal scene. What was real? The danger her intrusion into his life surely represented, or the muted stirrings of desire he felt as he watched her? He felt momentarily suspended between two worlds: the dark one he'd thought he'd left behind, and the bright, gentle one represented so improbably by a beautiful woman and the garden he'd created.

She turned off the hose and began to move carefully along the rows, plucking weeds. Her movements brought him reluctantly back to reality. Whatever she was *really* here for, she was obviously taking her role as "housekeeper" very seriously. The garden looked well tended, and so did the house, insofar as he could tell.

Why would she be so conscientious about a fake job? And how the hell had she managed to get the assignment in the first place? The service said that they'd been unable to find a replacement for Mary, and yet here she was, having obviously assumed that role.

Lucas began to think that nothing she could do or say would surprise him. If she walked into the house and greeted him as though she had every right to be here, he'd probably just smile and nod agreeably.

He shook himself out of his reverie as he recalled that purse in the kitchen. With considerable reluctance, he turned away from the doors, found the purse and began to search through its contents. After finding what he sought, he replaced everything and returned to his study.

The closet door showed no signs of having been forced, but when he opened it carefully he saw that the thread he kept in the space between the door and the frame had fallen to the floor. The door had clearly been opened.

He checked the safe without much concern and saw that no attempt had been made to open it. That didn't surprise him; nothing short of explosives could accomplish that. He wondered if she might just have been curious about the locked closet. Some people simply couldn't resist locked rooms or closets. But the lock was good enough that it would certainly have taken some expertise to get it open without damaging it, and that suggested that either she was a pro herself or she'd had help.

Lucas was well aware of the fact that her intrusion into his life and his home should be producing more than just curiosity. Even if he'd been unable to find any tie to his past, he still had plenty of reason for anger and concern. And yet he felt neither.

He had just returned the gun to the drawer when he heard the back door open.

SUSAN WASHED HER HANDS at the kitchen sink. It was a good thing she'd decided to come up again. It still hadn't rained, and his garden had begun to wilt.

Teddy had argued noisily against her making this last trip, but she hadn't wanted Lucas to come home to a dead garden. The excuse she'd given Teddy was that she didn't want to put his housekeeper's job in jeopardy, and there was truth in that. But she also remembered how he'd spoken almost wistfully about his newfound interest in gardening, giving her in that moment a tantalizing glimpse of the inner man beneath that polished, urbane exterior.

But she knew she couldn't risk coming back again, since she had no idea when he'd be returning from his trip. As soon as he returned, he was bound to find out from the domestic agency that no housekeeper had been sent. Furthermore, she really didn't have any business here at this point. Teddy and Greg had decided to end the investigation, since it appeared that nothing more could be learned about Lucas Andrews's mysterious past. A report had already been sent to Natalie Kroft, informing her of that fact.

But Susan was having a very difficult time accepting that. Lucas Andrews intrigued her, in a way no other man ever had. Somehow she'd gone from mere curiosity about an attractive man to something deeper. She was wondering how long it would take her to forget him when she heard a sound—and whirled around to face the object of her thoughts!

She simply stood there paralyzed, her wet hands dripping water onto the tile floor. Just as he had done earlier, Susan now began to wonder if she could be hallucinating. She was so stunned that for a moment she actually forgot that she didn't belong here.

He stopped just inside the doorway. He was wearing a conservative glen plaid suit, but his tie was loose and the top button of his silk shirt was undone...and he was smiling.

"Sorry if I frightened you," he said, a trace of amusement in his voice. "I'm Lucas Andrews, and I assume you're not a thief."

"Oh! I was told you were in Europe." Her mind raced. He didn't recognize her! Could she hope to get away with this? Did she have a choice?

She turned away to dry her hands, using that brief time to will herself to calmness. Then she turned back to him with a bright smile.

"I'm Sherri Thomas. Mary had to go away. Her daughter is sick." She was glad she'd learned his house-keeper's name.

"I see." He leaned casually against the door frame. "Well, I saw you watering the garden. Thanks for not forgetting it. It looks as though it's been dry since I left."

"Yes, it has." She still couldn't quite believe her luck. She felt herself beginning to relax, or at least come out of that paralyzing fear. Relaxing around this man was simply not possible.

"Well, I think you'll find everything in order, Mr. Andrews," she said brightly as she picked up her bag and began to move toward the doorway, and him.

He stepped aside, but she could not have felt his presence more strongly if she'd walked right into him. The lure of his maleness was so powerful that she could easily envision herself doing just that, and it mixed explosively with the lingering fear that he might grab her and demand to know the truth.

He followed her to the front door. She walked casually, her steps far slower than the pounding of her heart. The door seemed at least a mile away. Susan wanted to escape, and yet she didn't want to leave. She knew she should leave and consider herself lucky to have gotten away with this, but what she wanted was to turn around, look him square in the eye and demand to know who he really was.

"When will Mary be returning?" he asked as she reached the door.

"She wasn't sure." Her mind spun, trying to decide how to answer what she knew would be his next question. She *should* tell him that she was only filling in temporarily and he should call the service for a replacement.

"Will you be able to come until she returns?"

She hesitated, then turned to face him, nodding even as she told herself this was madness. "Yes, I can do that if you like."

"Thank you. I'd appreciate that. Could you give me a number where I can reach you, Sherri, just in case I need to change the days?"

He seemed genuinely grateful, and there was certainly nothing in his manner to suggest an ulterior motive for his question, but she felt a renewed stab of cold fear anyway. Had he recognized her, after all? Did he just want to be able to find her?

"Yes, of course," she said, digging into her bag for a paper and pen. "I'm staying in the city at the moment, with my cousin. Just until I can find a place up here."

She expected more questions, but he remained silent as she wrote down Teddy's number, transposing the last two digits in a last-minute burst of brilliance. She'd had to admit to living in the city, because she didn't know this area well enough to name a town, and neither did she know the local exchanges—something he very well might know.

He took the paper from her, apparently not noticing her trembling hand, then said he'd see her on Thursday and thanked her once again. She smiled, nodded, and escaped.

She was almost back to the city before she began to think clearly. Could she really hope to pull this off? Success breeds success, she told herself, and she'd gotten away with it thus far. Lucas Andrews had no reason to suspect anything, and she was only feeding her ego if she thought he'd remember her. Besides, if playing housekeeper for a time was the only way she could unravel the mystery of this man, then she would do it.

"He is *not* a criminal!" she stated emphatically to the empty car. "I know he isn't, and I'm going to prove it."

Her professional reputation was at stake here; a psychologist was supposed to be insightful, to see what others missed, and to know when she was dealing with a liar.

Chapter Four

Lucas watched as she walked to her car, expecting to see her break into a run at any moment. Unsettled as he was at having found her in his home, he still saw the humor in the situation. And he was inordinately pleased to know she'd be back. It was possible that she wouldn't be, but his instincts told him she'd appear on Thursday. Whatever it was that she wanted from him, she hadn't gotten it yet.

She was certainly no professional at deception, but she was fast on her feet. He admired that, and liked what it told him about her: that she was as bright and resourceful as she was pretty.

As soon as her car had disappeared from view, he went back to his study and called HomeClean. He told them that he could manage until Mary returned, then asked if they might have a number where she could be reached. Fortunately, they did. She'd given them her daughter's phone number. So he called there.

He hung up from that conversation and sat there chuckling. So it had been nothing more than a case of her being "Susan-on-the-spot." His admiration for her quick-wittedness grew.

He'd assured Mary that everything was fine and that her job would be waiting for her when she returned, although that probably wouldn't be soon, given the problems with her daughter. He got out his checkbook and wrote Mary a check, then enclosed a note telling her it was for a well-deserved vacation, even though he knew her present circumstances made it anything but that. Mary was a good person, struggling with problems that were not of her own making. He knew, of course, that the gift wasn't altogether altruistic. It might encourage Mary to stay away longer, which meant that Susan Trent could continue her charade.

Next, he dialed the number Susan had given him. A woman with a strong West Indian accent answered. Several kids were screaming in the background. She'd never heard of either Sherri Thomas or Susan Trent. So he called the performing artists' union again, and found that there was indeed a Teddy Trent listed on their rolls as a comedian. When he got his number, he saw that she had simply transposed the last two digits.

But that still told him nothing about the reason for her interest in him. To discover that, he had two choices: He could wait until she gave him the reason, wittingly or unwittingly, or he could try to find out more about her brother, on the assumption that he, too, was somehow mixed up in this.

He thought about it for a while, then decided to wait and see if she would reveal her purpose. It was obvious that despite her rather impressive efforts, Susan Trent found this game she was playing to be against her nature. She'd slip up at some point, especially if he gave her a push in that direction.

He knew he was taking a chance by letting her continue this game, but he was convinced that she meant him no real harm. And in any event, what harm could she possibly do? She was no more than a talented novice; he was a grand master.

Still, harm could take many forms, and he was uneasily aware of his growing interest in her, and the dangers that posed.

"ARE YOU NUTS?" Teddy stared at her, aghast.

"That's a distinct possibility," Susan admitted, laughing rather uneasily. How could she justify to herself, let alone to her brother, what had surely been a rash action? It must be the result of all those years of academic drudgery, and the consequent need to put some excitement in her life.

"Listen, Susan, for once, I'm serious!"

She could tell that he was. He never called her Susan at any other time. And he certainly had a point. Signing on as the housekeeper for Lucas Andrews wasn't one of the brighter things she'd ever done. On the other hand, she believed in following her instincts, and they hadn't gotten her into trouble yet.

"For God's sake, you're a psychologist! They're supposed to be sane and rational and careful!"

Susan sighed. She decided not to tell him that from her observations, psychologists were sometimes anything but, at least in their own lives. Some of the most talented clinicians she'd met led appallingly disordered personal lives.

"Look, Teddy, you haven't met him, and I have. I've also met people who work for him, including his real housekeeper, who speaks very highly of him. So how bad can he be? All I want to do is to get to know him better, to see if I can prove I'm right about him. And it won't be for long."

"Has it occurred to you that he might know you're faking it, and he's just waiting for the right time to attack?"

"He had that chance today. And stop being so melodramatic! Even if he does recognize me, the worst he's going to do is throw me out."

She adopted a placating tone. "Anyway, the only crime he's committed is to lie about his military service and have no credit history. And own a gun with an illegal silencer," she added quickly, knowing he would bring that up. "Everything else is just speculation on your part, and as I said, you haven't met him. If you had, I think you'd see him differently."

"I sure as hell would," Teddy scoffed. "I wouldn't be drooling over him the way you are."

"That's not fair! I'll admit that I'm attracted to him, but when have I ever made a fool of myself over a man?" She raised her eyebrows challengingly. She knew she had him on that point. She might have chosen an unorthodox manner of getting to know Lucas Andrews, but she wasn't about to fling herself into a swoon at his feet.

"What about job hunting?" he asked, obviously deciding to try another tack. "And I have a couple of new cases I might need your help with."

"It's only two days a week," she pointed out. "Besides, I've decided to broaden my job search. I've already applied for two jobs in Connecticut."

She saw the look on his face and hastened to assure him that it had nothing to do with Lucas Andrews. The truth was that she really liked the area.

"One job sounds interesting, and I thought that I might have a better chance up there."

What she didn't tell him was that she wanted a position that would afford her the opportunity to try unconventional approaches. Nothing she'd looked at had really offered that. So far, the jobs she'd found would have meant using standard clinical approaches. She wanted to work exclusively with kids, and to use the different techniques she'd used in graduate school—not just talk therapy, but art, music and play therapies, as well. She'd seen kids respond to these approaches.

Besides, she was beginning to suspect that she'd never really be comfortable living and working in the city. New York continued to overwhelm her. She thought about Lucas Andrews's statement about dreams turning to dust. Her own dream of living in Manhattan wasn't exactly turning to dust, but it *was* changing. Being close enough to immerse herself in the city's many pleasures without being forced to live in it was beginning to sound good to her.

"Look at the practical side of this," Teddy said, drawing her back to the issue at hand. "You can't expect to get away with it. He's bound to find out that you weren't sent there by the domestic service."

"Maybe," she admitted. That *was* the one stumbling block.

"Not maybe—for sure! You don't even know whether he pays you directly, or whether you get paid through the agency."

"Good point. I'll call them and see how they work."

She made the call, then gave him a triumphant look. "They're just a placement agency. The employer pays the employee directly. So unless they actually come up with someone, which isn't likely at this point, there shouldn't be a problem. Why would he call them? As far as he knows, they've already sent someone."

"I stand by my original assessment. You're nuts!"

WHEN SUSAN ARRIVED at Lucas's home, it was just after ten o'clock, more than an hour later than she'd intended. She knew his shop opened at ten. He hadn't specified what time he expected her to be there, but she'd decided to show up at nine. After all, she could hardly get to know him if he wasn't there.

Unfortunately, what she was certain had to have been every car in the state of Connecticut, plus some from neighboring states, had chosen to join her on I-95. Now, she let herself into the house and went straight to the kitchen, clutching her road map. There had to be a better way of getting here, and she was determined to find it.

As she walked into the kitchen, she immediately smelled coffee, and she blessed Lucas Andrews when she saw that the coffeemaker was still half-filled. She'd gotten up late and hadn't yet had her morning fix of caffeine. She poured herself a cup of coffee, spread the map out on the table, then suddenly remembered the alarm system. She'd forgotten to switch it off! Mary had said it had to be turned off within ninety seconds. Surely more time than that had passed. The alarm must be silent, and the police were probably on their way! It was not an auspicious beginning to her work day.

She ran headlong from the kitchen toward the foyer, and didn't make it. Lucas Andrews chose that moment to step out of his study into the hallway. She cried out in surprise and tried to stop, but her momentum carried her straight into him.

They both crashed against the wall, then slid to the floor in a tangle of arms and legs. Susan was horrified. Her mind was registering her embarrassment, but her body was doing something else entirely as it collided with that warm, solid wall of flesh.

"Oh, I'm sorry!" She exclaimed as she tried to extricate herself from her awkward position half on top of him, a position that threatened to give rise to some very erotic fantasies that were scarcely appropriate at the moment.

He merely grinned, pulling himself into a sitting position at the same time as he lifted her off him. Any doubts she might have had about his fitness vanished as she braced herself against the taut muscles of his arms. She scooted away from him, having decided not to test her legs just yet.

"Was it a mouse or a spider? I know I have both from time to time." He continued grinning at her and made no move to get up.

She was mildly affronted. As far as she was concerned, his amusement reeked of sexism.

"Neither," she said formally as she got to her feet. "It was the alarm system. I'd forgotten to turn it off."

He got up, too, filling entirely too much space in the narrow hallway. "It's already off."

"Oh. Well, I didn't know you were here."

"I often work at home in the mornings," he replied. "Are you all right? You didn't get hurt?"

"I'm fine," she lied. "What about you?"

"Nothing that a cup of coffee won't cure."

She followed him back to the kitchen. "Well, I hope you're not in critical condition, because I drank the last cup. I'll make some more."

She moved toward the coffeemaker just as he did, and they collided again, though much more gently this time. He backed away with a smile, then gestured to the map she had spread out on the table.

"Did you get lost?"

She refilled the coffeemaker. "No, I was just trying to see if there's another way to get here. I-95 is a mobile parking lot and Route 7 is under construction."

"There is. Let me show you."

Standing close together, they bent over the map as he explained the alternate route. The pleasant, homey smell of coffee wafted about them. His arm brushed lightly against hers as she put out a hand to follow the route. She murmured her understanding, even though she'd barely heard a word he said.

She cast a sidelong glance at him. Either the attraction was one-sided, or he was one very cool customer. As he refolded the map for her, she watched him covertly, trying to decide. If he *was* interested in her and could hide it that well, what else could he be hiding? The fact that he had recognized her, perhaps? But then, why would he have encouraged her to stay?

The telephone rang, startling her. He picked up the kitchen extension, then handed it to her. "It's for you."

She took it with some trepidation. Teddy was the only one who could be calling, and she had warned him not to call unless she received a call about a job interview. But she wasn't really expecting him to call this soon, and she was half-afraid he was calling merely to check up on her.

At least, she thought as she took the receiver, he must have had the sense to ask for Sherri Thomas. She'd propped signs with that name written in large letters next to his phones.

It *was* about a job interview. An agency in Stamford that served children and youth wanted to talk to her the next day. Susan was elated; they must have only just received her letter of application. Furthermore, of all the ads she'd seen, it was the one that interested her most.

"Good news?" Lucas asked after she had hung up. He was leaning casually against the counter, sipping his coffee.

She could not contain her pleasure, which in any event had been evident in her conversation with Teddy.

"Yes, a job in Stamford. They must have just received my résumé, so that's a good sign, I think."

"What sort of job is it?"

Susan thought fast. Why should she continue to lie? If she wanted the truth out of him, shouldn't she start being honest herself—or at least as honest as possible, given the circumstances under which she was here?

She felt keenly the burden of all the lies: the phony names and disguises, and following him and searching his house. At the moment, she wanted to be as honest as possible.

"Well, actually, Mr. Andrews, I'm a psychologist." She stopped as he raised his dark brows in surprise. "Yes, well, I know it might seem strange for a psychologist to be working as a housekeeper, but the truth is that I need the money. You see, I've just finished three years of graduate school, and now I've got to find a place to live and get some furniture. I sold mine before I moved here. I haven't had any luck finding work in the city, and it was either this or bartending, which is what I did while I was in grad school. But I didn't want to bartend here, because I don't know the places like I did at home and, well, it can be unpleasant for a woman bartender in the wrong kind of bar."

She stopped to draw a breath, hearing her rambling explanation echo embarrassingly in her ears. He continued to lean against the counter, watching her with obvious amusement as he drank his coffee. She wasn't exactly sure what the source of his amusement was, and that made her nervous. In her attempt to tell at least some of the truth, had she dug herself into an impossible hole?

"I imagine bartending would probably be good experience for a psychologist."

So *that* was it. She relaxed. "Tell me about it! I told my professors that I was getting better experience there than I was at the clinic. It was also really good money. You wouldn't believe some of the tips I got."

"I don't doubt it," he replied dryly. "So what is this job?"

"It's an agency that works with children and youth. They want a psychologist to set up and run programs for kids at risk, and I've been working with kids like that for years. I worked for Children and Youth Services before I went to grad school."

As she explained, she belatedly realized that she was touching upon what had to be a difficult subject for him. But if it was, he gave no indication. She was well trained in the art of reading body language, but she saw nothing at all to indicate that her words were bringing back memories of his own tragic childhood.

"The problem is that it's only part-time, but the ad said it would become full-time in the fall."

"Where are you from originally?" he asked, still betraying nothing more than a mild interest.

She hesitated, but only briefly. He wasn't likely to remember that the journalist, Susan Todd, had been from Indiana, and she also recalled that he'd said he was good with accents. "Indiana," she finally replied.

The phone rang again, and this time it was for him. He returned to his study and asked her to hang up the kitchen phone. As she did so, she heard him speaking what sounded like German. How many languages did he speak, and what did his multiple fluency mean, if anything?

She was still unnerved by his failure to react in any way to her mention of her past work in children's services. What did that tell her about him? Had he really suppressed those memories of his own childhood that completely? Or was he simply the best she'd ever seen at concealing his true feelings?

She wondered, too, if she had now forfeited any chance she might have had to learn more about him by admitting that she was a psychologist. Even people with little or nothing to hide often became wary around shrinks, fearing that their every word or action had "deeper meanings."

She sighed, deciding that it was time to play housekeeper. As she headed upstairs, she heard his low voice coming from the study, still speaking in German, or whatever it was. He sounded as fluent in that language as he had in French.

LUCAS PUT DOWN THE PHONE and leaned back in his big leather desk chair. The call had been productive: a fifteenth-century bible chest had been located for his client. But at the moment he was too preoccupied to take more than a passing pleasure in that.

A psychologist! He chuckled softly at the irony of it. He knew that many people were uneasy around members of that profession, but he had more to hide than most of them. A lot more.

He thought about her previous work, and his mind began to drift, going back to a time when he had dealt with people in her field. He'd hated them all then, and hadn't thought about them since. Now, however, he could recall a few who had tried to be helpful and kind to a scared and confused kid.

Susan Trent was prying open the lid on feelings that both intrigued and scared him. That collision with her a little while ago had proved beyond a shadow of doubt that he wanted her. It had been all he could do to control himself then, and later, when they'd stood there looking over the map. She knew it, too. He was as good at reading body language as she probably was. And she didn't control her reactions as well as he did. A lot of tension had been humming away between them.

Under normal circumstances, he would have been happy
to let nature take its course. But these weren't normal circumstances. Still, she'd opened the door on her own secrets just a crack, by admitting her real profession. Lucas
drummed his fingertips restlessly on the desktop as he
considered the situation. One thing was certain: He wanted
to keep her close to him, and that in itself was unique in his
experience. He was not a man who craved closeness.

It would have aided his peace of mind to believe that it
was only because he wanted to learn why she had thrust
herself into his life, but he knew that wasn't the case.
Somehow he kept going back to that moment when he'd
discovered her in his garden—to how right it had felt that
she should be there in the midst of what he often thought
of as a symbol of his new life.

Even if she had opened up a bit to him, she was still being very cautious, and it was going to take time to get past
that wariness. Mary could return at any time, and then her
reason for being here would cease to exist. Of course, he
could see her after that, through the simple expedient of
asking for a date. But what if she refused? What if she just
slipped out of his life as quickly as she had come into it?

After some time, he got up and went to look for her and
found her in his bedroom. He walked in casually and sat
down on the bed, watching her as she polished the furniture. She turned and gave him a definitely wary smile. That
tension was humming away again, more powerfully this
time, because of the inherent intimacy of the scene. He
decided to play it very cautiously.

"I've been thinking about something," he said slowly.
"There's an apartment over the garage that's been empty
since I bought the house. The previous owners had a live-
in housekeeper, and I'd originally planned to find one, too.
But Mary has a home of her own and wasn't interested."

He was shocked at how tense he'd become, a sure indication of just how much he wanted her to agree to this. He hurried on, while she stood there uncertainly.

"I'm in the city a couple of nights a week, and I travel fairly often, as well. There's no major crime problem here, but I'd still feel better if I had someone here. Do you think you might be interested in taking the apartment?"

About halfway through his monologue, Susan began to realize what he must be getting at. When he'd walked into the room, she'd been certain that he was rather tense and she'd begun to steel herself for the inevitable confrontation about her identity, even as she'd silently prayed that it wouldn't come yet. She didn't want it to end this way; in fact, she didn't want it to end at all.

The apartment! She'd already seen it, although he didn't know that. Her mind spun crazily. Teddy's apartment was tiny, and she was sleeping on a sofa bed, with practically no space for her belongings. And if she got the job in Stamford, it would be only part-time for a while, which probably meant she would have to stay with Teddy even longer.

Oh, yes, indeed, it certainly made sense for her to accept his offer. There was no doubt about that. But there was also no doubt that she was taking a big risk, as well. And shouldn't she be suspicious? If he'd really wanted someone in that apartment, he could have rented it long ago.

"How much rent would you want?" she asked, trying to gain some more time to think.

He shrugged. "I'm more interested in having someone here. How does rent-free sound?"

"Are you serious?" Susan was stunned, and her suspicions were growing, even if they couldn't quite convince her to say no.

"I'm serious," he said with a smile. "Would you like to see it?"

They went outside and then through the door hidden behind the shrubbery. Sunlight was pouring in through a window at the top of the staircase, and she saw the faint marks in the dust where she'd failed to cover her tracks completely during her earlier, clandestine visit. But he apparently didn't notice them, since he merely commented on the dust, saying that no one had been in here since he'd moved in.

"It's not very large," he said as they reached the top and entered the small living room. "But it's fully furnished, and if you get that job in Stamford, it would certainly cut down on the commuting."

He walked over to the bedroom, and she followed him, still trying to decide what to do. Maybe he was just being generous. Maybe he had no ulterior motives at all. He certainly hadn't shown any interest in seducing her, and why would he make the offer if he knew she was here under false pretenses?

"I couldn't really rent it," he said as he looked around the bedroom. "There's a covenant in my deed that stipulates it can only be used by household employees or family members."

"But I won't be working for you when Mary returns," she pointed out, still struggling with her decision. How much of her eagerness to accept his offer was a desperate need for a place of her own, and how much was a desire to stay in his life?

"Can you cook?"

"Well, yes, of course. Actually, I'm rather good."

"Okay, then, you can cook for me a couple of times a week. Mary usually fixes something for me the days she's here, but the rest of the time I either eat out or I'm reduced to eating UFTs."

"UFTs?" she asked with a frown.

"Unidentifiable Frozen Things," he said, with a grin that softened the harsh planes of his face.

She laughed, watching as he ran a hand through his hair and shook his head ruefully.

"You know, it's pretty damned ridiculous that I haven't learned how to cook. My sister reminds me of that regularly. She got divorced about a year ago, and she said that if she can learn how to fix her own car, I could learn how to cook. But I've traveled all the time, and I've never really had a home before this one."

"Does your sister live around here?"

"No, she lives in Pennsylvania. If she were here, I could fix her car for her and she could cook for me, except that she'd probably find that too traditional. She's the director of a women's center, and she never misses an opportunity to let me know about my shortcomings."

"I see," Susan said with a smile. "She considers you to be a male chauvinist?"

He made a flip-flop motion with his hand and grinned again. "Borderline. She gives me a *C* for effort."

Abruptly his tone changed, and became more formal. "Well, what do you think? You don't have to let me know today, of course."

Entranced by that glimpse into a persona she hadn't seen before, Susan had been about to accept his offer. But with his retreat into formality, she, too, became more cautious.

"Let me think about it," she replied. "But it's really nice of you to make the offer."

"THEY HIRED ME on the spot!" Susan announced to Teddy the moment she returned from her interview. "Well, actually, they asked me to call back in an hour so they could check my references. So I went to lunch, then called them back, and they said the job's mine. I start next week.

"It's only twenty hours a week for now, but it'll be full-time beginning in September. And it's just the kind of job I wanted, too."

She kept pacing around Teddy's tiny office, unable to contain herself. The salary wasn't great, but the job was perfect. The director of the agency was giving her free rein to develop an after-school program for kids at risk.

"Congratulations," Teddy said sincerely. "Do you mind that it's not in the city?"

She shook her head. "I wanted to live and work here, but what I wanted most of all was a job I could really enjoy. Besides, Stamford isn't all that far away."

"Yeah, the commute shouldn't be too bad."

She stopped pacing and tried to gather her thoughts. She hadn't yet told Teddy about Lucas Andrews's offer, because she hadn't decided what to do about it. But now that she had the job, the decision seemed easier—part of a package, as it were. She knew, however, that Teddy wouldn't exactly see it that way.

"Actually, I have an apartment, too," she began. As she told him about it, his expression went from incredulity to a stubborn lack of acceptance, so she hastened to make her case, knowing as she did that she was trying to justify it to herself as much as to him.

"Teddy, it's perfect. Forget about who he is for a moment. I can't afford an apartment on a part-time salary, and this place is too small for both of us. Besides, Amanda will be home next week, and I can't imagine that you want a chaperone around."

"How am I supposed to forget who he is? How can *you* forget it?"

"We don't have one single bit of proof that he's anything other than what he says he is. Besides, if he's suspicious of me, or if he's engaged in criminal activities, why would he make such an offer? That wouldn't make sense."

Teddy had no answer to that, although it was clear that he wished he did. And as far as she was concerned, that was the deciding factor. Only a fool would invite someone to live in such close proximity if he suspected that person of deceit, and Lucas Andrews was no fool.

Susan had never been one to leave things to chance or fate, but she had begun to feel that this was all of a piece somehow... that each step from the time she'd agreed to help Teddy by spying on Lucas Andrews had led inexorably to the next step and the next.

WHEN SHE ARRIVED at his house on Monday morning, she found a note in his neat handwriting telling her that he'd be in the city for the next two days and giving the number at his apartment there. She called and caught him just as he was about to leave for an appointment. She told him quickly about the job and said that if the offer of the apartment was still open, she would accept.

He congratulated her on the job and assured her that the apartment was still hers. Then he startled her with a rather formal invitation.

"Would you allow me to take you to dinner to celebrate your new job? Since I'm in the city, we could make it tonight, if you're free. And I'd be happy to have your brother join us, as well."

"Oh, that's very kind of you," she replied, "but Teddy's wearing two casts at the moment, so I don't think he could come."

"I'll meet him another time, then. Have you been to Windows on the World?"

Susan knew where it was. She'd eaten a hot dog at the cafeteria in the other tower of the World Trade Center, but she quickly decided that the view must be much better if it was accompanied by fine food. She told him that, and he laughed.

"I think you'll like it. Give me your brother's address and I'll pick you up at seven."

After she had hung up, Susan danced around his kitchen for a while, laughing to herself. A new job, a new home, and a dinner date with an intriguing man! What more could she ask for?

Then she stopped abruptly, and her happiness drained away, to be replaced by a chill. Hadn't she told him that she was staying with a cousin, not her brother? She tried to remember. She should have written down her stories so that she could keep them straight.

Finally she decided she must have mentioned her brother this time and the cousin had been a previous story. Otherwise, how could he have known?

After she had done a few chores in the house, she set to work on the apartment. When she had rid the place of its accumulated layers of dust and pulled the covers off the furniture, she surveyed it critically and decided that it could really be quite charming once she'd added a few decorative touches.

Her concerns about Lucas Andrews and the tangled web of her lies were shoved to a back burner for the time being.

"TO YOUR NEW LIFE," Lucas said, raising his wineglass and touching it to hers. It was a subject he knew something about himself.

She gave him a radiant smile that transformed a pretty face into a truly beautiful one. Her happiness washed pleasantly over him. Despite her lies, he thought she was a wonderfully uncomplicated woman, and essentially very honest and open.

He had actually surprised himself when he'd made that offer of the apartment. It had been an impulsive gesture, and he had never been one to act on impulse. In fact, he'd almost regretted it for a time and had felt considerable relief when she seemed to be hesitating. Now, however, he was glad for his uncharacteristic behavior.

As he listened to her talk about the apartment and then about her job, it occurred to Lucas that finding out why she had thrust herself into his life was definitely taking a back seat to simply getting to know her. Not even the fact that she was a psychologist troubled him now, although it had certainly given him pause when she'd first told him. He'd tried to figure out how that could fit in with whatever her game was, but he'd been unable to make any connection.

Something in Susan Trent was reaching out to him, reaching deep inside him. He was almost ready to accept her appearance in his life as nothing more than the act of a kindly fate.

"I'm sorry to be rambling on like this," she said, drawing him out of his reverie. "But it's just that everything seems to be falling into place so perfectly. A job I'm going to love. A place to live."

She hesitated after that, and he saw a faint flush creep through her fair skin. What had she been about to say? That he, too, was part of it?

"It happens that way sometimes, doesn't it?" he said into the small silence. "Everything seems to be going wrong, then you make one different move, and suddenly it all goes right."

She nodded, meeting his gaze across the small table for a moment, then lowering her eyes beneath long lashes. He nearly reached out to her, holding back at the last possible moment as he forced himself to remember the barriers between them: her lies and his own.

As they ate, she asked him about his travels—places he'd liked, and those he hadn't. She'd never been to Europe, she told him, and her questions seemed innocent of any hidden agenda. So he gave her a carefully edited version of his travels, all the while waiting for any hint that she was trying to pry the lid off his past.

The secrets between them held a certain allure, he thought, but it was an allure he could have done without. There was already seduction in the atmosphere, enough to make him think briefly about other nights and other women, when the outcome had been far more certain.

But none of those memories could hold his thoughts for long as he watched her struggle with her attraction to him. She was far less capable of hiding it than he was, and that knowledge made him feel old and cynical.

She mentioned her brother in passing, and he smiled to himself, thinking that she must not have realized that he shouldn't even know about him. The invitation he'd extended to include him tonight hadn't been a calculated ploy; he'd gotten mixed up, too. He was certainly going to have to be more careful in the future.

Lucas sensed that one wrong move on his part would send her out of his life, the apartment notwithstanding. He would simply have to bide his time until she was ready to tell him the truth. But he thought that time might not be far off.

They left the restaurant and rode alone in the elevator. Her closeness was torment. Instead of dropping her at her brother's apartment, he wanted to take her to his. But he'd promised himself that he'd go slowly and not give her any excuse to bolt from his life.

His hand rested lightly against her back as he ushered her from the elevator, and he could feel her sudden intake of breath. So he wasn't the only one thinking about the possible ending to this evening.

All the way uptown, he thought about ways to prolong his time with her. There was a small, quiet bar near his building. It could be an intermediate step. The apartment had a great view of the Fifty-ninth Street Bridge, and she'd already mentioned that she loved the city's many bridges.

He could easily envision them there now, with all the lights off so that they could enjoy the sight beyond the windows. He could even hear the soft whisper of her dress as it slid to the floor. But he drove her back to her brother's instead, helped her from the car and held her hand just a little too long, then watched as she disappeared into the building. There was no invitation to come inside, and Lucas wondered if she might be keeping secrets from her brother, as well.

ON A BRIGHT, warm Saturday morning, Susan pulled into the driveway of her new home, her car loaded down with her possessions. Lucas had told her he would be home in the morning, and only on the way up here had she suddenly realized that Natalie Kroft might well be here, too.

She'd somehow managed to push all thoughts of his fiancée from her mind, and now that she was forced to think about her again, she was amazed at how easily she had done that. But the more she got to know him, the less she could imagine him with Natalie.

Wishful thinking, she told herself disgustedly as she got out of her car and peered into the double garage, fully expecting to find a second car there. When she didn't, she realized that Natalie might not even have a car; many people who lived in the city didn't. Still, that empty space gave her hope. Maybe Teddy's report had ended their engagement. More wishful thinking. She was certainly living in cloud-cuckoo-land today.

She rang the doorbell, but there was no response. Her mind began to conjure up some very unwilling images of the two of them in his big bed. She dug out her key determinedly. He knew she was coming this morning, and she was right on time. Besides, she didn't have the key to the apartment.

She opened the front door, calling out to him while she fought down those persistent images. There was no response. She stepped hesitantly into the house.

"I thought I heard you drive up," a voice said from behind her. "I was out in the garden."

She turned to find him standing in the doorway, wearing gym shorts and a T-shirt and looking so sexy that visions of Natalie dissolved into imaginings of another sort.

He got the key, then helped her carry her things up to the apartment. Then he asked if there was anything she needed.

"I thought I might get some plants," she told him. "Would you mind if I put some hooks in front of the windows?"

"Do you know how to put them up?"

"Uh, no. But I'm sure I can figure it out. Will I need a drill?"

"You will, and I have one." He cocked his head to one side and grinned at her. "If I offer to put them up for you, am I going to get a lecture about male chauvinism?"

She shook her head. "No, I'm perfectly willing to admit that I'm a real klutz when it comes to tools. You may get a lecture at some point, but it won't be over that."

His dark eyes gleamed wickedly. "So you choose your battles carefully?"

She nodded, returning the look measure for measure. "Yes. It's too hard on my ego otherwise."

He told her that he had some plant hooks and would put them up now. As soon as he had gone, Susan began to unpack. But his comment about choosing her battles carefully remained in her mind. Had there been a hint of a double meaning there, something in his tone that suggested he already knew she had chosen unwisely in the past?

Once again she considered, then discarded, the possibility that he'd seen through her charade from the beginning. But something about that exchange troubled her; it seemed out of character for him. He just didn't seem like the type to engage in standard male-female bantering.

He returned a few minutes later and put up the hooks. She commented that she would have thought Saturdays would be a busy time at the shop for him.

"They're busy in terms of traffic," he told her as he climbed down the ladder, "but not that good for sales. Shops that sell less expensive things tend to do better on weekends. I'll go in soon, but if I spend the entire day there on weekends, my patience begins to wear pretty thin."

She almost commented that, from what she'd seen, he was very good with customers. But just as she opened her mouth, she remembered that *she* hadn't seen him with customers, Susan Todd had. He folded the ladder and started to leave. She thanked him distractedly as she wondered how many more near misses she'd have before she really blew it.

A half hour later, while she was examining the living room drapes and trying to decide if she should replace them, he drove off. Her thoughts returned to his fiancée.

Since both of them had shops, perhaps they didn't see each other on weekends. That made sense, she thought, although she wished it didn't.

It didn't take her long to finish her unpacking, and after that she drew up a shopping list, then ran down the stairs, eager to get on with the business of making the apartment hers. Just as she opened the door at the bottom, a large English sheepdog came bounding around the corner, followed by a woman's exasperated voice calling, "Reggie! Get back here!"

Susan bent down to pet him as an attractive blond woman appeared, clearly surprised to see her. Susan introduced herself as Lucas's part-time cook and new tenant. The woman turned out to be his nearest neighbor. Her name was Barbara Hunt.

"I'd forgotten all about the apartment," she commented. "It's been empty since Lucas bought the house. Since he's away so often, he must be happy to have someone here."

Then she explained that she'd come over to borrow some lawn chairs that Lucas was lending her for a cookout the next day. They found the chairs stacked in the garage, and Susan offered to help her carry them back to her house.

As they walked down the street, Barbara began to ask some pointed, if subtle, questions about how Susan happened to be here. Remembering Lucas's remark about the restrictive covenants in his deed regarding the use of the apartment, Susan gave her the same story she'd given Lucas, emphasizing that she was working for him.

"So you're a psychologist? How interesting. The Handelmans, just down the street, are both psychologists. Why don't you come to the cookout tomorrow and meet them and the other neighbors?"

Susan hesitated briefly, uncertain how Lucas would feel about that. Her status in this neighborhood was a bit unusual, although Barbara certainly seemed to accept her presence. She wondered, too, if Natalie would be coming. It might be interesting to see the two of them together; maybe it would even help her get over her hopeless attraction to him.

Barbara apparently noticed her hesitation. "Oh, for heaven's sake, Sherri. I'm sure Lucas won't mind."

Susan thanked her and accepted the invitation. They carried the chairs around to Barbara's lovely yard. Flowers bloomed in profusion in free-form beds, and a large pool, complete with cabana, helped create an atmosphere straight out of *Architectural Digest*.

"Are you interested in Lucas?" Barbara asked suddenly, then smiled self-deprecatingly. "I'm sorry. That's awfully nosy of me. It's just that I've already introduced him to every single woman I know, but he doesn't seem interested. I've given up."

"Um, well, I really don't know him all that well," Susan responded. Didn't she know about Natalie? What was going on here? "Besides," she added, "I thought he was already involved with someone."

Barbara's surprise mirrored that of the antiques dealer Susan had questioned earlier. "Well, if he is, he's certainly keeping her a secret. He didn't say anything about bringing a guest tomorrow. We see him fairly often socially, and he's never brought anyone."

"Perhaps I was mistaken, then. As I said, I don't really know him very well."

"He's awfully attractive, though, don't you think?" Barbara persisted. "There's something rather...mysterious about him."

Susan tried to hide her surprise. "Really? In what way?" she asked in a casual tone as she helped Barbara unfold the chairs and arrange them.

"Oh, I don't know." She waved an arm negligently. "Just an aura about him."

Susan could tell that she was slightly embarrassed, so she dropped the subject. It occurred to her that Barbara might be entertaining some fantasies of her own about her neighbor.

She smiled to herself as she walked back to Lucas's house. So she wasn't alone in finding him mysterious. And it wasn't likely that Barbara knew what she herself knew about him, so her opinion wouldn't be tainted by that.

As she drove off to do her shopping, Susan thought again about Natalie Kroft. It was strange indeed that Lucas's neighbors knew nothing about his engagement. A suspicion began to form in her mind. It was helped along, no doubt, by her desire to make it the truth. What if Natalie had lied about her relationship with him? She had seemed to know so little about him, and even Teddy had thought that a bit strange.

It seemed that she might now have *two* mysteries on her hands.

SUSAN WAS UNCOMFORTABLE, and wished that she'd declined the invitation to the cookout. But it simply hadn't occurred to her that in coming here she would be forced to spread her lies even farther. That unpleasant reality had struck her as her hostess introduced her to the Handelmans, the neighborhood's husband-and-wife team of psychologists.

She breathed a quiet sigh of relief when she learned that their practice was in Danbury, not Stamford, where she worked, but she was still concerned about the possibility of future problems there. She certainly could not afford to let her lies affect her professional life.

As she circulated among the guests, Susan couldn't help feeling that there was a huge arrow suspended over her head, with LIAR written in bold letters on it. What had begun as an innocent adventure was rapidly becoming a colossal blunder, and she had no one to blame but herself.

The other source of her discomfort was the result of her arrival at the party with Lucas. This morning, while she was still shambling around the apartment in her raggedy old terry robe, he had appeared at her door to ask her if she wanted to come to the cookout with him. He said he'd forgotten about it until he had come home and noticed the chairs were gone. Clutching the ends of her robe together and wondering if she could possibly look as bad as she thought she did, she'd explained that she had already been invited.

So they'd come to the party together, and it was clear to her that the other guests viewed them as a couple. This seemed not to bother Lucas at all, although she was beginning to think that her ability to read his moods was virtually nonexistent.

That it *did* bother her was probably the result of her newfound punctiliousness about honesty. She stayed as far away from him as possible, hoping to dispel that impression. It soon developed, however, that she was not to be permitted even this minor attempt at belated honesty.

Lucas managed to catch her alone. "Sherri, are you uncomfortable about being here?"

She was startled, both by his sudden appearance when she'd been avoiding him and by his question. It made her wonder if she'd been transmitting her thoughts to one and all.

"No, of course not," she said, too quickly. "Why should I be?"

"You shouldn't be, but you seem to be avoiding me, so I thought maybe you were uncomfortable."

Remembering her vow of honesty, she said, "Well, I just didn't want to create the wrong impression . . . about us, I mean."

"I see," he said as a smile curved its way into his mustache. "Well, actually, you could be doing me a favor. There aren't many single men around here, it seems, and I've found myself in some, uh, difficult situations in the past."

Susan liked the direction this conversation was taking now, although she was certainly aware of the possible pitfalls.

She returned his smile. "Yes, Barbara mentioned yesterday that she's introduced you to every single woman she knows, with no apparent success." Growing even bolder, she went on. "Does that mean you're just being very selective, or is there already someone in your life?"

"There isn't anyone," he said, meeting her gaze levelly.

Several other people joined them then, and Susan let the conversation flow around her. Even though she'd already admitted to herself that the man was impossible to read, and even though she'd already half suspected that Natalie Kroft was lying, she still found it difficult to completely accept. Why on earth would the woman lie? And why would she be willing to spend so much money to gain information about him?

Later, they walked home in the velvet darkness under starlit skies, serenaded by spring peepers. In the magic of such a night, it was too easy for Susan to drift off into a make-believe world in which the man at her side was far more than an employer and landlord.

Suddenly several large, dark shapes leapt out of the woods onto the road just ahead of them. Susan gasped and turned to him.

"Deer," he said in a low voice, just as she identified them herself. His arm came quickly around her waist, lingered for a warm moment, then dropped away as she laughed in embarrassment.

"I'm sorry. It isn't as though I haven't seen them before. But I'd never seen them up here."

"There are quite a few of them," he said as the deer disappeared into the woods again. "That's why I put a fence around the garden."

He went on to talk of neighbors who'd lost shrubbery and gardens to them, but she barely heard him, because she was still lost in the sensuality of that moment when he'd held her. How easily she'd turned to him, and how naturally his arm had come around her! For that moment, it had seemed to be part of the magic of the night.

That magic lingered even after they'd said good-night in the driveway and gone their separate ways. It seemed to her that each moment she spent with him drew her ever deeper into something both wonderful and dangerous, something wholly new.

But the situation was impossible, and it was unlikely to improve with time. There were just too many lies between them. He had lied about his past, and she was lying about her present . . . and that didn't augur well for any future.

Chapter Five

By the end of her first full week of work, Susan was feeling well pleased with herself. The disorientation that always accompanied a new job had worn off, thanks to a friendly, supportive staff and a heavy work load. She had worked more hours than she would be paid for at present, but the challenge of developing the program was more than adequate compensation for that, especially since she knew she would be working full-time soon.

She had seen little of Lucas during the week. He had gone to the city on Monday and hadn't returned until late Wednesday evening, rekindling her thoughts of Natalie Kroft.

On Thursday, she'd come home early and fixed dinner for them both, her mother's favorite chicken casserole. The kitchen in the apartment was barely adequate, so she'd prepared it in his kitchen, then left it for him, after taking a portion for herself. With the continuing mystery of Lucas's past now compounded by the mystery of Natalie Kroft's involvement with him, Susan had decided rather belatedly that it was time to extricate herself as much as possible from his life.

It was, she thought, a classic case of not being able to see the forest for the trees. She had become so enmeshed in his life and so seduced by the man himself that she had lost all objectivity. Teddy had been right. It was past time for her to back off a bit, and the fact that she was now deeply involved in her work made it much easier.

Lucas had called her later that evening. Her phone had now been installed, so there were no more unexpected knocks at her door. He'd complimented her on the dinner, then informed her that he had a dinner engagement the following evening and could manage for himself over the weekend.

Susan had hung up, feeling hurt. He'd been pleasant enough, but she'd thought he seemed rather distant. It didn't matter that she herself had decided their relationship should be kept on a more formal footing. She'd wondered what he'd meant by "dinner engagement." Was that his euphemism for a date? Or was it business-related? When he came home the next evening shortly before nine o'clock, she felt more relieved than she should have.

On Saturday morning, she decided to go shopping for a work wardrobe. She'd put off this expedition, partly because she disliked shopping in general, and partly because she had needed to see what was acceptable office attire. Fortunately, the office was quite casual, which meant that she didn't have to spend her limited resources on expensive suits.

If she disliked shopping in general, she hated shopping in giant malls in particular, so she chose instead to go downtown. In her teens she'd been as much of a "mall rat" as her peers, but now she preferred the charm of smaller stores.

Shortly before noon, she was walking down Main Street, burdened with the results of her shopping and trying to decide if she should go back to that last shop and buy a hand-crocheted cotton sweater she'd passed up because of its price. Her pleasure at her self-control was rapidly giving way to the greater pleasure that owning the sweater promised. With her thoughts thus occupied, she was slow to notice the dark green Mercedes as it passed by.

When she finally did spot it, she stopped on the sidewalk and stared. It was definitely Lucas, and there was someone with him. If it hadn't been for the slow-moving traffic, she might never have seen them at all. But, as it happened, she caught a quick glimpse of a sleek, dark head that she was instantly certain belonged to Natalie Kroft.

They drove on, and she belatedly realized that she was causing a minor pedestrian traffic jam as she stood there in the middle of the sidewalk. So she hurried on to her car, the sweater now forgotten.

Susan tried to tell herself that it could have been anyone with him, but the attempt failed miserably. She *knew* it was Natalie. And now she knew that Lucas had lied again.

She'd spoken to Teddy earlier in the week about her suspicions that Natalie had lied about her involvement with Lucas, but in response Teddy had raised the question she had already asked herself and could not answer. Why would Natalie have spent so much money having him investigated if she wasn't involved with him? Then Teddy had reminded her that they already knew that Lucas had lied, making it very likely that he was simply lying again.

Susan tossed her purchases into the trunk, then got into her car. She pulled out and began to drive about aimlessly. No wonder he'd said he could manage for himself over the weekend. He would have Natalie to cook for him. But why hadn't he just said that he was having company? Not that he was accountable to her for his social life, but he'd certainly been forthcoming about it up to this point.

She thought about driving down to the city to stay with Teddy for the weekend, then remembered that Amanda was back in town and he was spending the weekend with her, having just been set free from his casts.

There was nowhere for her to go. For the first time since coming here, Susan felt totally alone. There were several women at the office who were potential friends, but she couldn't think of presuming on those budding friendships just yet. But how could she go back to her apartment, knowing that sooner or later he would show up with Natalie?

Jealousy over a man was something Susan had never felt before, and she was appalled at experiencing it now. But then she knew that jealousy wasn't the *real* problem. The real problem was that she'd allowed herself to fall for a man she'd known from the beginning was a liar and possibly even worse. She, who supposedly knew so much about the workings of the mind and the emotions, had behaved as foolishly as anyone else. Maybe Teddy was right; maybe she *was* going through a long-delayed adolescence.

She found herself on Route 7 and made a quick decision to go down to Stamford and visit the Town Center shopping mall. Being surrounded by anonymous crowds seemed definitely preferable to returning to her apartment. She continued on even as it occurred to her that she was showing still more signs of retreating into adolescence.

LUCAS WAS SITTING on the darkened terrace, nursing his second Scotch, when he heard her pull into the driveway. He was always careful about his drinking, mindful of his father's legacy and also of the fact that alcohol loosened tongues, something he'd never been able to afford in his business. Or rather his *former* business. Tonight was one of those times when his past and his present seemed perilously intertwined.

When he heard her pull in, he set down the drink and started to get up, then sank back into the chaise and glanced at his watch. Only 9:15—too early, he thought, with an inordinate amount of pleasure, for her to be returning from a date. Unless, of course, she had someone with her. He listened, then smiled with satisfaction when he heard only one car door slam.

His plan had been to find some excuse to talk to her when he returned from the shop, then casually suggest that they go out to dinner. An invitation to dinner to celebrate her job was one thing, but a formal request for a dinner date was quite another. Her remarks at the cookout seemed to suggest that she was taking her "employment" with him far too seriously, so he knew he had to be careful.

In the silence he heard her open and then close the door to her apartment. Then it opened again a moment later, and his hopes soared. She must be coming to see him. He listened for the sound of the doorbell, but what he heard instead was the sound of a car trunk being closed. She must have been shopping. The door to the apartment closed again, and all was silence.

He wondered if he'd made a mistake in offering her the apartment. At the time, it had seemed like the perfect way to keep her here until he could pry the truth out of her. Or at least that was the excuse he'd given himself. Now, however, he was beginning to see the arrangement as sheer torment.

Lucas sank lower in the chaise and sipped his Scotch slowly. It irritated him to have so damned many questions and no answers. He'd read enough psychology to know that he was a control freak, one of those people who had to know everything that was going on around him in order to exercise complete control over his life.

Now it seemed that too much had slipped from his control. He didn't know what the hell was going on, and, worse still, he didn't know how to find the answers and regain that control.

Furthermore, things had become even more confusing when Natalie Kroft had suddenly reappeared today. He grimaced as he thought about her showing up just before noon at the shop, claiming to be visiting some friends in the area.

His curiosity had led him to invite her to lunch, which in retrospect appeared to have been a mistake, since it had undoubtedly encouraged her to believe that he was interested in her. At the time, however, he had thought that he might gain some information that would explain Susan.

But he hadn't learned a damned thing. If there was a connection between Natalie and Susan, he hadn't found it, and he was beginning to doubt that it existed. He tended to doubt coincidences, but perhaps in this case, that was all it was.

He finished his drink, listening to the subtle sounds of the night. His mind drifted between Susan and his past. He'd been wrong to believe there was no connection. It was there, all right. Not that she herself was connected to that past, but her presence in his life brought it uncomfortably close to the surface for him. He'd carefully constructed his new life, and just as carefully locked away his past, but now his dreams were expanding, changing, and that part of him he'd always believed to be invulnerable was being threatened by Susan Trent.

SUSAN WAS AWAKENED by the sound of the garage door beneath the apartment opening, and then his car starting.

She jumped from the bed and dashed to the living room windows, then peeked out cautiously between the drapes just as he began to back down the driveway. He was alone in the car. That meant that dear Natalie must still be in the house, perhaps lingering in bed after a night ...

No, dammit, she wasn't going to torment herself with those images anymore. Lucas Andrews was nothing more than an attractive man with a mysterious past and questionable taste in women. He'd been kind to her, for whatever reason, and she was grateful for that. She would stay here until she could find a suitable place to live, and then she'd get on with her life and let him slip away into her memory, to be looked back on someday as a minor figure in her personal history. She'd probably even enjoy telling the story to new friends someday.

She went back to the bedroom and glanced at the clock, surprised to see how late it was. She'd slept much later than usual, thanks to the emotional torments she'd subjected herself to. He was probably headed to his shop.

That meant that Natalie would probably be lurking about the place all day. Susan wondered if Lucas had mentioned her presence. A mischievous smile curved her lips. Jealousy could work both ways, couldn't it?

She stripped off her nightshirt and put on shorts and a T-shirt, then laced up her sneakers. She preferred bicycling to running, but since she hadn't been able to bring her bike with her, she had settled for running until she could get a new one.

The morning was comfortably cool, with the sun temporarily obscured by high, thin clouds that were slowly melting away. Along her regular route, she ran into several neighbors out walking, running or cycling. She liked being part of a neighborhood again; it was something she'd missed during her weeks in Manhattan.

"It's better sometimes when you don't get to touch your dream." She frowned, wondering where that had come from. An old song, she thought, then abruptly recalled that it was from Harry Chapin's "Sequel to Taxi," an old favorite.

She slowed her pace. How long had she dreamed of coming to New York, only to end up here? And what about her fantasies regarding Lucas Andrews—now gone, as well?

But she *did* have a job she liked, and that would sustain her. As far as the city was concerned, she could still visit it any time she wanted. And as to Lucas Andrews, well, he had just been a mistake, that was all.

By the time she got back to the house, the last of the wispy clouds had vanished and the sun was gloriously bright. It would be a good day to work on her tan—carefully, of course. And with Lucas gone for the day, there was no reason why she couldn't use his terrace, was there? The yard on her side was in shade, and how was she to know that he had company, when he hadn't seen fit to mention it?

Ah, yes, there was definitely some evil lurking in her thoughts, and more than a little resentment of Lucas for having lied to her. If she couldn't confront him with the full extent of his lies, she could certainly gain *some* satisfaction. Never mind the fact that she had lied to him, as well.

She showered and ate breakfast, then put on the bikini she'd bought the day before. She'd told herself that it would be perfect for sunbathing, but the truth was that she also knew it looked very good on her. She'd even fantasized a bit about Lucas discovering her on his terrace.

Now, instead, she thought about Natalie Kroft discovering her, and grinned shamelessly. She spared only a moment in self-recrimination over her cattiness, then put the bikini on, grabbed a towel and her sunscreen and ran down the stairs.

There seemed to be no sign of life from within the house. Could Natalie still be in bed? Susan stretched out on a chaise, expecting to see Natalie appear at any moment and demand to know who she was.

But when she had allowed herself as much sun as she dared and Natalie still hadn't appeared, Susan began to wonder if she could have been wrong. She was still sure it was Natalie she'd seen with Lucas yesterday, but perhaps she hadn't stayed over.

She went back up to the apartment, took another shower and put on a light cotton sundress. She had to know if the woman was here, so she sat down and composed a menu for the upcoming week. Lucas hadn't asked for one, and had in fact told her that he ate anything and everything. But it provided an excellent excuse for her to be in his house.

Clutching the menu, she let herself in through the kitchen door, still expecting Natalie to be there, probably wearing the little smile of someone who has just spent a very pleasant night. But the kitchen was empty, and there were no sounds in the house. She left the menu on the counter, then crept softly toward the front of the house and paused to listen once again. Surely, if she was here, she'd be awake by now. With all the nervous energy Natalie exuded, she couldn't possibly be the type who would spend the day in bed.

Finally Susan went upstairs. His bedroom was empty, and the bed was neatly made. She peeked into the master bath and saw only one damp towel. A lingering trace of his cologne teased her nostrils pleasantly and set her nerve endings to quivering almost as much as his presence did.

She stood there smiling. So she'd been wrong, after all. Could she also have been wrong about yesterday? No. The fact remained that he'd been with Natalie yesterday. It would be foolish for her to pretend he was innocent in this, and she'd promised herself there would be no more such foolishness.

She left the house by the front door. As she was crossing the driveway, she heard someone calling her, and she froze, thinking irrationally that it must be Natalie. But then she saw her neighbor and former hostess, Barbara, approaching on a bicycle. Susan walked down the driveway to meet her and was invited over for a swim.

She thanked Barbara and accepted with pleasure. Then, as she was about to open the door to her apartment, she heard a car pull into the driveway and screech to a halt. She stepped around the corner to see two police officers with their guns drawn! The alarm system! She'd forgotten about it again.

They demanded to know who she was, and she almost gave her real name, then caught herself just in time and quickly explained the situation. The one officer asked her for identification, sending shards of ice through her. But the other one suggested they go into the house and call Lucas.

"If he's at his shop, the dispatcher will have contacted him by now," he explained. "And the alarm needs to be reset."

Susan hurried to let them into the house before they could ask her for identification again. She quickly reset the alarm, then led them to Lucas's study, so that they could call him. She could only hope they would think her nervousness was the result of fear that Lucas would be angry with her.

"Let me talk to him," Susan requested after one of the officers had spoken with Lucas and confirmed that she was who she said she was. She felt she had to give some explanation for her behavior.

"Lucas? I'm really sorry. I came in the back door just to leave a menu for you, and I completely forgot about the alarm system."

His response was both amused and soothing. "Sherri, it's all right. I'm sorry if they scared you. And thanks for the menu, even though it wasn't necessary."

A few minutes later, she watched the patrol car drive away and breathed a sigh of relief. What if they'd been unable to reach Lucas? Once they'd seen the discrepancy between the name she'd given and her license, it would have been all over for her. At the very least, Lucas would have found out.

She wondered just how much longer she could keep up this deceit before she made that fatal error that brought it all crashing down upon her.

WHEN THE DOORBELL RANG, Susan was bent over with her head in the refrigerator, trying to decide what to have for dinner. The sudden, shrill sound startled her. She'd spent most of the afternoon at Barbara's swimming pool and was still wearing her damp bikini. A belated realization of her scanty attire, combined with the certainty that her visitor must be Lucas, brought her to a halt halfway down the stairs. She was poised to run back up again and find something to cover herself when the bell rang again. She went down and opened the door.

He was just returning from the shop and was dressed in one of his conservative suits, and as a result she felt positively naked. But if she'd originally bought the suit with the notion of impressing him with her charms, it obviously wasn't working. Not a flicker of interest showed in his dark eyes; she might as well have been wearing a full-length flour sack.

"You must have been swimming at Barbara's," he said, proving that at least he'd noticed she was wearing a swimsuit.

She nodded. "It's nice to have a neighbor with a pool."

"Actually, you might have one even closer. I've been thinking about putting one in myself. I have a builder coming next week to discuss it."

"Oh? That would be great!" She gestured upstairs. "Would you like to come up and see what I've done with the place?"

He followed her up the stairs and seemed genuinely impressed with the small efforts she'd made thus far. She found his presence in her home unnerving now that she'd truly made it hers, and she also found his apparent lack of interest in her annoying. She certainly didn't think of herself as being an outstanding beauty, but she knew that men always found her attractive. Thoughts of Natalie Kroft intruded once again, reminding her of the alarm disaster. She repeated her apology, but he waved it aside.

"Actually, I was more concerned about you. You sounded scared to death when I talked to you earlier."

How right you are, she thought, even if you don't know why.

"Well, I was on my way back up here when they arrived, and when I walked around to the driveway, there they were, with their guns drawn and pointing at me."

He chuckled. "Don't worry. I would have bailed you out."

Maybe not, if they told you I was a fake, she thought, but all she said was a dry "Thanks."

"I, uh, stopped by to see if you had any plans for dinner," he said. "I have some steaks, and I do know how to use a grill."

Susan was startled to realize that he actually sounded rather nervous. Surely it must be her imagination.

"That would be nice. Thank you. I can bake some potatoes and make a salad."

He told her he'd see her later, then left, rather hurriedly, she thought. When the door closed behind him, she frowned thoughtfully. He *was* nervous. How very interesting. But that scarcely gave her any advantage in this game, since his presence unnerved *her*. And if this was to be a battle of nerves, she had no doubt at all that he would be the winner.

She showered quickly, then put on a comfortable strapless sundress in a coral shade that showed off her golden tan, telling herself, of course, that she was dressing for comfort, not for seduction. Then she put together a salad and took out some potatoes to be baked in his microwave.

She found him on the terrace, dressed casually now in an open-necked silk shirt and loose cotton slacks that had a European look to them. Lucas, she'd noticed—both from his appearance and from her investigation of his closet that time—tended to dress with a certain elegance that seemed rather at odds with his rugged appearance.

And once again he seemed not to notice *her* appearance. What would it take? she wondered. Should she show up naked sometime?

He fixed drinks for them at a rolling bar cart, then began to talk about his plans for the pool.

"It's probably going to mean taking down some trees, but I'm hoping they can design one that will fit into that space over there." He indicated the far side of the big yard.

"With all these woods around, that seems like a small sacrifice," she commented. "How long will it take to put it in?"

"Probably no more than a few weeks." He gave her an amused look. "Would it be fair to say that you like the idea?"

She felt somewhat embarrassed, because she was already imagining the pleasure of having her own pool. But it wasn't hers, and she rather belatedly reminded herself of that little fact.

"Of course I like the idea, but I wouldn't want to intrude upon your privacy."

"You won't be. Feel free to use it anytime."

They were standing side by side at the edge of the terrace, and she turned to thank him. But the words were caught in her throat. His expression quickly became unreadable, but not quite quickly enough. In that moment when she first turned, she caught his gaze on the top of her sundress, where gentle swells of golden skin gleamed in the lowering sun. And something of what he was feeling remained in his eyes for just a moment when he raised his gaze to meet hers.

Susan felt a voluptuous rush of heat that owed nothing to the warmth of the day. Maybe it was only because he'd hidden his desire so well before, but she felt somehow transformed by this unmistakable evidence of that desire. She was totally, achingly aware of her body, of the heated flesh chafing against the confinement of her clothing.

Her mind ran through all the arguments against letting herself feel this way: Natalie Kroft, her own deceit, his dark past...and perhaps even his present. But all of it was burned away in an instant by the flames of passion that crackled and roared through her.

That brief, unguarded moment seemed to have set the tone for the evening. Social conversation came easily to them both, and only those skills prevented the silences from lengthening to an unbearable tension. Even so, words seemed often to hang suspended between them in an atmosphere laden with the unspoken.

Susan was conscious of her every word and movement. He often used gestures to accompany his words, a habit picked up in Europe, she supposed, like his wardrobe, and her gaze was drawn again and again to his strong, long-fingered hands, with their light sprinkling of red-gold hairs.

After dinner, they carried things into the kitchen, and what had once seemed like more than adequate work space for two now became cramped by her aching awareness of him. She was actually thinking about thanking him for dinner and escaping to the lonely safety of her apartment when he suggested after-dinner drinks on the terrace.

In the soft darkness, their families quickly became a safe topic of conversation. He told her that his sister and her five-year-old son would be visiting him next weekend. Susan was pleased at the possibility of meeting her, and also couldn't help seeing it as an opportunity to learn more about him.

Lost in these thoughts, she failed to react right away to his question about her brother.

"He's a comedian," she replied. "He's really talented, but he's finding it hard to break into the business in New York."

And even as the words left her mouth, an icy fear was creeping through her. Had she told him about Teddy? She must have. She thought she could even recall the conversation, but hadn't that been when she was Susan Todd, the journalist?

Her blood turned to ice water. The lies were getting all mixed up again. She couldn't remember what she'd told him, or who she'd been.

"New York is the world's toughest market," he commented. "Like the song says, if you can make it there, you can make it anywhere."

"Yes, that's why Teddy decided to come here." She began to relax a bit. Obviously she'd made it through yet another potential disaster.

"I suppose he must do something else then, too?"

"Um, yes. He works for a friend who has a computer business. I'm not really sure what he does. Computers and I are barely on speaking terms."

"I noticed those pictures in your apartment," he went on, in the same casual tone. "So you've done some acting yourself?"

Oh, God! Why had she put them up? How could she have been so dumb? But they were on the wall in the bedroom, and he'd only glanced in there.

"Yes," she said quickly. "But it was strictly amateur stuff. I'm not really very good, and I never got the roles I wanted."

"What do you mean?"

"Well, I wanted serious dramatic roles, but I always ended up playing the ingenue—someone's kid sister, or the leading lady's best friend."

He smiled at her. "Your nose and eyes."

She nodded and twisted her mouth wryly. She was glad that they'd moved away from the subject of Teddy, but not at all happy to hear him refer to the two features she'd been unable to disguise.

"Has your brother been up to visit you yet?" he asked.

"No, not yet. He had an accident and was in casts, but he just got them off a few days ago." Panic was nibbling away at her again. Had she said that about her nonexistent cousin, the one she had supposedly been staying with?

"I'm sure he'll be up soon," she went on. "Along with his bra-model girlfriend."

"Bra model?" Lucas threw back his head and laughed, then made a placating gesture. "I'm sorry. I didn't mean to be insulting, but . . ."

She laughed, too, having thrown that in in a desperate attempt to change the subject. "You should have heard me when he told me. Actually, she's graduated to modeling sportswear now."

He nodded with mock solemnity. "That seems like a career advancement."

Their shared laughter allowed her panic to recede once more. Either she hadn't mixed up her stories, or he'd simply failed to notice.

"Teddy and I are only a year and a half apart in age, and we used to do comedy routines when we were just kids. We'd stage plays for everyone in the neighborhood. We even studied magic. I was never very good at doing tricks, but Teddy is.

"You see, both our parents were frustrated show-business types. Dad had always wanted to be a comedian, and Mom had done some acting. Then they got married and had us, and that was the end of those dreams. But they always encouraged us. In fact, I think they were just a bit disappointed when I decided to become a psychologist instead."

"It sounds as though you have an interesting family," he commented.

She nodded, lost in thoughts of her childhood. "Our house was always filled with friends. Some of them liked our home better than their own. When I look back at it now, I think we were a lot more interesting than most TV sitcoms.''

He was silent for a time, and she began to feel guilty. She knew that he must be making comparisons with his own sad childhood, and she didn't want to cause him pain.

''We were lucky,'' she said finally. ''I know that not many kids grow up with all that we had.''

She waited in a tense silence, hoping he might say something to open the subject of his own family. But instead he finally asked how her job was doing.

So she told him about it, knowing they were still treading on difficult territory. The program she was developing was for kids much like the boy he had once been.

''What we'll try to do is to give them the support and the skills they'll need to cope with their families, because if they don't get that help now, they'll carry those scars into adulthood.''

He merely nodded, but she thought she could feel a subtle shift in the atmosphere. Of course, it might have been nothing more than her awareness of how he might be feeling. He asked her if she'd like a refill, and she declined, telling him instead that she had some work-related reading to do. It was true enough, but it was also true that she had succeeded in driving away the sensual tension that had existed between them. And now, in its aftermath, she knew just how dangerous it had been.

She stood up, thanking him for dinner, and he stood, too. The terrace was dark, illuminated only by the light from inside the house. Susan hesitated, knowing she should leave, but wanting to stay. The desire she had only a moment ago declared to have fled now came rushing back with a force that actually made her tremble.

How it happened, she could not have said, not at that moment and not even later, when she relived it endlessly.

One moment they were simply standing there, a few feet apart, and in the next moment she was in his arms. There seemed to have been no subtle signals, no slow, cautious movements. One moment blinked to the next, and flames were roaring in her ears.

His arms encircled her as though they'd been there forever, her hands were clutching the taut muscles of his shoulders and their mouths were on each other with a devouring passion.

She strained against him, and he lifted his hands, threading them through her curls and holding her head in a gentle vise as his tongue met hers with demanding thrusts. She pressed still closer and felt her nipples harden as they met the solid wall of his chest through thin layers of fabric.

Then his hands slid slowly downward, tracing her curves with sure fingers, digging into soft flesh to force her against him. She made a strangled sound as her own hot need met the unmistakable evidence of his desire. The velvet darkness grew heavy with sensual promise. Their lips drew apart to seek other flesh and found the soft lobe of an ear, the graceful curve of a neck, the tiny hollow at its base.

It was not enough, and they both knew that. With each indrawn breath and with each soft exhalation, they knew that they came closer to the moment when there could be no going back. Sparks had been ignited, and a conflagration was imminent. They both knew it would be fierce and wild and all-consuming.

But they stopped, somehow, neither of them certain just how the decision had been reached or who had made it. He released her slowly as they both drew in shaky breaths. Something clearly needed to be said; to pretend that it had been merely a kiss would be to deny the obvious. But all either of them could think in that moment was that it shouldn't have happened. Their secrets hung in the night air, weighing them down and keeping them silent.

Susan backed away from him, then managed to say good-night in a husky, choked voice and turn away. When she knew she was out of his sight, she ran headlong for the safety of her apartment.

LUCAS STOOD THERE, running a shaky hand through his hair. The taste of her was still on his lips. The feel of her was imprinted on his body. His arousal was painful, reminding him of adolescence, because since then there'd been no time when he'd had to stop.

Had he stopped or had she? It wasn't very clear. He wasn't even sure how they'd let it happen in the first place. It had seemed to him that they both had some pretty formidable barriers in place. Certainly *he* had; after all, he'd survived that trip to her apartment, following her up the stairs when she was wearing that bikini.

Furthermore, seduction hadn't really been on his mind this evening. He'd managed to shove those thoughts aside while he tried to elicit some information from her. Hadn't he told himself that that was the evening's game plan? When in his life had he ever deviated from a plan like that? And when in his adult life had he ever allowed his gonads to rule his brain?

Lucas stood there, shocked at his behavior and slowly coming to the conclusion that he was in deep trouble. What had happened hadn't happened because of mere lust. If it had been only that, he *would* have controlled it.

He thought of her in his garden, even as he could still taste the sweetness of her on his lips. That moment began to take on the quality of a premonition. He'd felt the rightness of her being there, just as he'd felt it a few moments ago.

When he'd decided to build a new life for himself, he had thought briefly about having someone to share that life with. But he'd pushed the thought away; there were too many complications. The women in his past hadn't much cared who or what he was, but he knew there was a very big difference between that kind of woman and one he might want to keep.

As a measure of calm returned to him, Lucas was suddenly struck with a renewal of the fear that had prompted him to offer her the apartment. What if she decided to walk away, just vanish from his life, as quickly and mysteriously as she'd entered it? At some point, she might realize that she'd exposed some of her lies and fear the consequences enough to run away.

She was clearly as nervous about involvement as he was. How long could they continue this charade before it all came crashing down on them?

Chapter Six

"Sherri, I want to apologize for last night."

She forced herself to relax her death grip on the phone. "There's no need for you to apologize, Lucas."

"Yes, there is. I don't want you thinking that I'm taking advantage of our, uh, situation."

She was shocked at his tentative tone. He actually sounded fearful. At the very least, he didn't sound like his usual self.

"I don't think that at all," she assured him. The truth was that she still didn't know who had really been responsible for making the first move, even though he clearly seemed to believe it had been him.

"I'm not planning to file charges of sexual harassment against you, Lucas," she teased.

He chuckled, and when he spoke again, his voice was more normal. "I hadn't actually thought about that," he admitted, with a smile in his voice. "I just didn't want you to feel uncomfortable living there."

"I don't," she lied glibly. "It was just something that happened. That doesn't mean that it has to happen again." She wondered if her tone might betray her own desire for him.

"It won't," he replied.

After they had hung up, Susan stood there staring at the phone. Could he be feeling guilty because of Natalie? Could she have been on her way to his apartment even as they'd spoken?

She didn't want him to feel guilty. *She* didn't feel guilty. She knew it had been a mistake to let it happen, given what could only be a disastrous outcome, but *he* couldn't know that. And she was not going to feel guilty about something that had touched her, however briefly, with magic. No man had ever made her feel that way—and she was determined to cherish the memory.

She frowned, thinking about his apparent concern that she might leave. It wasn't likely that it was only because of her skills as a housekeeper and cook; he could find that anywhere. And if he'd been so keen on having someone in this apartment, he could have done something about it long ago.

She shivered with remembered pleasure as she relived those moments once again. With each replay, she felt ever more strongly the heat of his desire, the driving force of his need. But she knew, as he could not, the fragility of that need, based as it was on her lies.

She should get out of here. She'd started telling herself that last night as she ran away from him. After work, she'd even gone to look at a new apartment complex someone had recommended, and she'd brought home the Stamford newspaper to search for other possibilities.

But she didn't want to leave. If she did, she'd never see him again. What was the point of leaving, if not to get him out of her life?

She knew that deep down inside she was irrationally hoping that he would come to care for her so much that he would accept the truth and not hate her for her deception.

She'd played out the scene many times in her mind, and he always forgave her.

But the other half of that scenario remained murky. He would also have to be honest with her, and Susan just wasn't sure what her own capacity for forgiveness was.

LUCAS TOLD ANNE that he'd be taking a long lunch, then drove home quickly. He knew Susan would be at work all day today; she'd mentioned a daylong conference when they'd met while they were both out running this morning.

He pulled into the driveway, walked around to the apartment entrance, then rang the bell, even though he knew she couldn't be there. After waiting a few seconds, he took out his key and let himself in.

He didn't really hold out much hope for finding something that would explain her sudden appearance in his life, but he was ready to try anything. His patience was wearing thin.

As he stood in the small living room, which had been transformed by her personal style, he chuckled to himself. Here he was, doing exactly what she'd done while he was in Europe. He hoped that the day would come when they could both laugh about it.

Unlike his own home, hers displayed her past. He'd glanced at the photos on the wall in her bedroom before, but now he took the time to study them more closely. There was a collection of pictures showing her in various theatrical roles, including one with her wearing a wig and makeup remarkably similar to the disguise she'd worn as a journalist. And there was a collection of family pictures, as well, several candid shots, and a formal portrait that had probably been done about the time she'd graduated from high school. He thought she didn't look all that much older now.

Lucas stood there for a long time, staring at the family pictures and recalling her description of her family. She'd said that she knew how lucky she'd been, but he wondered if she did. He rarely thought about his own childhood anymore, but seeing these pictures brought it back too vividly, and he turned away. He'd never been one to wallow in self-pity, and he wasn't about to start now. But he *was* uncomfortable with the sharp differences between them that these pictures indicated.

He searched the desk drawers and found nothing of interest. There was a recent bank statement, and he scanned that, looking for any large deposits that could indicate payment for spying on him. But there was nothing. She was living on dwindling savings.

His search of the closet and dresser drawers revealed nothing but her personal tastes and the meager wardrobe of someone who had spent the past few years living the life of a student. In one drawer he found a pale peach teddy, and he held it up, smiling to himself. It still bore a sales tag, and it was definitely out of place among more utilitarian things.

But nowhere did he find anything that hinted at a reason for her presence in his life, and his frustration grew as he left the apartment and returned to the shop. The game, it seemed, would have to continue under her rules.

CAROLYN ARRIVED for her weekend visit with her brother just as Susan got home from work. In fact, Susan followed her down the winding street and failed to notice the Pennsylvania license plates until the station wagon pulled into Lucas's driveway just ahead of her. The moment it came to a halt, the passenger door flew open and a small, dark-haired boy bounded out, then flung open the rear door to release a golden retriever.

Seconds later, Lucas appeared at the front door. He had managed to take only a few steps before he was set upon by the boy and the dog. Susan got out of her car slowly, watching Lucas's reaction to the boisterous greeting. He picked up his nephew quickly, managing at the same time to pet the dog, then carried him down the walk to the driveway. There was, she noted, something not quite natural in his actions. He was laughing and talking to his nephew, but it was obvious to her that young children were alien creatures to him.

"Hi. You must be Sherri."

Susan turned her attention to the woman who had gotten out of the wagon. There was no doubting that they were brother and sister, even though Lucas's rugged good looks were somewhat softened in his sister. Carolyn was far from beautiful, but she was still quite striking, with strong features and short, dark curls.

Susan nodded and extended her hand. "I'm glad to meet you, Carolyn."

Lucas had reached them by that time, and he set down his nephew to embrace his sister. Susan couldn't quite prevent a tiny pang of envy when she saw the warmth that lit his eyes. Obviously the long separation hadn't alienated brother and sister. It occurred to her that Carolyn might well be the only person to whom Lucas Andrews had ever felt truly close. That, of course, made her a perfect source of information, albeit one who would have to be questioned very discreetly.

Susan was quickly introduced to Jason, Carolyn's son, and to Norman, the golden retriever, who grinned at her and extended a silky paw. She chatted with them for a moment, and then was about to excuse herself when Lucas asked her to join them for dinner at a local restaurant.

She hesitated, thinking that the invitation had been extended only out of politeness, but Carolyn spoke up quickly.

"Come with us, Sherri. Give me a chance to talk you into taking me shopping tomorrow—that is, after I talk Lucas into baby-sitting."

She agreed, the thought of Lucas baby-sitting bringing a smile to her face. Then she went upstairs to change. It seemed that Carolyn had presented her with the perfect opportunity to gain some information, but she was beginning to feel rather guilty about it.

Still, she rationalized, what was a little guilt compared with a lifetime of wondering who Lucas Andrews really was?

DINNER PROVED to be interesting. Susan quickly came to like Carolyn, and regretted that she'd probably never see her again, not to mention the fact that she was seeing her under false pretenses now. She was reminded of that each time one of them called her "Sherri." It was a pity that she hadn't had the forethought to use her real first name, at least.

Lucas had chosen a restaurant that was rather too elegant for a small, active boy, but Jason managed to behave himself quite well. Carolyn proved to be open and honest, and that observation served to remind Susan of the lack of those qualities in her brother.

Lucas himself was indulgent toward his nephew, warmly affectionate to his sister, and politely formal toward her. Several times Susan caught Carolyn looking from one to the other of them with a slightly quizzical expression, as though she were uncertain just what their relationship was.

Susan could scarcely blame her for that, but she realized that she'd better be prepared to answer some questions herself.

CAROLYN apparently was not one to ease herself gradually into a subject that intrigued her. She and Susan had barely driven away from Lucas's house the next day when she spoke up.

"So what's the story with you two? Are you really just a part-time housekeeper and cook, or is something else going on? When Lucas told me about you, I had the impression he was holding something back."

Caught unprepared by Carolyn's rapid plunge into the matter, Susan hesitated, and Carolyn shrugged.

"Listen, he could be madly in love with you and I wouldn't know it. Lucas, as you might have noticed, isn't the easiest person to read. But I thought he was trying just a little too hard to pretend there's nothing going on."

Susan smiled to herself. Ever since last Sunday, Lucas's behavior toward her had indeed been very formal. It was clear that he'd meant what he'd said about not kissing her again, and she wished she could feel more pleased about that.

"It's really just what it seems," she told Carolyn. "I haven't known him long, and I don't know him well."

"Sherri, *no one* knows my brother well, not even *me.*"

Susan turned briefly to stare at her. "Really? I thought the two of you seemed quite close."

"We are, or I should say that he's closer to me than to anyone else. I don't know if he's told you anything about our childhood, but it wasn't too pleasant, especially for him. Our parents are both dead, and we were raised separately. And then, of course, he spent the past fifteen years traveling."

"Yes, he mentioned that, with a company that imports antiques."

Carolyn made a sound that drew Susan's attention to her sharply. "So he says," she stated doubtfully.

"You don't believe him?" Susan felt her worst fears begin to materialize, when what she'd been hoping was that Carolyn could lay them to rest.

"If you want the truth—no, I don't believe him."

"Then what do you think he was doing?" Susan asked, mentally bracing herself.

"I don't know, and I don't think I *want* to know, either."

A chill swept through Susan, and she had to struggle to hide it.

"We didn't see much of each other until Lucas was in college. He went to Michigan and I went to Penn State and we used to visit each other. That's when I really got to know him. He was a big football star, and the sportswriters used to say that he was so good because he took chances. It's a miracle that he was never seriously injured.

"He was recruited by the pros and offered a lot of money, but instead he went to work for that antiques firm. It seemed like a really strange thing for him to do, but he said he wanted to travel, and they were offering him really good money.

"Before I got married, he used to send me plane tickets to meet him in various places: Paris, Rome, Athens, Vienna. It was wonderful, because I could never have traveled like that otherwise. But when I'd get there, he'd be so...so distracted and edgy at first. His excuse was always that he'd been working too hard."

"But you don't believe that?"

"No. I don't think I ever did." She shifted in her seat, leaning toward Susan. "Please don't tell him I've told you this. Whatever he might have done, he's my brother and I love him. And anyway, that's all over now. He seems more relaxed and settled than he's ever been.''

"Don't worry. I won't say anything," Susan assured her. "But what do you think he could have been doing?''

"Something illegal, if you want the truth," Carolyn said unhappily. "For a while, I used to imagine that he was a spy or something, an American James Bond. But that's pretty farfetched.''

Susan privately agreed that it was, but could scarcely blame her for wanting to believe it. She would have liked to believe that, as well.

"It's hard for me to think of Lucas as having been some sort of criminal," Susan said tentatively, trying to give careful voice to her own roiling emotions.

"It is for me, too, believe me," Carolyn responded. "But when I try to look at him objectively, I'm not so sure. I told you about what a risk-taker he was, and he has a lot of money. What does that add up to?'' she asked plaintively.

Susan could think of nothing to say. She kept her eyes on the road. Carolyn could love him even if he had been a criminal; she was his sister, after all. But how could she herself ever accept that?

"I suppose I feel safe telling you all this because you're a psychologist and I know you understand confidentiality. I've always worried about him, and there was never anyone I could talk to who knew him.

"Besides," she went on, in a determinedly lighter tone, "in spite of what you said, I think you *are* interested in him, and I think he feels the same about you. He even came pretty close to admitting that last night.''

She was silent for a moment, then said ruefully, "I guess I'm not really helping the romance along by telling you all this, am I?"

Susan wanted to level with her, to tell her the truth about how she'd come into Lucas's life, and to admit that, yes, she did indeed care for him. But she settled for a small part of that.

"You're right, I *do* care for him. But there needs to be some honesty between us that just isn't there."

The two women spent several hours at the Danbury Mall, then returned to Ridgefield for lunch and more shopping. Carolyn wanted to stop by Lucas's shop, and Susan agreed, although she was somewhat concerned about seeing Anne, his assistant, again. The woman had seen her twice before now, once as herself and once in disguise.

Anne was thankfully occupied with customers when they walked in, but she greeted Carolyn immediately, then gave Susan a tentative smile that seemed to suggest she knew she'd seen her before.

Carolyn walked around the shop, examining the merchandise carefully, then stopped and looked around with a smile and a shake of her head.

"Well, whatever else can be said about my brother, he *does* have taste."

"Maybe you're wrong about him, Carolyn," Susan suggested gently. "After all, doesn't this indicate that he was doing just what he said he was—working in the antiques business?"

"Oh, I *know* he was working for them. I had their number so I could always reach him, and I called it once, when I wanted to tell him I was getting married."

"I don't understand, then. If you knew he was telling the truth..."

Carolyn shrugged. "I know. I'm probably being ridiculous."

Susan wondered if they were *both* being ridiculous, but she had no opportunity to discuss it further, since Anne came over and began to talk to Carolyn. The two women chatted for a few minutes before Carolyn realized that Anne didn't know who Susan was. She belatedly introduced them.

"Of course. Lucas has mentioned you, Sherri. Have you been in here before? I know we've never met, but you look familiar."

"Actually, I *was* in here, but it was some time ago. Before I met Lucas. You must have a good memory for faces," she added, hoping that flattery would defuse the situation.

Anne smiled. "I try to remember customers, but I'm nowhere as good as Lucas is. He never forgets a face or a name."

The smile froze on Susan's face. This was definitely something she did *not* want to hear. Today was proving to be full of unpleasant revelations. She was forcibly reminded that bad things always happened in threes when Natalie Kroft walked into the shop just as they were leaving.

Natalie's sharp gaze swept over them both, but lingered on Carolyn. Anne chose that moment to ask Carolyn to have Lucas call her later. Natalie had stopped near them, but Carolyn's glance passed over her without recognition. Susan held her breath until they had left the shop.

Then, as the two of them walked down the street, Susan kept expecting Natalie to rush up and introduce herself. She was sure that Natalie must know by now who Carolyn was.

Just as they reached the car, Natalie did come out of the shop. She stopped on the sidewalk and stared in their direction, but made no move toward them.

As they drove home, Susan pondered the situation. Would Natalie show up at the house? Surely she would, if she really was engaged to Lucas. He'd certainly want his sister and his fiancée to meet.

But it just didn't make sense that Carolyn would know nothing about Natalie, even if she hadn't yet met her. And if Carolyn knew that Lucas was involved with someone, why would she seem to be encouraging Susan?

Natalie Kroft failed to appear. Lucas went into the shop for a few hours, but returned alone for dinner. By the time she said good-night and went up to her apartment, Susan had reached the inescapable conclusion that Natalie Kroft had definitely lied. But *why* had she lied? And why had she been willing to spend a considerable amount of money to gain information about him?

Susan lay awake far into the night, asking herself that question. At some point, it got all mixed up in her dozing brain with Carolyn's speculations about Lucas's past. Was it possible that Natalie was somehow involved in that? Could she possibly represent a threat of some sort to Lucas?

DURING THE NEXT WEEK, Susan came to cherish her job even more than before, because it was only during working hours that she managed to set aside her concerns about Natalie Kroft's intentions. She felt torn every which way. Problem solving was a skill well known to all therapists, but when Susan tried to apply those skills to her situation, she was unable.

She could move—sever her ties with Lucas and begin the process of forgetting him. Toward that end, she went to look at a few apartments, but with little enthusiasm. It seemed wrong to abandon him, carrying with her information that could be of great importance to him if Natalie *was* somehow mixed up in his past. She had a strong sense of responsibility in this matter, since it was she who had helped Natalie gain information about him.

On the other hand, if she stayed, she would have to tell him what she knew, and how she knew it. And however valuable her information might be to him, he was certain to regard her in a very unpleasant light.

Fortunately, while she debated with herself over this matter, Lucas was absent. He spent the early part of the week in the city, then flew to Chicago to attend an estate auction. Construction began on his swimming pool, and she went down each day to check on its progress, certain that one way or the other she would be gone before it was completed. The pool became a symbol of everything she would be giving up if she made either of the choices, but it was Lucas she would miss most of all.

There was also a third option—to do nothing and say nothing, while continuing to live here. It was certainly the most attractive, but Susan knew that it was impossible. At some point, she would surely make a slip of the tongue that would bring it all crashing down upon her. And she knew what that "all" was. She was dangerously close to falling in love with him. She could no longer write her feelings off as mere physical attraction.

He returned Thursday evening, and she went down to see if he'd had dinner, her decision not yet made. She found him out in the yard, examining the ugly mess that was on its way to becoming the pool. He turned and saw her, and she felt, beneath their restrained greetings, the crackling fire of mutual desire. Neither of them seemed able to conceal it very well now. It was as though the very air around them became denser, charged with a hot sensuality.

He began to describe what the finished pool would look like, while she stood beside him in the soft twilight, and she felt such a yearning to stay here with this man that tears began to well up in her eyes and she had to keep her face averted. It didn't help at all that he was asking her opinion about the landscaping, almost as though she had a right to approve or disapprove such choices.

"Susan?" he said softly, his low voice filled with concern.

She made a hurried swipe at her eyes before turning to face him, and the fact that he'd called her by her real name didn't register until their eyes met. And then everything else was swept away in a mind-numbing wave of panic.

"What's wrong?" he asked, staring at her, the concern still in his voice.

"Nothing," she said quickly. "It's just been a long, difficult week, and I wish it were over." Then, taking what she knew to be a very great risk, she hurried on, giving him a sympathetic smile. "You must be tired, too. You just called me Susan."

"Did I?" He seemed genuinely shocked. "Sorry. It *has* been a long week, and you've reminded me from the beginning of someone I knew years ago named Susan."

Was he telling the truth? His explanation seemed as genuine as his shock at the mistake, so perhaps he was. But it still seemed entirely too much of a coincidence.

"Mary called while I was away, and left a message saying that she'll be back next week, so that should ease the burden on you a bit," he said as they started back toward the terrace.

"Oh? That's good news," she replied, but she interpreted it as another sign that her time here should come to an end. "It hasn't been any trouble for me, but I'm sure she's a much better housekeeper than I am."

"I haven't noticed any difference," he said with a smile. "And your cooking is better."

She thanked him distractedly, then hesitated when he asked if she'd like to join him on the terrace for a while. He apparently noticed that hesitation and misinterpreted it.

"Sherri, I meant it when I said that there'd be no repetition of that other time. And I enjoy your company."

They had stopped at the edge of the terrace and were standing close together in the gathering darkness. The voluptuous softness of the night seemed to mock his words.

"Come on," he said, taking her arm lightly. "It sounds as though you could use a drink, and I could, too. I need some liquid courage to convince myself that I made a wise purchase."

He dropped his hand as she followed him across the terrace, but the imprint lingered, tingling with warmth. If a casual touch like that could do this to her, what would happen if they made love?

"What purchase?" she asked.

"Let me get the drinks and I'll tell you."

He disappeared inside, and she stood there, rubbing the spot he'd touched and remembering those moments in his arms. How could she leave him? And how had she managed to let this happen? She'd always been so sensible about her life.

He brought the drinks and they settled themselves on the terrace, and he told her about the Hepplewhite dining suite he'd bought, for what he admitted was an outrageous price. Susan knew Hepplewhite was a style, and vaguely recalled that the secretary she'd seen in his shop had been that style. Considering the price of that piece, she wondered what constituted "outrageous."

"Normally I wouldn't buy something like that unless I had a definite customer for it," he went on ruefully.

"And you didn't this time?"

"Unfortunately, the only person I had in mind was *me*. I had a Hepplewhite secretary recently, and I let it go, even though I wanted to keep it. So I suspect this is a case of self-indulgence. Would that be your diagnosis?"

She laughed. "We all need to indulge ourselves from time to time. It's healthy."

"For the mind, maybe, but not for the bank account." He chuckled. "So what happened this week to upset you? I thought everything was going well."

"It was," she replied, struggling now to manufacture some sort of plausible difficulty at work, and discovering to her dismay that she just couldn't dissemble any more.

"It doesn't have anything to do with work," she said suddenly, the words tumbling out before she could stop them. "Lucas..." But she stopped, unable to take the plunge that would end it all. "I don't want to talk about it," she said finally, then sipped her drink.

When he said nothing, she heard in the silence the echoes of her abrupt statement. "I'm sorry," she said. "I didn't mean to sound so rude. Thank you for your concern."

She drained her glass quickly and stood up. "What I really need is a good night's sleep." Before he could respond, she almost ran across the terrace, around the back of the house, and into the tenuous safety of her apartment.

Her trembling legs carried her as far as the sofa, where she collapsed and let the tears flow. How could she have let herself get into such a situation? She was appalled. How many times had she listened to people talk about the messes they'd made of their lives, then felt oh-so-superior in her certainty that she had her own life firmly in hand?

How innocently it had all started out! She'd come to New York full of dreams, and had succeeded in creating a nightmare. She thought about Lucas: his genuine concern, his statement about enjoying her company. They *had* something. It was tentative and fragile right now, but the beginning of something was definitely there. She recalled Carolyn's parting request that she "give him a chance." But that wasn't the issue right now. The issue was her deceit.

She began to think seriously for the first time about how she could explain herself to him. Could she get away without admitting what she knew about his past? Certainly she couldn't reveal anything Carolyn had told her, but what about the things Teddy had learned?

After thinking about that for a time, she switched to a contemplation of his probable reaction. It was very difficult for her to guess. Did he care for her enough to laugh it off? Or was it possible that he would be so grateful to her for telling him about Natalie Kroft that he would forgive her deceit? And what was Natalie up to, in any event? Would he tell her that?

She pulled herself up from the sofa and all but ran down the stairs, counting on the physical momentum to carry her straight to him before she could change her mind. When she closed the downstairs door behind her, she saw a patch of light shining on the grass and realized that it must be coming from his study. The study was in a part of the house that jutted out just behind the garage. She crept quietly in that direction.

He was seated at his desk, his back to her, opening his mail. He'd removed his jacket and tie and rolled up his sleeves. Then, as she watched, he pushed the mail aside impatiently and rested his elbows on the desk. His hands began to sweep through his thick hair, the motion repeated several times before he finally lowered his hands and simply sat there.

Something was clearly troubling him. She wondered if it was that purchase he'd made, or *her*. He hadn't really seemed all that concerned about the purchase. In fact, she'd thought it seemed more like a conversational gambit than anything else.

She took a few steps back from the window and walked determinedly toward the front of the house. Then she rang the doorbell and held her breath.

LUCAS LIFTED HIS HEAD at the sound of the doorbell. It had to be her. No one else was likely to appear on his doorstep at this hour of the night. All along he'd been betting on her being unable to maintain that false facade for very long. And then, tonight, he'd slipped himself. At this point he wouldn't be willing to place any bets on *either* of them.

He got up to answer the door. She might simply be coming down to apologize for her abrupt departure, or she might by now have concocted some tale to explain her mood. Or she might be coming to tell him the truth.

As he reached for the doorknob, Lucas decided that if she didn't volunteer the truth, he was going to force the issue. The game had gone on long enough.

BY THE TIME the door opened, Susan was poised for flight. But she managed to keep her feet planted firmly on his doorstep, and she even met his gaze levelly.

"I have to talk to you, Lucas." Her voice was firm and didn't waver even in the face of his slightly wary scrutiny.

He stepped back and gestured for her to come in, then led her down the hallway to his study, where she perched, rather than sat, on the handsome leather sofa across from his desk. He walked back to his desk chair and sat down, tilting the chair back slightly as he studied her.

He was definitely not making it any easier for her. Had she offended him by her abruptness earlier? She glanced around the room, wishing he'd chosen the living room instead. The study was intimidatingly masculine, with its dark woods and brass-studded leather furnishings. Then she remembered the gun in the desk drawer. She suppressed a shudder, telling herself that she had no cause to fear anything more than his anger. She began to fumble about mentally for an opening, realizing belatedly that she should have rehearsed it.

After looking everywhere but at him, she faced him squarely and took a deep breath. "Lucas, I've been lying to you about a lot of things."

She waited a moment to see how he would take that, but nothing at all showed in the dark eyes that continued to gaze steadily at her. God, he could be so intimidating, with that poker face and that utter stillness. It made him seem like a stranger, a stranger with a past she couldn't afford to think about now. Her gaze strayed involuntarily to the desk drawer before returning to him.

"First of all, my name isn't Sherri Thomas. It's Susan Trent." She thought about the strange coincidence of his having called her that, but let the thought go quickly.

"Some of what I told you is true. I am a psychologist, and I did just move here recently from Indiana. When I arrived, I discovered that my brother—who *is* a comedian, by the way—had broken an arm and a leg in a skiing accident a month before."

She paused again, still hoping he'd say something—anything. Or maybe at least give her an encouraging look. But he said and did nothing. He might as well have been carved from stone.

"Teddy's had trouble breaking into comedy, as I think I told you. So he's been working for a friend. But I told you that his friend had a computer company, and that's not true. He's a private investigator."

Aha! She finally saw something flicker in his eyes—surprise, she thought—but it was gone quickly.

"Well, what happened is that Teddy talked me into helping him with his investigations. Greg, his friend, had been getting a lot of requests from women who wanted to check out their prospective husbands. Apparently it's become a big business, and Teddy had been doing it for some time.

"Anyway, just as I arrived, Teddy had gotten this case, and the woman wanted a lot of information. Since Teddy couldn't get around, I agreed to help him with it. And that's how I met you."

He was by now frowning slightly, not in anger, but in thought. Or so she hoped. It had just occurred to her that she would be breaking confidentiality by giving him Natalie's name, and she didn't quite know what to do. She'd been so concerned that Natalie might pose a threat to him that she'd failed to consider that aspect.

Then, to her utter amazement, a smile began to spread slowly over his face. He raised his arms to clasp them behind his head as he began to chuckle.

Her astonishment gave way to confusion. She was certainly glad that he wasn't angry, but why should he be laughing? She hadn't even told him enough for him to understand it all yet.

Then she began to get angry. What if Natalie was a friend of his who had played some sort of elaborate trick on him? That could certainly explain his amusement.

"Natalie Kroft," he said, shaking his head and still smiling.

She nodded, her anger growing. But when he spoke again, that anger soon dissolved into astonishment once more.

"The yellow rain slicker. I assume that was the first time you followed me. Then there was the middle-aged woman on the subway. It was a good disguise, except for the nose and the fact that you were so obviously avoiding eye contact with me.

"Then, let's see . . . Next was the journalist—I've forgotten her name. That wasn't a bad disguise, either. I assume you must have been in the shop before that and found out from Anne that I like scrimshaw." His gaze left hers for a moment and flicked to the collection on the bookshelf.

"And finally there was your *real* stroke of luck, that you happened to come here when Mary was expecting someone from the agency and was probably so distracted that she didn't question you very much. Good marks for opportunism there," he added with an amused nod.

He continued to watch her steadily as he recited all this. Susan simply sat there in openmouthed amazement.

"I knew your real name from the day I came home and found you here playing housekeeper. You'd left your purse on the kitchen counter, so I just checked in there."

He didn't really sound smug, but she chose to believe he was anyway. She bristled at his amused expression.

"Then why did you let me get away with it?" she demanded angrily, thinking about all the times she'd been so careful, so constantly on guard against mistakes. She thought, too, about her slipups and how she'd thought he simply hadn't noticed.

"Because I figured that sooner or later you'd tell the truth."

"Well, now I have," she said coldly. "I'll move out this weekend." She stood up to leave.

"Sit down, Susan," he said gently. "I'm not asking you to leave."

"Well, you said you were waiting to find out the truth, and now you have. So what's the point in my staying?" She lifted her chin defiantly, but her voice had a tiny quaver she couldn't control.

He grinned at her. "Well, for one thing, you're a good cook."

She stared at him, unsmiling. She was still smarting over the wound to her ego and annoyed at his smugness, real or imagined.

"I'm not *that* good, Lucas. You could very easily find someone else who'd be happy to have that apartment in return for so little work."

He said nothing for a moment, and then his smile softened until it began to edge very close to seduction. She stood her ground, but she was beginning to regret her challenge.

"I told you before that I enjoy your company," he said, with what she thought was just a touch too much casualness.

"And now that there are no more lies between us, your company should be even more of a pleasure."

She nodded and turned to leave before she would be tempted to tell him that she knew there *were* more lies between them. But his lightly teasing tone stopped her at the doorway.

"Aren't you curious about Natalie Kroft?"

She turned back, allowing herself a tiny nod intended to suggest that it was certainly nothing more than minor curiosity. The truth was that she'd simply forgotten about her for the time being.

"I assume she lied to Teddy," she said, once more taking a seat on the sofa. "I'd begun to suspect that, since you hadn't mentioned any fiancée." She told him about seeing Natalie in the shop when she'd stopped by with Carolyn.

"But Carolyn didn't know her, and when she didn't come here, I decided she *had* to have lied. I was afraid that she might be some sort of threat to you."

"More of an annoyance than a threat, I'm afraid," he said with a rueful chuckle. "I met Natalie some time ago at a party. She, uh, came on pretty strong. Anyway, I took her out to dinner and decided pretty quickly that I wasn't interested.

"She called me a few times to invite me to various things, then showed up here one weekend, uninvited." He paused and gave her a slightly embarrassed look.

"In all honesty, I didn't know what to do about her. Her attention was flattering in a way, and I'm no more immune to that than the next guy, but I just wasn't interested. Anyway, I probably wasn't as forceful as I should have been, but after a while she finally stopped calling, and I thought she'd gotten the hint."

"But I saw you with her a week or so ago in town, and then she was at your shop last Saturday."

He nodded. "I took her to lunch that time you saw us. She made it difficult for me not to invite her."

"You have a very strange way of telling her to get lost, Lucas. And I'm having some trouble seeing you as a wimp."

He laughed. "I took her to lunch because it was the first time I'd seen her since you appeared on the scene, and it occurred to me that there could be a connection between the two of you. I wanted to see if I could find out what it was. And now that I know, I promise you it won't happen again—Scout's honor." He held up his fingers in the traditional salute.

They smiled at each other, but then Susan shook her head.

"I can't believe she'd go to such trouble and expense. She must be obsessed with you." Her voice ended on a rather uncertain note, as she was beginning to feel entirely too much empathy toward Natalie Kroft.

"I guess so, but you'd know more about that kind of thing than I would."

Indeed I would, she thought, hoping that he was referring only to the fact that she was a psychologist.

"Well, now that we know the lengths to which she's gone, should I be worrying about her? The movie *Fatal Attraction* comes unpleasantly to mind."

"I don't think so. That movie was really pretty extreme. But I *do* think that you've got to be firm and stop sending her mixed messages if she shows up again."

"Thank you, Dr. Trent. I'll certainly take your advice. No more wimpiness."

They both laughed. She got up again, and this time he did, too. When they had reached the front door, he turned to her, his expression once more serious.

"I meant what I said, Susan. I want you to stay."

"Then I will. Thank you."

He opened the door, and she started to walk through it, then stopped. Acting totally on impulse, she stretched up and kissed him on the cheek. The edge of his mustache tickled the corner of her mouth and set off little explosions of heat. She backed away quickly.

He started to lift a hand toward her, then subsided. They both said good-night hurriedly. When he had closed the door behind her, the warm night air felt almost icy against her heated skin.

She half ran and half danced her way back to her apartment, almost unable to believe her good fortune. Only as she lay in bed, thinking about their conversation, did she remember that remark of his about there being no more lies between them.

Chapter Seven

"So he knew that I was following him right from the beginning. I know I shouldn't have told him about Natalie, Teddy, but I *had* to. I was really afraid that she could be some sort of threat to him. And anyway, he promised me that if he sees her again he won't tell her that he found out she hired an investigator."

Susan leaned forward to emphasize her point. She was still very uncomfortable about having broken confidentiality in that way. She'd called Lucas the next evening at his city apartment and extracted that promise from him. The conversation had been brief, with both of them retreating into a careful formality. "One step forward and two steps back," she'd thought after they hung up.

The waiter arrived with their soup. They were dining at Teddy's favorite Japanese restaurant. Amanda was out of town on an assignment, and Teddy had wanted to celebrate the removal of his casts, while she had wanted to explain herself.

"Greg would be pretty upset," Teddy admitted when the waiter had gone. "But I guess I won't mention it to him. I'll just have to hope that Andrews keeps his word." He didn't sound too sure of that.

"So now *he* knows the truth," Teddy went on after he tasted his soup. "But *you* still don't. Don't you think it's kind of strange that he spotted you following him that quickly?"

"Come on, Teddy. I was an amateur." But it *had* bothered her, once she'd gotten over her initial euphoria at his acceptance of her lies.

"Maybe so, but I thought your disguises were pretty good. You could have followed *me,* and I wouldn't have recognized you. And I'm your *brother,* for crying out loud. Besides, you're looking at this through small-town eyes. City people don't ordinarily pay close attention to the people around them. It would drive them nuts. A New Yorker could walk down the street and not notice a four-foot-tall green man from Mars—even if he was dressed in fluorescent pink!"

She said nothing. He was right; she'd even remarked upon that fact herself. The only people-watchers here were out-of-towners.

"Well, he's not a New Yorker," she said halfheartedly.

Teddy snorted. "Look, the only way he could have spotted you that quickly is if he makes a habit of checking to see if anyone's tailing him. And normal people with nothing to hide don't do that."

"It could be a case of old habits being impossible to break," she said defensively.

"Ah! My point exactly! So maybe he's gone straight. I'll go along with that, if only because he seemed not to be upset by being investigated. But what does that tell you?" He raised his brows questioningly, then answered his own question when she remained silent.

"It tells *me* that he's *really* buried his past. And why would he do that, unless there's something pretty bad there?"

He waited a beat, then pressed on. "Of course, the other possibility is that he's worried that you've found out something, and he's just waiting for you to spill *those* beans. After all, you said he told you he let you get away with it because he figured you'd 'fess up sooner or later. So now he's waiting for you to come up with the rest of it."

"You're forgetting a third possibility, Teddy, which is that he has nothing to hide and that we're making mountains out of molehills." Her tone was defiantly insistent, but deep inside she didn't believe that. How could she, when his own sister feared that he'd been a criminal? She could just imagine what Teddy would make of *that*.

"Talk about love being blind," Teddy replied scornfully. "Look, Susan, even if he *is* being Mr. Nice Guy about all this, you're still playing with fire. You know, you're a perfect example of why women probably *should* hire investigators to look into a guy's background."

Despite her irritation, Susan had to smile at the irony of that. She recalled with some chagrin her scorn when Teddy had first told her about this trend. "What ever happened to the notion of actually getting to *know* each other before you decide to get married?" she'd proclaimed self-righteously.

"I'm not planning to marry him," she pointed out, though not without a little twinge of uncertainty. If Lucas loved her, if she were sure she loved him....

"Right," said Teddy sarcastically. "You're so wrapped up in him you don't now which end is up. And that's not like you."

She could tell that he was genuinely worried about her, and that did little for her peace of mind.

"I met his sister, by the way," she said brightly, hoping to ease his concern. "She came to visit with her son. I liked her. And she happened to mention that she'd gotten in touch with him a few times when he was overseas, through that company he worked for."

"What's the name of the company?" Teddy asked quickly. "Maybe we can check them out."

"I didn't ask. It would have seemed strange. But he must have been working for them, just like he said."

"No doubt he was," Teddy nodded. "The company was probably a front for some gang of international criminals. Look at the BCCI mess, for heaven's sake. He could have said he was working for a multinational bank, and that would have sounded innocent, too."

He had a point. She shrugged, trying to make light of it. "Well, at the first sign that he's involved in anything illegal, I'll be outa there. I promise."

"Hmph! By that time, you'll probably be married to the guy and trailing a couple of his kids after you."

"Oh, Teddy! Stop being ridiculous!"

He leaned forward until his nose was almost touching hers. "I am not being ridiculous. You're in love with him. Admit it!"

She stared at him steadily, unwilling to let him win the game. But finally she drew back a bit. "Okay. I may be *falling* in love with him, but I'm not there yet. And anyway, I have no idea how he feels about me."

But she did, didn't she? She knew he wanted her, and she knew he cared enough to want her to stay even though she'd lied to him.

"In that case," Teddy said, "I think it's time for an objective appraisal of the situation. Invite me up to meet him and I'll give you one."

"As a matter of fact, he said that he'd like to meet you. But I'm not going to invite you up there so you can subject him to some third degree."

"I'll be the very soul of discretion. You can invite Amanda and me up when the pool's finished."

"Ah, so you're finally willing to let me meet Amanda? Well, in that case, I'll see what I can arrange. But it's his pool, after all. I'm just the hired help."

Teddy rolled his eyes heavenward.

IF SUSAN HAD EXPECTED that her truth-telling would result in a change between them, she appeared doomed to disappointment. Having once been certain that Lucas would order her out of his life when he learned how she'd deceived him, she had moved quickly to an equal certainty that he would now declare his feelings for her.

But he didn't. She, of course, was far more relaxed around him now, but she brooded just as darkly when she was alone, wondering if Teddy could be right and Lucas was just waiting for her to admit that she knew more about him.

In the meantime, he had managed to find precisely the perfect balance between formality and familiarity, between letting her know he enjoyed her company and still withholding true intimacy. He was so good at it that she couldn't begin to guess if it was natural or contrived. She decided that Lucas Andrews could provide an intriguing subject for a psychological case study, if only she could retain the objectivity necessary to conduct one. But that objectivity had been absent almost from the beginning, where he was concerned.

Often his gaze would touch hers for just a moment too long, edging close to seduction and then veering off quickly, leaving her to wonder if she hadn't misinterpreted it in the first place.

Their conversations, as they sometimes sat on the terrace on the soft summer nights, tended to remain in more or less impersonal realms. She began to learn about antiques. He seemed interested, but not emotionally involved, in her talk about her work. There were a few heated discussions about politics; he was rather conservative, while she was an unapologetic liberal. But his interests lay in foreign affairs, while hers were the domestic issues, so they each carved out their spheres.

Occasionally talk would move toward the personal. The subject under discussion might itself be of a general nature, but a glance or a comment or even a silence would create a fragment of intimacy. One evening, when she had gone on at some length on a pet topic—America's failure to care for its children, and what could be done about it— he gave her an indulgent smile.

"You're idealistic, Susan. I'm not saying that's bad, but you make me feel old and cynical."

"Maybe that's because you've seen too much of the wrong things," she retorted challengingly, knowing that she was stepping into a mine field.

He stared at her in silence for a moment, and she could almost feel his mind probing hers questioningly, seeking that secret information.

"What 'wrong things' do you mean?' he asked mildly.

She struggled for something close to the truth, or what she feared might be the truth. "I think you're distrustful of people and their motives, and there has to be a reason for that."

He steepled his long fingers in front of him and smiled. "So, Dr. Trent, what does your psychological portrait of me tell you could be the reason?"

His tone was light and teasing and nothing more, but by now she knew just how good he was at hiding his true feelings. She proceeded cautiously.

"Well, it's often a result of some betrayals of trust in childhood. Of course, it can also be the result of working in certain professions. Police are frequently like that, for example." And criminals, she added silently, unhappily. Even reformed criminals.

"I see." He lapsed into a silence that went on for so long that she was sure he had no intention of pursuing the topic further. But just as she was about to announce her intention of going up to her apartment, he ended it with a question.

"Did Carolyn tell you about our childhood?"

At the moment, Susan couldn't recall what Carolyn had said, since she had her own knowledge of it. "A little. I think she said something about the two of you having been separated because of the deaths of your parents."

The story unfolded in a flawless narrative that suggested he might have rehearsed it, or perhaps told it many times before, though she somehow doubted that. And there was little hint of any emotion in the telling. It was essentially what she already knew.

"If he hadn't been killed in that accident," Lucas said, referring to his father, "I would probably have killed him myself when I was old enough. Certainly I wanted to."

"But you must have felt guilty about his death," she said, knowing that was usually the case. "At that age, children often believe that wishes come true, and you were wishing him dead."

"I don't remember feeling anything but relief," he said succinctly. "There are times when the death of one bad person can change many things for the better."

Susan felt a chill descend upon her as his unemotional words echoed through her brain. "But people can't set themselves up as judge and jury like that," she protested.

"In the case of my father, the judgment was rendered by God or fate or whatever," he reminded her.

A storm had been building in the distance as they talked. The deep rumblings of thunder and distant flashes of lightning had seemed so appropriate to the conversation that she'd paid scant attention. Now, however, a few fat raindrops began to pelt them.

They said good-night quickly, and she hurried back to her apartment, just escaping the deluge. But his words stayed with her, along with the uneasy sense of a conversation sliding inexorably into a dark abyss.

When Susan thought about it again the next day, it seemed to her that Lucas had led her close to the edge of something, then let her take a few steps on her own to peer into the darkness of his past.

THE NEW POOL was constructed with amazing speed. Susan was charmed by the design he'd chosen, a free-form shape that prevented much tree cutting. In less than two weeks, it was finished.

The two of them stood in the yard, staring at the glistening water, which was tinted a soft blue by the pool lining. Lucas had just returned from the city, and the builders had departed only hours earlier.

Susan was thinking how she'd believed, only a short time ago, that she would be gone from here before it was completed. Yet here she was, living in a situation in which a delicate balance persisted between friendship and love. A very peculiar situation, she thought. All her instincts told her that it could not continue this way.

"The landscapers will be here tomorrow," Lucas said, breaking into her thoughts. "If the weather holds, they'll be finished by the weekend. I was thinking of giving a party on Sunday."

"That sounds like a good idea," she said, thinking about Teddy's request for an invitation. Now that the possibility existed, she wasn't quite sure she wanted them to meet, despite Teddy's promise of discretion.

"I'll ask Mary to come in to handle it so that you can enjoy yourself."

She was touched by his thoughtfulness, but felt compelled to point out that she was already doing very little in exchange for her apartment. Several people at work to whom she'd explained her living arrangements had been openly astonished. The cost of apartments in this area was such that it was always a major topic of conversation.

"Cooking was only part of the bargain," he replied, waving away her objections. "The main thing is just having you here."

She cursed silently. He was doing it again. Did he mean having someone in the apartment or having *her* here? She suspected that he was well aware of the double meaning. And she was also becoming aware of the inequity of their relationship. He was both employer and landlord, however unusual their relationship. And it was *he* who set the tone for that relationship.

The temptation was growing within her to confront him about this, to demand to know just what he had in mind for them. But since she wasn't prepared to deal with the consequences, she hadn't yet pushed it. Fortunately, he went on before her annoyance gave her an intemperate tongue.

"Is there anyone you'd like to invite besides your brother? I assume you'd like to have him up, with or without the bra model," he finished with a chuckle.

"With her, I suspect. It's time I met her, so that I can try to take her seriously. She can't possibly be the ditz-brain

I'm imagining, or he wouldn't be dating her. And there are a few people from my office I could invite."

"I'll call the neighbors and a few other people," he went on. "And we'd better decide what to do about your name."

She gave him a blank look, and he laughed. "You can't be Susan to some of the guests and Sherri to others."

"Oh!" She'd somehow managed to forget that. They hadn't actually spoken about her "confession" since that night, and now that he'd raised the issue, she was more interested in asking some questions than in finding an answer to the problem of her names.

"Why did you take all that so well, Lucas? I'm not sure I could have been so forgiving toward someone who'd lied to me like that."

"You forget that I knew you were lying from the beginning and just went along with it until I could find out why."

"Still, you have every reason to be angry."

The smile he gave her was dangerously close to a caress. "I'm not. It was actually pretty amusing."

She saw an opening yawning before her, dark and threatening. But she leapt into it anyway, albeit with some care. "Most people would consider what I did to be an invasion of privacy."

"I suppose that's true, but in this case no harm was done."

How can you be so sure of that? she asked silently. And yet she was convinced that he *was* sure. Teddy must be right; whatever was in his past had been covered very well. She no longer believed Teddy's other suggestion, that Lucas was simply keeping her around until he could determine if she knew anything else. He'd had ample opportunity to question her discreetly, and he hadn't taken it.

"There is one discovery you must have made that perhaps I should explain," he went on in a neutral tone.

She didn't look at him, fearful that he would see how eager she was to have him explain himself. "Oh?"

"The guns you undoubtedly found." He chuckled. "I saw you glancing a few times toward my desk drawer while you were making your confession. Surely you didn't think you were in any danger from me?"

"No, of course not. It's just that guns make me nervous." Especially when I've been told that they're the weapons of a professional killer, she added silently.

"I've had them for years. There are several more in that safe in the closet. I used to be something of a collector until I lost interest in them."

"I see" She wanted very badly to believe he was telling the truth. He *could* be. Many people collected guns, and from what Greg had told her, they were good ones. That might even explain the silencer. Perhaps it had simply come with the gun.

He had moved slightly so that he was now facing her. She looked up to find him watching her intently.

"Is there anything else you'd like me to explain?"

She stared at him, startled by the question that seemed to imply she had a right to know. Was he really issuing an invitation? And if so, did she dare take him up on it? She took one small step.

"Well, Teddy seemed to think it was strange that you had such a brief credit history. He checked that." Coward, she castigated herself. Put the blame on Teddy.

He nodded. "I assumed he had. I spent virtually all of the past fifteen years out of the country, in Europe. So there was just no need to have credit here. When I was in the U.S., I used an apartment in the city owned by the company, and company credit cards, as well.''

"I guess Teddy should have thought of that," she said, nodding. It certainly sounded reasonable to her.

"Perhaps. But the very fact that Natalie asked him to check up on me would make me sound suspicious. And my guess is that your brother isn't too happy about your living here."

"Um, well, you know how brothers can be. I'm sure he'll change his mind when he meets you."

"I hope so. But my chief concern is that *you* aren't suspicious of me."

She looked him straight in the eye, protesting. Of course she wasn't suspicious of him! Why should she be? He had more reason to suspect *her*, given her past behavior, than she did to suspect *him*. She could only hope that she'd convinced him. After all, she *wanted* to believe that.

If her performance was less than adequate, he gave no indication. He merely nodded, then returned to their former discussion. "So what are we going to do about your change of names?"

She chewed her lip thoughtfully. "I don't know. It seems that I've exhausted my capacity for lying."

He laughed. "You *were* very good, by the way. But I'd suggest that if you decide to do this sort of thing in the future you write down your various stories, so you don't get them mixed up."

"Thanks," she said dryly. "I'll keep that in mind. You know, it's really annoying when I think of all the trouble I went to and all the times I worried about whether or not you'd caught my slips of the tongue. And anyway, how *did* you recognize me so easily? Those disguises were pretty good."

"I happen to have a good memory for faces, especially pretty ones with upturned noses and big eyes. Otherwise you might have gotten away with it."

His voice was more teasing than seductive, but she could still feel heat stealing into her face, not to mention into the rest of her. Embarrassed at her overreaction to a perfectly ordinary compliment, she asked him if he had any suggestions.

"For your future career in investigative work?"

"No, for getting me out of this mess. My career as a private eye is over."

"Why don't we just make some vague allusions to its all having been a joke?"

"I don't think *I'd* buy that," she said doubtfully.

"*You* don't have to buy it, *they* do. I think we could carry it off. Hints of some sort of secret between us—that kind of thing."

"Well, in the absence of anything better, it'll have to do," she sighed. "I just can't believe that I got myself into this situation."

"Sometimes people can take a few small steps, then discover too late that they've walked into quicksand," he said. "It must have sounded exciting and different."

She nodded, suppressing a shiver. Once more she was sensing multiple layers of meaning. Had he gotten into something innocently, then been unable to extricate himself?

She said good-night and left him there, staring out at his new pool. She wondered if she'd gotten any closer to the truth about him. Everything he'd said *could* be true, and she certainly wanted it to be. But that was the danger, wasn't it? She wanted to believe him, and he might very well know that.

Layers beneath layers. Boxes within boxes. Circles within circles. She was reminded suddenly of the bathroom in her grandmother's home, where a large mirror hung opposite the mirror on the medicine cabinet and the two reflected each other endlessly. All was real, and nothing was real.

She wanted the Lucas who seemed to be slowly emerging from beneath that armor: a man of wit and kindness and gentleness. But what if there was yet another man beneath that?

LUCAS STARED AT THE POOL and let his mind drift for a few seconds until he began to envision the two of them swimming together in the moonlight, their naked bodies glistening, moving toward each other.

He was having one hell of a time keeping his hands off her, and an already nearly impossible situation wasn't being helped by his certainty that she, too, harbored such desires. It was beginning to seem to him that by the time something *did* happen between them, if it ever did, they'd burn each other up with the heat they generated.

And it was much worse since she'd made her confession. Before that, he'd only glimpsed the real woman beneath the lies; now he was confronted by her all the time. Lucas was half embarrassed to admit even to himself that she was everything he'd ever wanted in a woman: bright, funny, warm, vulnerable in some ways, but strong in others.

And understanding and accepting. He didn't know if that was a result of her profession, or the reason she'd chosen it in the first place. But what it meant to him was that if he had a chance to build a life with any woman, Susan Trent was the one.

Something was keeping them at arm's length, though, and it wasn't just him and his fears. She couldn't really know the truth about him, but she suspected something. He wondered if her suspicions could be worse than the truth. It was a thought worth considering.

ABOUT THIRTY PEOPLE were gathered to celebrate the new swimming pool, and about half of them were already in it. The weather had cooperated by remaining warm and sunny, and on this day there was a light breeze that held the afternoon heat at bay.

Lucas's guests included neighbors, other antiques dealers, a local attorney, and a few other people whose connection to him Susan hadn't yet learned. Her guests consisted of Teddy and Amanda and several people from her office. The two groups seemed to be meshing well, drawn together by the beauty of the day, the setting, and, of course, the pool.

The Lucas Andrews she saw today was the urbane, charming man she'd first encountered in her journalist disguise. He played the role of host with ease and divided his time between his guests and hers. Watching him, Susan found it nearly impossible to imagine that he could be harboring a dark, secret past.

Teddy and Amanda had been the first to arrive, and Susan had nervously introduced the two men. Lucas thankfully did not mention Teddy's role in her deception, while Teddy gave the impression that no such thing had ever occurred.

And yet it was clear that the two men were taking the measure of each other in that subtle way men so often exhibited. What they actually thought of each other at this point was impossible for her to guess, but she suspected that Teddy might be having some difficulty sustaining his image of Lucas in the face of the reality. She'd caught him watching Lucas several times, a slightly puzzled expression evident on his handsome features.

She was both surprised and pleased to discover that Lucas's suggestion regarding her two names appeared to be accepted. Teddy's presence during one of these "explanations" had discomfited her, because she'd forgotten to warn him. But he'd gone along with it smoothly, even adding a remark about his not being the only practical joker in the family.

Lucas himself had displayed a surprising talent for acting when he'd casually hinted at some private joke between them, his arm draped lightly around her shoulders. It was then that Susan saw what she'd failed to grasp when he'd first proposed that explanation—that their listeners would be titillated, assuming some sort of romantic involvement between them.

It occurred to her too that that assumption might already have been made in any event, simply because Lucas was treating her in every way as his hostess. She was both pleased and uneasy about this. Surely he knew the impression he was creating, and yet there was no suggestion that he found it troubling.

When she thought about his behavior toward her, both before and after her confession, Susan found herself wondering just what was happening. Was it all an act, a plan to pry from her the full extent of her knowledge about him? Or was it an elaborate, slow game of seduction? And how could she trust her own judgment, when she was in his thrall?

It was for this reason that even when his touch sent spirals of heat curling through her, another part of her held back, certain that the proverbial "other shoe" would drop at any time. She wanted him, but she could not forget the danger in that wanting.

A rather embarrassing moment occurred when two of Lucas's guests arrived. The woman turned out to be the dealer Susan had talked to at the time of her first visit to Ridgefield, before she'd taken to disguises. Susan recalled that the woman had been surprised at her statement that Lucas was about to marry, and that she herself had hinted at an interest in Lucas.

Unfortunately, the woman remembered her and mentioned the visit. Lucas noted her chagrin with amusement, but, fortunately, neither he nor the woman said anything to deepen her embarrassment. Later, however, when the woman caught her alone, she proved that she had recalled their conversation quite well. Susan began to wonder if these people remembered everyone who stepped through their doors.

"So you must have been wrong, after all, about Lucas being engaged," the woman said with a smile.

Susan flushed slightly. She wanted badly to put all those lies behind her, although that hadn't really been a lie at the time.

"Yes, I guess I was."

The woman leaned close and put a hand on her arm. "Well, between you and me, he's quite a catch. I introduced him to every single woman I know, but he never seemed interested."

Her words echoed those of Barbara, their neighbor, and Susan wondered silently if there could be any single woman within a fifty-mile radius who *hadn't* been brought out for his inspection. Lucas and women was a subject about which she speculated endlessly. Not once had he ever mentioned an old girlfriend. Of course, he rarely spoke of his past in any but the most general way. Still, no man of his age and attractiveness could *not* have a past littered with women. And surely, among the women he'd been introduced to by these would-be matchmakers, there must have been at least one who appealed to him.

She wondered if he'd sworn off women for some reason. She could understand that; after all, she'd avoided any entanglements during graduate school. But what could be his reason? A love affair gone bad, perhaps? Maybe she was wrong to think that his careful avoidance of intimacy with her had anything to do with his uncertainty about her knowledge of him.

She walked over to the pool. She hadn't gone swimming yet, though she wore her suit beneath a long, gauzy cotton dress. Teddy and Amanda were among those in the pool, and they swam over to her.

Amanda had turned out to be something of a surprise, and Susan was now feeling guilty about having made fun of her. She was bright and funny and very down-to-earth. Instead of the usual model's sculptured perfection, she exuded an air of healthy outdoorsiness and athleticism.

"C'mon in," Teddy urged her, reaching out to grab her bare ankles with a cool, wet grip. "We're getting up a game of volleyball."

Susan obligingly slipped off the dress and joined them, gasping a bit at the water temperature, which was probably perfect for swimming laps, but was a bit cold after the heat of the sun.

Lucas had strung a net across the pool earlier, and a game now developed quickly. People began to gravitate to one side or the other, and Teddy announced loudly to one and all that his sister had been a high school and college volleyball star, drowning out her protests that that had been years ago and on a gym floor, not in a pool. Then he counted heads and stated that one more person was needed on the opposing side.

"Hey, Lucas, get in here!" he called. "You look like a man of many talents."

Susan, who hadn't noticed Lucas at the side of the pool, turned toward him, with her brother's double entendre ringing through her head. She could cheerfully have killed him for that, but Lucas merely laughed and stripped off his shirt and pants to join them.

Her stomach clenched at the sight of the long, ragged scar that traversed his broad chest from the shoulder to a spot near his heart. The glimpse of it before he jumped into the pool actually made her forget the pleasure of seeing his nearly naked body.

Beside her, Teddy muttered that it must have been "one hell of a fight," then wondered if his opponent had survived.

The game began quickly, but for a time Susan was too rattled by the sight of that scar and the change wrought in his appearance by bare, muscled flesh and hair slicked down by the water. He no longer looked like the sophisticated antiques dealer. Instead, he'd been transformed into the kind of man who walked far more dangerous paths.

Thanks to Teddy's noisy urging and her longtime love of the game, she soon regained her skills. On the other side of the net, Lucas proved Teddy's assessment to be correct. What he lacked in skill, he more than made up for with a natural athleticism. Susan tried not to watch him, but she could hardly help being aware that they soon established themselves as the stars of their respective teams.

The game ended with Susan's side the winners by two points and Susan herself the top scorer, although Lucas had come close. As the others scrambled out of the pool to get some refreshments, she and Lucas stood on opposite sides of the net, with Susan having to tread water lightly to keep her head up.

"Congratulations," he said. "You obviously haven't lost your skills."

"No, but I'll be paying the price for it tomorrow," she said ruefully, thinking of all those abused muscles.

She stared at him through the net, and that earlier impression returned to torment her. It seemed that a layer of civility had been peeled away with his elegant clothes, and she shuddered inwardly at what remained.

He slid under the net to join her, and she tried not to stare at that jagged scar. The tiny ripples created by the others in the pool and by her motions as she continued to tread water seemed to be pushing them together.

"You were pretty good yourself," she told him. "You scored almost as many points as I did."

"Like Teddy said, I'm a man of many talents." He smiled, then wrapped a long arm loosely around her waist. "Come on. Let's get something to drink."

They paddled over to the ladder. He climbed out first, then reached back to assist her. Wet bodies touched fleetingly, and the feeling lingered on in a melting warmth as she toweled herself dry and then walked with him over to the refreshment table, where guests were helping themselves to cold smoked turkey and roast beef, pasta salad and a huge platter of perfect strawberries. The affair had been catered, but Mary was there to supervise.

Small tables were scattered about the big yard, and after they had gotten some chilled white wine and filled their plates he led her to one away from the crowd.

As soon as they were seated, he remarked that everyone had seemed to accept the explanation about her two names.

"Yes. Thank you for that," she replied. "But now half the people here think we're having an affair." She was striving for a light note, but couldn't quite prevent a slight huskiness from creeping into her voice.

"Does that bother you?" he asked with a half smile, then lifted the towel he'd slung over his shoulders. He started to toss it aside, but he saw her staring at the scar.

"No, not really," she said, her voice trailing off slightly.

"Knife fight," he said casually as he let the towel fall into place again, obscuring the scar. "In Istanbul, a long time ago. I happened to be in the wrong place at the wrong time. It wasn't as bad as it looks. I'm not sure that the guy who stitched me up was even a doctor, let alone a surgeon."

"I wouldn't have guessed that the antiques business could be that dangerous," she said, with another attempt at lightness.

"It isn't, but I was young and stupid and out to sample the nightlife." He paused a moment to taste the wine. He laughed softly.

"Just as you were drawn to New York, I felt an urge to see the world, to try everything just once. And believe me, no matter how dangerous parts of New York can be, there are places far worse.

"And early on in my travels I discovered that I have a real gift for languages. I pick them up very quickly. So instead of sticking to the usual tourist spots, I'd go where the natives went. That's what happened the night I got into the knife fight."

"How many languages do you speak?" she asked curiously, recalling that she'd heard him speak both French and German—or what she'd thought was German.

"Four fluently, besides English. And I can get along well enough in four or five others. It came in very handy in my business, especially since Europeans are accustomed to Americans who can't speak any other language.''

"I'm impressed," she said sincerely. She'd barely survived college French herself. Was a criminal likely to be multilingual? And an antiques expert, as well? It seemed that she could not resist tormenting herself with these questions.

Their eyes met across the small table, and she was once again aware of their near-nakedness as they sat in the warm sun. But the heat that pulsed through her had nothing to do with the day. These moments of intense awareness lent an almost surreal quality to their encounters, making it seem as though two very different conversations were being conducted simultaneously. Sensuality whispered just below the surface of more mundane discussions.

He began to talk about the pool, wondering aloud if perhaps he should have put in a diving board. He'd chosen not to do so for esthetic reasons.

Susan sat there, only half listening to their spoken conversation, and wondered suddenly if the day would come when he would tell her in that same low, almost hypnotic voice that he'd once been a hired killer.

But how could he be? It simply wasn't possible. He was a man who could wax eloquent over fine old furniture, who collected exquisite carvings, who had a deep appreciation for all things fine and beautiful. She'd seen his small kindnesses to Mary, his housekeeper, who clearly adored him. And she'd watched him with his nephew. He was clearly unaccustomed to small children, but he tried hard to overcome that.

But he was also a man who had triumphed over a terrible childhood, re-creating himself in the process. Did that mean he could have done the same thing a second time, casting aside the shell of a criminal to become the man she saw now?

They finished eating and began to circulate separately among the guests. From time to time their gazes would lock, and before they slid away again Susan would become aware of the fragility of that thin veneer of civility that kept the human animal in check. If it weren't for that, the primitive mating call of male to female would surely prevail.

It was dusk by the time people began to take their leave. Lucas surprised her by inviting Teddy and Amanda to stay over, offering them his guest room, since her apartment had none. But Amanda had a modeling assignment in the morning, and Teddy had to see a club manager in the Village about a possible job.

Curious about Teddy's reaction to Lucas, Susan managed to get him alone for a few moments before he left for the city. He shrugged in response to her question.

"Okay, so he's not what I expected. But all that proves is that if he's a criminal, he's a class act. So maybe he's an art thief or a jewel thief."

She made a sound of disgust. "You've watched too many movies, Teddy. Just admit that you *could* be wrong."

"I *could* be wrong," he said obediently, though not very convincingly. "Did he say where he got that scar? It looks like a knife fight to me."

"It was." She told him what Lucas had said, including his explanation of how his facility with languages had led him astray.

Teddy nodded. "He has a handy talent. For a lot of things."

She rolled her eyes, even though she had to acknowledge the truth of what he'd said.

"One thing I can say for sure," Teddy continued. "He's got designs on your body, Peggy Sue. No doubt at all about that. Even Amanda remarked it."

She couldn't very well deny it. "But he's not pushing—quite the opposite, in fact."

"So he's just being patient for now. Successful criminals have to be careful. Otherwise they get caught." He shrugged. "Okay, I admit I could be wrong about him. I hope I am, because, actually, I kind of like the guy. But I'm still worried."

He frowned thoughtfully. "You know, you were right when you said that there's something dangerous about him. I mean, he's a class act and all that, but there's something about him that makes me think I wouldn't want to meet him in a dark alley."

"Teddy, he's lived in places you and I have never even dreamed about, and I doubt if that knife fight was the only danger he ever faced. He admitted that he often went to places that are off the usual tour routes. Most Americans don't do that because they can't speak the languages."

Teddy raised his hands in mock surrender. "Okay, okay, I give up. I have to, anyway, because here he comes."

Lucas and Amanda joined them, and they all said goodbye. The last few guests departed shortly after that. Mary had done most of the cleaning up before she left, leaving only a few things for Susan and Lucas to carry back into the kitchen as dusk turned to night.

After having so many people around, Susan now felt a disquieting sort of intimacy between them. It was all she could do not to start nervously when Lucas brushed against her casually as they finished the cleaning up in the kitchen.

Lucas broke the silence by saying that he liked Teddy and Amanda. Susan admitted that Amanda had been something of a surprise to her, since she failed completely to live up to the stereotypical image of the fashion model.

"You and Teddy are a lot alike," he observed as he put the last of the glasses into the dishwasher.

Susan groaned. "That was always our problem. If only one of us had had more sense, we would never have gotten into so much trouble. It's lucky for us that we have such understanding parents."

She hadn't been referring to their joint efforts as private eyes, but was quickly reminded of that when she saw him smile.

"Well, you've already seen an example of that, haven't you? It was like that when we were kids, too. One of us would think up something, and the other would carry it even further. Neither of us was ever very good at applying the brakes, I'm afraid."

Lucas laughed. "In this case, I'm glad neither of you did."

They exchanged smiles that had just begun to edge toward something more when Lucas suddenly suggested they go for a swim.

"The water temperature should be perfect by now, thanks to all those bodies in it all afternoon."

Susan could not say no. The idea was irresistible, even if it did reek of danger. Ever since he'd first mentioned building the pool, she'd thought of such a scene. But she'd permitted her fantasies to go far beyond what she intended this night. That, after all, was what fantasies were for.

Susan was not alone in her fantasies. Lucas, too, was aware of the dangers. The term "safety in numbers" had never been more applicable than on this day. He'd found it very difficult to keep his eyes off her, and several times had seen Teddy regarding him with brotherly suspicion.

No doubt he was warning her against any involvement. Lucas couldn't really blame him, since if their positions were reversed he would be doing exactly the same thing, and probably even more strongly than Teddy was.

He switched on the pool lights, and as they walked across the lawn toward the shimmering water Lucas found himself at the mercy of some very strange and contradictory emotions.

He wanted Susan more than he could ever recall wanting any woman before, but he also felt this overwhelming need to protect her—from *him*. And he knew he'd never felt that before.

What he wanted, he realized, was for it to be different for them. As much as he wanted her, he didn't want a frantic coupling that might leave them both physically satisfied but nothing more.

That sudden realization brought him up short, and he glanced at her with something approaching awe. How had he gotten to this point? How had curiosity and amusement and simple pleasure in her company brought him so close to the brink?

She stepped out of her cover-up and he began to fumble with the buttons of his shirt, his fingers strangely uncoordinated as he thought about all this. She turned briefly to smile at him, then jumped into the water and began to swim, becoming nothing more than a dark blur in the shimmering water.

Lucas thought about other women and other nights and tried to reach back to remember how he'd felt then. But the faces and the names were a blur, and if he'd had any feelings beyond getting them into bed, he couldn't recall them now.

He stood for a moment, poised at the edge of the pool, and stared at the shadowy figure now swimming laps. And he knew that, no matter what happened, Susan Trent would never be a blurred memory.

Lucas jumped into the pool, lost in a volatile mixture of wonder and fear.

Chapter Eight

The water temperature was perfect for serious swimming, just cool enough to dissipate the heat of hardworking muscles, but not so cold as to pose a risk of cramps. Susan succumbed quickly to the pleasures of stroking back and forth the length of the pool. It took her back to her high school days, when she'd done some competitive swimming and had spent long hours practicing in a nearly deserted pool.

But this pool wasn't deserted, and she was reminded of that every time she pushed off at one end and saw him at the far end or somewhere in the middle, a dark, powerful shape silhouetted by the lights. And even when she couldn't see him, she could feel the movement in the water as they passed each other, swimming in opposite directions.

She became sharply aware of both their isolation and their connectedness as they moved through this watery world, slipping past each other's mostly naked bodies. So she swam harder still, pushing against her limits in an attempt to ignore him.

Accustomed to a standard Olympic-sized pool, Susan had no idea how many laps she'd done before she felt the not-unpleasant sensation of exhaustion, as though her muscles had dissolved to become one with the water. She flipped over onto her back and floated for a time, her eyes closed, drifting with the tiny eddies and swells in the pool.

At first, when her head touched something solid, she thought she'd bumped against the edge. But even as she opened her eyes and simultaneously started to flip over to tread water, she knew she was mistaken. Instead of the smooth, unyielding pool liner, she felt almost equally unyielding warm flesh.

His arms came around her, sliding down from her shoulders and grazing the full undersides of her breasts as he held her while she righted herself. The sensation was electric, the current magnified by the soft lappings of the water around and between them.

"I thought you might have fallen asleep," he said. There was husky laughter in his deep voice.

"I think I could have," she admitted. Her hands had closed around his upper arms, and now she didn't quite know what to do about it. She was feeling clumsy in her body now, after the sleek grace of swimming and the out-of-the-body sensation of floating.

The water wasn't deep, reaching only just slightly above her waist and occasionally lapping at the lower edges of her breasts in a way that seemed to mimic his brief touch. Beneath the surface, his leg rested against hers, solid and bristly.

"You're a good swimmer," he said, his voice still husky.

"I used to do some competitive swimming, but I'm long out of practice."

Their words seemed disconnected from themselves, floating somewhere above them in the soft night air. The lights in the pool shimmered around them, adding to the sense of unreality.

"Lucas..." she began, when the silence had dragged on for too long. "You did *not* take advantage of me that other night, no matter what you seem to think. I'm not some innocent schoolgirl, and I *do* know how and when to say no."

She hadn't really known what she was going to say until the words were coming out, and she didn't tilt her head to look up at him until halfway through her little speech.

He had that harsh look again, with his hair slicked against his head and the planes and angles of his face made even more evident by the interplay of light and shadow.

She had issued an invitation to him to kiss her, but it didn't happen. In her mind she twined her fingers through his hair and drew his mouth to hers, but in reality she simply stood there, waiting for him to respond and feeling, with each ticking heartbeat of a second, that she had made a mistake.

He shifted slightly, keeping his hands curved around her waist, but moving his leg away from hers. Then he turned his head away, as well, and stared off into the darkness for a moment before turning to face her again.

"I'm, uh, trying to think of a way to explain this that doesn't paint too ugly a picture of my past," he said at last.

She tensed involuntarily, and knew that he felt it. At first it was because his initial words had suggested a rejection, a denial that he had any romantic interest in her at all. And then, as he finished, it was because the specter of his past had risen up in her mind.

"I traveled all the time, and that made it impossible for me to have normal relationships with women—to get to know them well."

He hesitated, clearly uncomfortable. In fact, he was more uncomfortable than she would have believed possible for him. But she was already relaxing, knowing now that he didn't intend to talk about his work. Instead of being threatening, the situation had become almost amusing, though she took care to hide that as she sought to make it easier for him.

"What you're saying is that your romantic past has been a series of one-night stands." She spoke the words evenly, with no hint of judgment, as much the psychologist as the woman at the moment.

"I'm afraid so. For the most part, anyway." A rueful grin curved into his mustache.

"And now?" She wondered where she'd gotten the courage to press on. The psychologist was still talking, no doubt. But the woman knew she was treading on very dangerous ground.

"I don't want that now, Susan."

"Good. Neither do I. So what do you propose we do about it?"

He chuckled softly. "I think I hear a psychologist talking."

"Well, it's difficult to turn off completely."

She lifted her hands and curved them lightly over the tops of his shoulders. "Lucas, I was attracted to you from the beginning. Don't ask me why, because I don't know. But I'm nervous, too. I spent three years burying myself in my studies, with no time at all for men.

"At first I told myself that my interest in you was because of that . . . because I was starting a new life. But that isn't it, or at least not *all* of it. I don't know what's happening here, but I *do* know that it isn't just the result of living without a man for too long."

He smiled at her. His was the soft smile of a man who has heard what he wanted to hear, what he'd hoped to hear. She was amazed that a face that only a moment ago had seemed so harsh could now be so gentle.

"No, it isn't." He lifted a hand slowly and touched a finger to her lips, tracing its outline and leaving a trail of warmth behind.

"For a while, when I didn't know why you'd suddenly appeared in my life, I was almost tempted to believe in magic. Maybe I still do."

His hand slid around her neck, and he drew her to him with a slow movement that let her savor the next moment. Instead of claiming her mouth, he buried his face in the curve of her neck. His tongue ran slowly, languorously, over her sensitive skin.

She arched against him, her fingers digging deeply into the corded muscles of his shoulders as she half stood and half floated against him. Nothing more than a few wisps of wet cloth separated them. His lips and tongue moved slowly, tracing the outline of her ear, then trailing lightly across her cheek until she turned impatiently and sought his mouth with hers.

Their tongues met instantly and began a sensual duet, touching and probing. The temperature of the water seemed to drop precipitously, causing her to shiver as the molten heat of desire throbbed within her.

He groaned, and the sound vibrated through her, as well. His hands slid down to cup her bottom, and his fingers kneaded her soft flesh as he drew her against him. That unmistakable hardness brought a gasp from her and sent her mind spiraling off into a realm where only the pure, white-hot heat of desire existed.

The water ebbed and flowed with their slight movements, adding its own sensuality to a scene that needed none. Susan felt herself drifting, her body supported by his as she floated several inches above the pool's bottom. In that peculiar, semiweightless state, Lucas Andrews became the only solid reality as his lips and hands roved over her.

Her wet, slick fingers moved over him, as well, tracing the harsh planes and taut muscles of his body and registering his essential maleness deep inside her female core. Only when her seeking fingers touched the slight ridge of that scar did a small, quiet note of caution force its way through the languorous heat. She struggled to ignore it, but it stayed there.

The change was subtle at first. They continued to kiss and caress and flow together in the water, and yet somewhere, somehow, the point of no return had been approached, though not crossed. Nearly lost in the engulfing waves of their mutual passion, they both somehow kept a small but important grip on the solid ground of their lives.

After a time, Lucas slowly lifted his face from hers. A rueful smile curved his lips. "It may kill me, or kill us both, but I want to enjoy the waiting." Once again he touched a finger to her lips, now achingly sensitive from his kisses. "Can you understand that?"

She nodded, even though every fiber of her being cried out for more... for that ultimate more. It was, she knew, proof that he wanted it to be different for them. She met his gaze and wondered if he had felt the hesitation in her. And, if so, whether he understood the reason for it.

A delicate and fragile balance existed between them now. Mutual need had been acknowledged, but secrets remained. The future whispered tantalizingly, but the past still lurked threateningly.

He leaned forward and kissed her softly, with aching tenderness. "Then I think we'd better say good-night."

SUSAN SEARCHED through Lucas's collection of software, found what she wanted and inserted it into his computer.

She was grateful for his offer to let her use his computer so that she could work on the brochure for the new program. The agency's office space was crowded and computer time was limited, and she needed to have the brochure ready for next week's meeting of the local mental health association. Besides, computers were hardly her forte, and using Lucas's, she didn't feel pressured.

Lucas had left for the city early on the morning following the party, then stayed there last night. When he'd called her, she'd feared that he was going to apologize again. But there was no apology this time. Instead, they had talked for nearly an hour, and more had been heard by them both than had been spoken. In fact, when they'd hung up, Susan could barely recall what they'd said, but that powerful desire had been reaffirmed.

He would be home later this evening, after a stop in Bronxville to consult with a client and her decorator. Already Susan's body was tingling with anticipation, and she wondered just how long they could maintain their control. They both seemed to need it just now, though for very different reasons. He wanted romance; she wanted answers. But they both wanted each other.

She sat there at his workstation, temporarily ignoring the task in front of her as she relived the night before last one more time. She hadn't really been surprised by his confession about his past relationships. She'd already speculated about the women in his past, and given what she knew of him, she'd guessed that his romantic life had probably consisted of little more than a succession of brief affairs.

His determination to change all that touched her. Lucas Andrews was clearly a man of many layers, and the more that fact was confirmed, the stronger her feelings for him became.

But those nagging fears about his past remained, and she was increasingly certain that he knew that. Was this all a plan of his? she wondered. Was he revealing himself with deliberate slowness, hoping that by the time he gave up his secrets their love would be so strong that she would accept whatever he had to tell her?

She could not fault him for that. In his place, she might well do exactly that. In fact, she *had* done exactly that. With the clarity of hindsight, she could see that she'd revealed the truth about herself only when she'd been reasonably sure he would accept it. If it was taking him longer to reveal himself to her, it was because the revelation itself must be far more damaging.

She shuddered as she thought about Teddy's insistence that Lucas was a criminal—or *had* been. Her glance strayed involuntarily to the desk drawer where he kept the gun. She got up from the workstation and went over to it. Still locked. But then, why wouldn't it be? Anyone who kept guns in the house should keep them locked away. She was making too much of this; millions of people kept guns in their homes, and he'd said he was a collector.

She went back to the computer, but now found herself staring at the closet door, thinking about his statement that he kept other guns in the safe. But what else did he keep in there? From what Greg had told her, it seemed an elaborate precaution just to store guns. Most men who collected them simply kept them in ordinary gun cases.

She turned to the computer with determination. Tormenting herself with questions that had no answers—and that might never have answers—was a waste of time. Lucas might never tell her the full truth about his past. Either she could decide that that past was an insurmountable obstacle and get out, or she could simply accept the man she knew now and bury the past, as he was apparently doing. It was a choice she didn't want to make, but one she knew she would have to make soon. For now she pushed it aside and got down to work.

Some time later, the phone rang. She got up to reach for the combination telephone and answering machine on his desk, thinking it might be him, but the machine was set to pick up after the first ring. It clicked on before she could pick up the receiver. His message was brief, and after the beep, an unfamiliar voice came on.

"Lucas, it's Jack. We need to talk. Something has come up, and we need you. Call me anytime."

The machine hummed and clicked and went about the business of resetting itself. Susan shuddered. The message replayed in her mind as clearly as if she'd hit the play button on the machine.

Something in that voice frightened her. The voice hadn't been menacing, but it had been urgent. And maybe there was a hint that the caller knew his message would not be welcome.

She sank into his desk chair, staring at the machine. The message light blinked implacably back at her. She *knew* it. No matter how hard she tried to interpret the brief message differently, she knew that voice had come from his past. They—whoever they were—wanted him back. Would they succeed? Did that damnably anonymous "they" have some sort of hold over him that would force him to do what they wanted?

She recalled how she'd once erased a message from the domestic agency. She could do it again, but what good would *that* do? He would only call again.

She forced herself to review her work on the computer, but the words meant nothing. She finally gave up and switched off the computer, then popped out the disk and took it back to her apartment.

When she heard his car pull into the driveway, Susan had no idea how much time she'd spent pacing about her small apartment, wrapped in the icy grip of her fears. He pulled into the garage beneath her, and she waited for the sound of the automatic door closing. But instead, her doorbell rang.

She got up slowly, wondering if she should mention the message. He couldn't have listened to it yet. And he would probably guess that she'd been there at the time, since the machine automatically recorded the date and time of messages. She ran down the steps and flung open the door, still undecided.

He hesitated only a second before reaching out to draw her into his arms, but even as she let herself be enveloped by his warmth she wondered if he might be regretting the other night after all. If only there were some certainty in her life right now.

But the only certainty was their mutual desire. His mouth sought hers hungrily as she laced her fingers through his hair and stretched up to meet his need with her own. She could feel his rigid self-control, that taut leash that was barely holding back his passion. She moved still closer to him, fitting her curves to his hardness and tormenting them both.

He released her slowly, his lips moving from hers to brush softly against her nose, her cheeks, her brow. By the time he withdrew, her fevered mind had already imagined those lips tracing fiery lines over the rest of her body. Her T-shirt and shorts chafed against her heated skin. She had a nearly overpowering urge to begin tearing off his suit right there.

"Did you get your brochure written?" he asked, his arms still circling her waist lightly.

"Mostly. I can finish it at work tomorrow."

"So my computer was friendly?" he teased.

"We reached an understanding. But as far as I'm concerned, if we were meant to communicate with machines, we'd speak in beeps."

He kissed the tip of her nose. "If you're finished working for the evening, why don't we go for a swim?"

She nodded. She'd thought about that earlier, and her fantasies had gone far beyond a swim . . . until that phone call.

He left, and she went back upstairs to change, thinking of the previous evening, when she'd worn nothing at all as she glided through the water in her solitary swim, hoping irrationally that he'd return early from the city.

When she came around to the side yard, she saw that he had already turned on the pool lights. But there was no sign of him. Was he calling that man Jack? Might he even now be agreeing to do whatever Jack wanted?

She hesitated for a moment as she started toward the pool. She'd left the window in his study open. If she were to sneak around there, she could probably overhear any conversation. She glanced back at the terrace, then started in that direction, taking only a few steps before she stopped again.

No. She would not sneak around. However much she needed to know who the caller was, she would not resort to such methods. Her past deception and her secret doubts about him weighed heavily enough on her without adding still more deceit.

She went to the pool, climbed down the ladder and began to tread water. That call could mean anything, really. The man could even be another dealer who simply needed Lucas's advice. Clinging tightly to that hope, she struck out for the far end of the pool, where big old trees overhung the sparkling water. By the time she started back, he was walking across the terrace. She swam over to meet him, hoping to glean something from his appearance or his words.

He said nothing as he climbed down the ladder to join her, then set off to swim laps. She stared after him. His very silence told her that her hopes had been misplaced. She watched as his powerful strokes carried him quickly to the far end of the pool. She resumed swimming herself.

But there was no relaxation to be found in exercise tonight. Her muscles were taut, and, fearing a cramp, she rolled over onto her back and began to float instead, staring up into the blackness of the night sky.

She imagined herself issuing some sort of ultimatum: Choose your past life or me. But she had no idea which he'd choose, and perhaps he didn't even have a choice. She rolled over and began to swim again, emptying her mind into the rhythms of her strokes.

He was still swimming when she finally gave up and climbed out of the pool. She rubbed herself with a towel as she watched him glide swiftly through the glowing water. Her despair nearly overwhelmed her. She loved him and wanted him . . . and she didn't even know him. She thought about the long, improbable chain of events that had brought her here to this place and time. A silly game, a few moments' foolishness, and now she was being swallowed by the darkness surrounding him.

He swam to the ladder, pulled himself from the pool, picked up a towel and began to dry himself. She sat down in one of the chaises, wondering if he would say anything about the call. His continued silence made her so tense that she began to cast about in her mind for some harmless conversation.

"I have to go away tomorrow," he told her as he, too, settled into a chaise. "I'm not sure how long I'll be gone. It could be a week or two."

"Oh?" She fought to keep her tone casual. "Where are you going?"

"To Europe." He hesitated, and she thought he would say nothing more, but after a moment he went on. "I had a call from the company I used to work for. They need my help with something. It's hard to say no, because they know I can use the contacts I built up with them over the years."

She said nothing. She simply filed away the information to examine it later. And she sensed that by remaining silent she was encouraging him to say more.

"I know it's not a good time to leave," he said after a long silence. "Not a good time for us, I mean. But I don't really have any choice in the matter."

The one thing Susan knew for certain—the *only* certainty in the midst of unasked and unanswered questions—was that he didn't want to go. She was sure he couldn't be faking that.

"Didn't you tell me that you've never been to Europe?" he asked after another hesitation.

"No, I haven't."

"Then we'll go as soon as you can get some time off. Fall would be a good time, because the tourist season will be over."

"I'd like that," she said, not doubting his sincerity, but unable to think that far ahead right now.

He was silent for another long moment. Then he got up and came over to sit on the edge of her chaise. She didn't look at him, because she felt the tears threatening. How could she explain being upset just because he had to go away for a short time?

He reached out and drew her face around, then leaned over and kissed her lightly. "I don't want to leave you now, Susan. It's... Everything feels so—" He stopped abruptly, then continued. "I'm half-afraid you won't be here when I return."

She stared at him, feeling the effort it had cost him to say that. He made a sound, as though laughing at himself.

"I'm not very good at talking about my feelings. I know a lot of men are like that, but I suspect I may be worse than most. But you've become... very important to me, and I want you to know that."

She reached out to touch his face. "I'll be here, Lucas. You've become important to me, too."

Where, she wondered, does being important to each other fit on the scale of things? Was it a small step, or a giant leap, from there to being in love? She loved him, and now she knew he felt the same, even if the words seemed to trail behind the feelings. And knowing now that he had his own fears somehow made hers easier to bear, even if they didn't fear the same things.

She dropped her hand, and he lifted it to his lips, running his tongue lightly across her sensitive palm. Belatedly she wondered if he might be telling her this now because he feared he might not come back. Could he be killed? Or sucked back into whatever he'd escaped from? It took every ounce of courage she had to ask the question.

"You said you were worried that I might not be here when you get back. Should I be worrying that *you* might not come back?"

His dark eyes bored into hers, seeking, probing. Then he shook his head. "I'll be back. There's nothing for you to worry about."

It was impossible for her to guess if he was telling the truth. What had she expected him to say? That he could get killed hunting antiques? All she'd done by asking that was to let him know that she knew, or at least suspected, that he had some secrets.

He was still holding her hand, his head bent as he stared at it. Then he looked up at her, and Susan made a decision.

"Make love to me, Lucas. I don't want to wait any longer."

She felt him tense and heard his sharp intake of breath. His eyes met hers and held them, weighing her words and testing them. What she feared most in those few seconds was that he would ask why, why now. How could she tell him that she feared he was about to be lost to her forever? That she wanted him *now* because they might never have another chance?

He stood up and extended a hand to draw her to her feet. She thought he intended to say good-night, a good-night that might really be goodbye, and she was determined that that would not happen. But instead, he continued to hold her hand as he led her across the yard, onto the terrace and into the house.

She thought he might be remaining silent for the same reason she had earlier: to encourage her to say more, to explain her urgency when they'd agreed to go slow. She, too, maintained her silence as they walked through the house and up the stairs.

His ploy, if indeed that was what it was, nearly worked. Susan began to have second thoughts. Was this *really* what she wanted? Not just the moments in his arms, but the aftermath? Was she sealing her fate, binding herself to him too tightly, when she still knew so little about him?

He stopped just inside his bedroom door and turned to her, raising his brows questioningly. She met his gaze defiantly and reached around with trembling fingers to undo the clasp on her bikini bra. It fell to the floor, and she shivered lightly, because her skin was still damp.

He stared at her, at the swelling fullness and the taut nipples. Beneath the damp bikini bottom, her skin radiated heat, chafing against the cool wetness. Then, with a groan that echoed endlessly in the silence of the room, he pulled her into his arms.

The flesh-to-flesh contact electrified her, sending tiny shock waves throughout her body as she strained against him. There was an all-devouring hunger to their kiss, a greediness for more than could ever be satisfied by lips and tongues alone.

The damp chill left her breasts, driven out by the contact with his solid, warm chest and teased to aching sensitivity by the tiny hairs that prickled her soft skin.

His hands slid down slowly, tracing her curves, then dipping beneath the band of her bikini pants. The sensation of sudden warmth against her chilled, wet skin set off shuddering explosions even before he pressed her against his hardness.

He pushed the damp scrap of cloth down, then lifted her slightly to help her struggle out of them. As she half stood, half lay across the corded steel of his arm, he lowered his mouth and surrounded a taut nipple. She gasped as the sensation traveled along the length of her body.

She could not have stood on her own, and her fevered brain wondered how *he* could, because she could feel the tremors in him, as well. But, somehow, he lifted her onto the bed, then stepped back to strip off his swim trunks.

He stood for a moment, staring down at her, glorious in his maleness, and at the same time somehow touching in his vulnerability and need. But if he was vulnerable, so was she. Her own need throbbed painfully within her, and she raised a hand, reaching for him.

It became a sensuous charade. He pretended that the object of his desire was the curve of her neck, the rosy crests of her breasts, their soft undersides, the hollow of her waist and the concavity of her navel.

She pretended to want nothing more than to caress with lips and tongue his hair-roughened chest, the small nubs of his nipples, the line of fine hairs that trailed down across his muscled stomach.

They avoided what they wanted most, in a mutual, unspoken conspiracy that served only to drive that need to ever greater heights. A wildness grew in them that welded them together in its heat even before they were fully joined.

"Please!" she gasped, trying to pull him to her.

He silenced her with a kiss, then began a slow, deliberate descent, sliding along the length of her body as his lips tasted her heated flesh. Her moans sharpened to a cry as his tongue found the very center of her throbbing desire. She writhed and gasped beneath his probing, driven to the very edge of her endurance, feeling her tenuous grip on reality slipping away.

Then he raised his head, slipped his hands beneath her and brought them together with slow, tentative movements, building the ancient rhythm by small degrees, moving more deeply into her with each thrust.

She clutched at him, arched to him and pulled his mouth to hers as the spasms began deep within her, then exploded for them both into mindless ecstasy.

He dropped heavily beside her and folded her into his arms, where they lay breathing raggedly and feeling the tiny quivers that were the gentle aftershocks of fulfilled passion.

As soon as she could begin to think again, Susan was searching for something to say. She wanted to tell him that she loved him, but feared giving voice to that truth. She wanted to beg him not to leave her now. Wasn't that what had *really* been behind her request that he make love to her? But she couldn't say that, either, because she knew what his answer would be, and she would only sound foolish if she objected to a brief separation.

His past seemed to be lying there between them, an almost solid presence in the bed. She moved still closer to him, fitting her body against his to drive that presence away. He ran a hand caressingly over her curves, and she felt his lips move against her hair. When he spoke, his voice was low and thick.

"I need you, Susan. I thought the need would go away now, but it hasn't." He propped himself up on an elbow and stared down at her. "Maybe you don't need to hear this, but I want you to know that I'm not going back to my past."

She stared at him and swallowed hard to relieve the lump in her throat, a lump made of pure fear.

"What do you mean?" she managed to say in a choked voice.

He hesitated, his eyes again boring into hers, seeking her secret knowledge and fears. Uncertainty flickered briefly in his features, and when he spoke again she was nearly certain that he wasn't saying what he'd intended to say.

"There won't be any other women. That's over. I just wanted to be sure you understood that."

She merely nodded, feeling as though she'd entered into a conspiracy with him, a conspiracy to ignore the dark presence between them.

They fell asleep in each other's arms, still lost in the soft sensuality of their lovemaking, warmed by bodies fitted so perfectly together.

SUSAN AWOKE WITH A START when she heard an unfamiliar voice, and only belatedly realized that it was coming from the radio on the nightstand. She always awoke gently to WQXR, the classical music station, but she knew by now that Lucas was a news junkie and so had tuned the radio to WINS, the all-news station. She groaned at the sudden assault on her senses as the announcer droned on about the latest upheavals in Eastern Europe as it struggled unevenly toward democracy.

A bristly mustache tickled the hollow where her neck joined her shoulder, and the announcer's voice faded away as she shivered with pleasure.

"How can you wake up to that?" she grumbled. "I need at least two cups of coffee before I can face the day's disasters."

He chuckled and reached across her to turn off the radio, then deliberately drew his hand slowly back across her breasts as he pressed himself against her back. Memories of the night just past shuddered through her awakening body. Sleep was quickly driven away by molten desire that flowed through her from her head to her toes.

He propped himself up on one elbow and stared down at her, a grin curving his mustache. "Something tells me that you're not a morning person."

"You're right," she replied. Her response lacked conviction, because he had grasped the covers and was dragging them off her. His lips and tongue followed the downward sweep of his hand.

"What I mean is..." she began, but ended with a moan as both mustache and whisker stubble rubbed against her stomach.

"I'm not big on conversation in the morning myself," he stated, his breath fanning softly against her thighs.

Their bodies picked up the conversation quickly, speaking to each other very eloquently in the special language of new lovers who mistakenly assume that they already know everything there is to know about each other, only to have new facets revealed.

Any lingering inhibitions were cast off as they flowed together, taking more time now to explore each other, and allowing their need to build until it threatened to consume them both.

Susan had never felt so voluptuous, so cherished, so free to let her body dictate its needs as he played upon her flesh with fingers, lips and tongue. Then she made him the instrument of her passion, thrilling to the planes and angles and hard muscles and unexpected softness and smooth skin stretched tautly over the bold evidence of his manhood.

Unable to take the torment any longer, he groaned and lifted her over him, and she took him into herself and brought their erotic symphony to a shattering crescendo.

Lucas held her quietly, feeling the aftershocks of their lovemaking tremble through them both. Thoughts of his trip kept trying to intrude, and he kept pushing them away. This was where he wanted to be—now and forever. He wanted to tell her that, but didn't. Some small amount of his normal caution remained, warning him that, in spite of what had happened between them, he still shouldn't trust these feelings.

He was poised on the border of two worlds: the one he'd been trying to leave behind, and the one he hadn't dared to let himself believe he could have until she had entered his life. One foot was in the past, and one was poised to reach for the future. It was a dizzying feeling.

As he lay there struggling to find some words—words that didn't come easily to a man who rarely talked about feelings—the sound of the front door opening intruded. She sat up quickly, a stricken expression on her face.

"Oh, my God! It's Mary! What's she going to think?"

He smiled at her, amused by her sudden prudishness, since it contrasted so sharply with her wild abandon of moments before. "She'll think exactly what she's *already* been thinking," he responded as he swept her soft, shining hair away from her neck and buried his face in her fragrant warmth.

"Oh?"

"She's been acting like a campaign manager for you ever since she returned," he smiled. "With varying degrees of subtlety."

He got out of bed reluctantly and put on his robe. "I'll let her know there'll be two for breakfast."

Smiling, Susan watched him disappear. The smile vanished when her gaze fell on the leather bag that sat just inside the door. She hadn't really forgotten that he was leaving, but she didn't want to be reminded of it, either.

He returned, shrugged out of the robe, then leaned over the bed to kiss her softly. "Will you join me in the shower?"

Of course she would, and the hot water ran out before they had finished washing each other. The process of drying off took even longer, with both of them just barely resisting the temptation to return to the bed.

The only clothing she had with her was the still-damp bikini, which had been abandoned on the bedroom floor, so he gave her a T-shirt and gym shorts that covered her sufficiently to allow her to run back to her apartment and grab some of her own. When she returned, Lucas was already at the glass-topped table on the terrace, sipping orange juice and perusing the *New York Times*. He put the paper aside as soon as she appeared. The smile he gave her warmed her clear through.

"Convincing you to take that apartment was a stroke of genius, if I do say so myself," he said as she bent to kiss him lightly.

"So you had designs on my body even then, did you?" she asked archly as she sat down and picked up her own glass of juice.

"No more than you had on mine," he replied, his dark eyes glittering.

"Um, well, there *did* seem to be a few pheromones flying about. Lust at first sight, I'd say." She grinned at him.

She was surprised to see the amusement leave his expression, to be replaced by a sudden seriousness. He reached across the table to take her hand.

"That was then, and this is now. It's more than lust, Susan, a lot more."

She nodded and tried to swallow the sudden lump in her throat. "Yes, I know."

Unspoken words hung in the air between them as they stared at each other in a mutual acknowledgment of excitement and fear. They were still holding hands and staring at each other when Mary appeared with breakfast, beaming at them both.

A little over an hour later, Lucas stood in the doorway, watching Susan drive away. When her car rounded a bend in the street and was lost to view, he felt a chill run through him. And in that moment he saw his past whirling by in a darkness that made him reach out for the solidity of the door. For one irrational moment, as he stared at the empty street, he was convinced that she had been only a dream... a lovely, tantalizing dream forever beyond his reach.

SUSAN LOOKED in her rearview mirror and caught one last glimpse of him before she drove around the curve and the house disappeared. Their actual goodbye had been brief, as though by tacit agreement. At the time, it had the benefit of making it seem as though this were nothing more than a brief business trip. But already she felt an emptiness and a fear that gave the lie to that charade.

A gray Jaguar approached her as she drove slowly down the winding street. There was very little traffic on this quiet cul-de-sac and her attention was drawn to it. She frowned, certain that she'd seen it before, and when they passed each other she recognized the driver.

It was Ted Rutledge, the attorney who'd been one of the guests at the swimming party. Susan watched curiously in her rearview mirror as he continued on toward Lucas's house. She had assumed from things he'd said, or perhaps from some remark of Lucas's, that he was Lucas's attorney.

She drove on, wondering why he should want to see his attorney now. There could be many reasons, of course. Probably it was something connected to his business. But she still carried the question with her as she drove to work. It seemed far less threatening than the question of where he was going and why.

Chapter Nine

Some time later, Lucas stood in the doorway again, now watching Rutledge drive away. He didn't like the fact that he'd felt compelled to take this step before leaving. It seemed to indicate a lack of confidence, and that was something he'd never felt before.

The difference, he knew, was Susan. As soon as he'd agreed to do what they wanted, he'd called Ted at home and told him he wanted to change his will, and wanted to sign it before he left. Ted hadn't questioned either the change or the reason for doing it now, but he surely must have wondered about the necessity for speed, since Lucas traveled regularly to Europe.

Reading it before he signed with Mary as witness, Lucas had felt a chill pass through him. But he'd signed it, knowing that if anything *did* happen to him, Susan would be taken care of.

Not that she really needed to be taken care of. Despite her current situation, she would do well for herself. But it seemed to be the only way he could tell her just now how much she meant to him.

He went upstairs to get his bag, turning his mind to the days ahead. It all felt so damned alien to him now, and while he knew that was good, it troubled him in that same vague way that his sudden insistence on changing his will had.

In the limousine on the way to JFK, and later, as his flight soared over the Atlantic, he kept returning to the question that had been haunting him. What did she suspect? Could it be worse than the truth? And how long did he really have before he would be forced to tell her that truth?

He was in love with her. There were no longer any ifs, ands or buts about it. For the first time in his life, Lucas knew how it felt to truly *need* another person.

And, for that reason, he wanted to bind her so tightly to him that the truth couldn't send her away. He also knew just how selfish that was. He might be a novice at love, but even he knew that love had to be built on trust...and he'd been betraying that trust from the beginning.

SUSAN THREW HERSELF headlong into her work, spending far more hours at the office than she was presently being paid for. It had already become obvious to her that this was a perfect marriage, from both the employer's and the employee's points of view. They had been seeking an unconventional psychologist, and she had been hoping for a job that would give her the latitude she sought to be innovative.

Already a number of the staff had remarked that they were glad she was "fitting in so well." She devoted herself to setting up her program and working out the training that would be given to her two aides. Her plan was to use play, art and music therapy, but in a far less structured situation than those forms were usually applied in. She stretched the program's supplies budget to the max to get art supplies and video games, then got a piano donated to the program and even persuaded a supplier of musical instruments to provide her with some instruments that had been traded in.

She visited the church near the office where the program would actually be held, and after seeing how drab the place was, asked if she might repaint the walls herself. The youth minister, caught up in her enthusiasm, recruited a group of teens to paint the place, including the battered wooden chairs and tables.

Susan met with the teens and, rather to their surprise, asked them what *they* thought should be done with it. After several meetings on the subject, they politely told her to stay away and set to work. She and the youth minister exchanged several worried phone calls, but agreed to leave the project in the hands of those who were far more likely than they themselves to know what would appeal to kids.

As she began to sift through the referrals that were already coming in for the program, Susan found herself thinking more and more about Lucas. She missed him.

Finally, she gave in to her impulse, and checked through his house again, hoping to find some clue as to where he'd gone. There were only two sets of slacks missing. Likewise, it appeared that only a few dress shirts were gone, although she was less certain about that.

Lucas Andrews was a man who paid attention to his appearance. In fact, Susan found his slight vanity rather amusing. His wardrobe, both business and casual, was extensive, not to mention expensive, and she had yet to see him not elegantly turned out. And yet he appeared to be traveling very light. Rather strange behavior, she thought, for a man who, insofar as she could tell, never wore a suit twice in the same week. But, having made these discoveries, Susan then told herself that experienced travelers often traveled light, and Lucas was certainly an experienced traveler.

Two weeks edged toward three, and Susan became more and more uneasy. She'd been sleeping in his bed some nights, the nights when Mary wasn't scheduled to be there in the morning, since she was too embarrassed over her behavior to want the housekeeper to discover it. And on one of those nights she suddenly thought about his guns.

That she had even thought about them was proof positive of just how nervous she was becoming over his continued absence. She lay in his bed, staring at the nightstand and wondering if the gun was still there. Then she turned away from it and tried to sleep, but to no avail. Instead, she played a game with herself. If the gun was still there, she would stop worrying about him. If either it or the one downstairs was gone, *then* she would worry.

She didn't have Greg's implements or his skill at opening locks, but as she sat there on the edge of the bed, staring at the nightstand, it occurred to her to just pick up the stand and shake it. So she got up and grasped the edges and lifted it. It turned out to be much heavier than she'd expected, but when she moved it there was a distinctive thump that she was sure must be a gun.

Next she went downstairs to his study, where she opened the desk drawer directly beneath the locked drawer that had held the gun and the silencer. Reaching inside the other drawer, she rapped against the wood, thumping it as hard as she could from such an awkward angle. She was rewarded by several dull thumps.

Her relief was just edging toward guilt over her spying when two things struck her that might have occurred to her much sooner if it hadn't been one o'clock in the morning. First of all, he had told her that he also kept guns in that safe, which she had no way of checking. And secondly, it wasn't likely that he could get a gun through airport security, and even less likely that he'd risk trying.

She ran a tongue over her abraded knuckles, feeling foolish and fearful in roughly equal measure. The truth was that he was gone, and she didn't know where he was or what he was doing or when he'd return. And she had absolutely no way of getting any answers, either.

Mary's concerns were soon added to hers, since Lucas had also told her that he expected to be gone only a week or so. And then Anne called from the shop, having been told the same thing. She did not improve Susan's state of mind by saying that in the past, when Lucas had been delayed, he had always called her.

Susan thought, but did not say, that this trip was different. In all likelihood, his past trips had been ordinary buying trips for his business. By contrast, this was a trip into his past, however much he had attempted to gloss it over to her.

She continued to sleep in his bed most nights, trying desperately to recapture that night of magic. But her dreams became increasingly troubled. She would awaken in the dark stillness of the house, certain that she'd heard the sound of his key in the door, and then fall asleep again to be tormented by dreams in which she always seemed to be fleeing from some ill-defined threat. It did not take her psychological training to know that the threat was his unknown past, which was now threatening their present and future.

Only at work did she remain relatively free of her fears, although even there Lucas and his terrible childhood were always with her, especially as she read the referrals to the program. Nearly all the children being referred came from alcoholic or otherwise addicted families and were struggling, just as he must have done, simply to be children.

The teenagers who had assumed the responsibility for preparing the church site for the program summoned her to see the results of their labors. Susan and the church's youth minister stood in the middle of the large room and smiled with genuine pleasure. The drab space had come alive with bold colors and huge murals featuring rainbows, Sesame Street characters and Teenage Mutant Ninja Turtles, plus a variety of other figures beloved by children, all mixed together to create funny and hope-filled scenes.

She decided to give a swimming party for the teen workers, who were carried to Lucas's home in the church's van. It did occur to her that she was taking considerable liberties with a home that wasn't hers, but she did it anyway. It seemed somehow appropriate to her that Lucas's home should be used for such a purpose, though of course he might not see it that way.

On the day of the party, Susan sat on the terrace with the youth minister and his wife, a junior high school teacher, while the teens enjoyed the pool. She explained her living arrangements to them and then went on to tell them something of Lucas's own background and her growing sense of this program as a sort of "gift" to him, though admittedly without his knowledge at the moment.

"Well," said the minister's wife, "he sounds as though he must be living proof that some children can triumph over incredible odds."

Susan nodded, but she feared that his supposed triumph was in great danger....

IN AN ANCIENT CITY in a land at war with itself, the Lucas Andrews of Susan's worst fears moved from shadow to shadow along darkened streets. A dull red glow could be seen over distant rooftops. It often seemed that half the city was on fire at any given time.

A curfew had been imposed by what passed for law in the divided city. The penalty for breaking that curfew was a simple one: death at the hands of whatever faction happened to catch the lawbreaker.

Barricades of burned-out cars had been erected at various intersections, and here and there the night's dead lay where they had fallen. In the morning when the fighting was usually less intense, relatives would seek them out and carry them away before going on to forage for food, too shell-shocked to grieve properly. Then, carrying whatever they could find, they would scurry back to the cellars where they now lived most of their lives. At nightfall, the shelling and the sniper fire would begin again.

United Nations peacekeeping forces had fled a few days before, because there was no longer any peace to be kept. The death and destruction was condemned by one and all, including those who continued to wreak it. It would stop only when various factions had exhausted themselves, then resume when they'd rested enough to remember how much they hated their neighbors' ancestors. Memories were long indeed in the Old World, something few in the New World understood.

But Lucas understood this. He'd been here many times in the past, when the might of the Soviet Union had suppressed the hatred with an iron fist. He and others had predicted all this when the Soviet Empire began to show its first cracks, but it gave him no pleasure to see his prognostications come true.

He paused in a shadowed doorway, his eyes carefully scanning the empty street and darkened windows above. Anyone looking down from one of those windows would have seen a rough-hewn man dressed like a manual laborer. Certainly, they wouldn't have seen a sophisticated man dressed in a Savile Row suit, silk shirt and hand-made Italian shoes. That Lucas Andrews was in the closet in Connecticut that Susan had recently searched.

And if anyone had chanced a word with him, no suspicions would have been raised. He spoke the language, even down to the accent of the social class he was pretending to belong to.

Lucas reached behind him and withdrew the slim, black German 9 mm automatic from his waistband, then stepped out onto the empty street. When he was halfway across, a sudden burst of automatic gunfire shattered the night. It came from behind him, only a few blocks away, and he guessed that it might well have been an area he had traversed only moments earlier.

Then he slipped into the shadows on the far side of the street, this time into a dark alleyway that lay between two buildings, barely wide enough for two men to pass each other without turning sideways. At the end of the corridor was a stone wall about six feet high. He hoisted himself over the wall, grunting slightly with the effort and thinking that only a few years ago he could have accomplished it effortlessly.

After dropping to the other side, he hunkered down and edged, crablike, along the wall until he was concealed behind some big trash cans. And there he stayed for several minutes, his eyes and ears and the sixth sense all his kind possessed seeking out any signs of life.

Finally he got up and sprinted across a small courtyard and ran silently down a short flight of steps to a heavy basement door. He rapped sharply on the door in a prearranged code. The door opened a crack almost immediately, and an automatic rifle was poked through the opening. Words were exchanged in low voices, and then the door was opened to admit him.

The room beyond was dimly lit and stank of cigarette smoke and unwashed bodies. Only three men were there, but Lucas immediately saw the one he sought. The two men embraced briefly, then got down to business.

When daylight came and the street was filled with people moving hollow-eyed about their business, Lucas joined them. After walking for nearly an hour, he came to the rear entrance of a hotel. He slipped inside and hurried up the back stairs to his room. There he picked up his watch and decided he could grab a few hours' sleep before setting out again in his foreign correspondent's guise.

He was exhausted, but sleep wouldn't come. Instead, his dozing brain became fixated on an image and a time that now seemed to belong to a different life... that *did* belong to a different life.

He pushed those thoughts aside reluctantly and considered instead what he'd accomplished thus far and what more he hoped to do. But his thoughts kept snagging on that ever-present awareness of danger he felt now. He'd never felt that before. Often, when it was over, he'd think about the narrow escapes, the consequences of being caught. But never before had he let such thoughts intrude at the time.

The difference, he knew, was Susan. He had a life worth preserving now. It shocked him to realize that he must not have believed that before. Or perhaps he had, after all, since he'd gotten out. But there was a much sharper sense of a different life now, a need to get back to that life. A need to get back to Susan.

Days and then weeks passed. He left one place and repeated his activities in another. People who had trusted him then trusted him now. None of them knew his real name. He wore a name that had been translated into several languages; in English, it was Eagle. The few who did know his real name were men like himself, and the ones who were still alive were doing much as he was.

Every time he saw a telephone, he wanted to call her. He even thought about calling and saying nothing, just listening to her voice. But he didn't do it, because he didn't want to frighten her. The thought of what she might have guessed was never far from his mind. It followed him around, just like his newly developed awareness of his own mortality.

EVERY DAY Susan expected him to return, or at least to contact her, and every day brought a new disappointment and deepening fears. She slept in his bed each night now, whether or not Mary was coming in the morning. The housekeeper was clearly concerned, too, and Susan was beyond caring whether or not she was behaving like a silly fool.

A dread grew in her that Lucas would *never* return. She didn't doubt that he had intended to return to her, but she feared now that he'd been irredeemably dragged down into his past. He had reinvented himself after a terrible childhood, into what she didn't know, but she was sure that he had. And then he'd left that life to create a new one here. With a history like that, what was there to stop him from repeating that transformation yet again, willingly or unwillingly?

She recalled seeing his lawyer arrive the morning he left. Her blood ran cold. She should have made the connection before. If he had planned to return to his old life, or even guessed that he might be forced to return to it, he would have to dispose of his business and his home, and surely that would require the services of an attorney.

"I'll be back. There's nothing for you to worry about." She thought about those words now and wondered if they'd been nothing more than the words of a desperate man who was trying to reassure himself as well as her.

After another largely sleepless night, Susan could stand her own inaction no longer. There had to be something she could do, some action she could take to find the truth. She thought about contacting his lawyer, but as one who dealt in client confidentiality herself, she knew she was unlikely to gain any information from him. She might be forced to try at some point, but there was one thing she could do first.

She found Carolyn's phone number on the Rolodex in Lucas's study. Her guilt over dragging his sister into this was outweighed at this point by her determination to take action. Carolyn was immediately frightened, and even as Susan tried to downplay her fears she felt a certain relief at being able to share them. It didn't really lessen the burden, but it did make it easier to bear.

As Susan had hoped, Carolyn still had the number Lucas had given her long ago, and the name of the company, as well. Since it was now Saturday, Susan had thought she would be forced to wait until Monday to call them. But Carolyn told her that the number was supposed to be answered twenty-four hours a day, every day, since the company had business interests worldwide.

She thanked Carolyn and promised to get back to her as soon as she had news, then hung up and punched out the New York City number for Antiquities International Corporation.

After four or five rings, it was answered by a rough male voice announcing the name of a delicatessen. Susan checked the number to be sure she had dialed correctly, then asked about the company. It was obvious that the man knew nothing about them, and the background noise certainly sounded like a deli.

She pondered what to do next. She could call Carolyn back to be sure she'd copied the number accurately, but she was sure she had. And calling her again might only upset her still more. Instead, she called Teddy.

From his groggy response, it was obvious that she'd awakened him, but she hurried on anyway, explaining the situation.

"Is there some way you can find out about this company? Maybe they moved out of the city."

"Yeah," he said with a yawn. "That's possible, but it's also possible that they've disappeared."

She already knew that, but hated to have her suspicions confirmed.

"Let me work on it," he went on. "I'll go over to Greg's office and see what I can do."

Susan spent the rest of the morning and most of the afternoon on tenterhooks, but tried to keep herself busy by cleaning her seldom-used apartment, weeding the garden and then going for a swim. When she came back from the pool, the message light was blinking on her machine, and she punched the play button, hoping against hope that it would be Lucas himself and not Teddy calling with news she didn't want to hear.

But it was Teddy, and his message was brief. "Call me at home."

She tried not to read too much into his abruptness, but her fingers were trembling as she punched out his number. He answered right away.

"It doesn't look good," he said unhappily. "They went out of business about ten months ago. I got one of Greg's people to help me, and we dug up some information, but what we found raises more questions than it answers. They were privately owned by another company that's privately owned by another company that's . . . Are you getting the picture yet?"

"No," she said, although she feared she was.

"The guy who helped me has done this kind of thing before, and he knows a lot more about it than I do. He says this is the way they go about hiding true ownership, and often the fact that the other companies are offshore points to some sort of criminal enterprise."

"Offshore?" Susan asked weakly.

"Meaning that these other companies are incorporated in countries that don't have the disclosure laws the U.S. has. That means that true ownership can be hidden."

She said nothing. Darkness was swallowing her. Despite all their earlier suspicions regarding Lucas, this was the first concrete evidence they'd seen of a criminal history. Teddy expressed that very thought as Susan sat there silently, struggling with this new knowledge.

"Stay out of it, Susan! The best thing you can do is to pack up and get the hell out of there—now! Come back here until you can find a place."

"I—I have to think about it. There's nothing more I can do, anyway, and they won't know I know this."

After a brief silence, Teddy went on, in a softer tone. "Look, I really did like the guy. And maybe he really *was* trying to get out of whatever he was mixed up in, but I think it's sucked him in again. Just be glad that things didn't go any farther with you two."

Any farther? A bubble of hysterical laughter welled up in her as she thanked Teddy and hung up, promising she would give some thought to his suggestion. How much farther could it have gone? She loved him, and she knew that he cared very much for her.

The rest of the day and night passed in a blur. She had wild fantasies of somehow rescuing him. She would go to the FBI and tell them what she knew and demand that they do something. She would search Europe for him. She would get Greg to blow apart that damned safe so that they could find the records he must keep there.

By the time Monday morning came, the wildness had gone out of her, replaced by a numbness and a hollowness she suspected would be there for a long time. Mary was arriving just as she was leaving for work, and she asked again if Susan had heard from Lucas. Susan merely shook her head, not wanting to talk about it.

Mary frowned. "I don't mind telling you, Susan, I'm getting real worried. I've been kind of worried ever since I saw the way he was that morning he left. He just wasn't himself."

"What do you mean?" It suddenly occurred to Susan that the housekeeper would have been there when the attorney arrived.

"He just seemed worried about something, and then he had a visitor, too. They were in his study for a while, and then he called me in to witness something."

"A legal document, you mean? I saw his visitor. He's Lucas's attorney."

Mary nodded. "I thought so. It was some sort of legal thing, but I don't know what it was. He just called me in and signed it, and then I signed as witness. But I don't know what it was."

Susan did her best to reassure the worried woman, then left for work, thinking about that legal document. Could it have been a power of attorney? Had he given the lawyer the power to sell his home and business?

She thought about calling Ted Rutledge, the attorney. After all, he knew her; they'd met at the party. But she was sure he would be unable to tell her anything, and given her own profession, she could hardly attempt to badger him into breaking attorney-client privilege.

She drove on to work, grateful that she at least had a challenging job to occupy her thoughts during the day. But the long, empty nights loomed.

LUCAS SAT IN THE SHADOWS at the back of the dimly lit, smoke-filled bar, nursing a glass of the potent local wine. His eyes burned from the heavy pall of cigarette smoke that hung in the air. Everyone smoked here; it was one of the things he'd noticed on this trip, although he'd paid it scant attention in the past. So many people had quit

smoking in the U.S.—including him—that he'd been surprised at first to see that that hadn't changed here. No
surgeon general's nagging in these countries.

Outwardly he looked calm, just another workingman
stopping off for a few before heading home, but there was
a knot of tension growing in his gut. Two nights ago he'd
slipped across the border into the old Soviet Union, not
into Russia itself, but into one of the other republics now
threatening to explode with newly released nationalism.
The tension in the country was palpable, even though no
actual fighting had broken out as yet.

Susan. He knew he shouldn't be thinking about her
now, but he'd long since given up trying to put her from his
mind. He saw her watering his garden. He saw her in his
study, nervously explaining the real reason for her presence in his life. And he saw her that last night, in his bed,
her lithe body an instrument perfectly attuned to his.

Lucas was alternately dismayed and awed by the
strength of his feelings for her—dismayed because something in him kept warning him against allowing himself to
be in thrall to another person, and awed because he could
not control it . . . and maybe didn't even *want* to.

This was the last and most dangerous of his multiple
missions. After he met his contact here, he would begin the
circuitous and difficult journey back to the West, and then
home to Susan.

He was thinking about a little shop he knew of in Paris
that designed perfumes to order, and wondering if she
would like such a gift, when two men appeared suddenly
at his table. They shouldn't have been able to get that
close, but he'd let his mind wander. His hand had already
begun to move toward the gun strapped inside his boot
when he looked up at them, then relaxed.

They pulled up two chairs and signaled the barmaid.
The conversation was casual, between old friends meeting

after a hard day's work. Then, after sharing a pitcher of the execrable local brew, they all got up and left.

Lucas and his companions walked through dark and nearly deserted streets, carrying on sociable conversations as they watched the shadows, feigning slight drunkenness, which allowed them to bob and weave and so survey their surroundings regularly.

They had reached the outskirts of the business district when the gunfire erupted.

SUSAN SQUARED her shoulders and marched into the attorney's office, prepared to do battle. Lucas had now been gone for nearly two months. She could tolerate the uncertainty no longer. And she reminded herself that she was not the only one who was frantic over his absence.

Carolyn called nearly every day. They consoled each other, but could do little else. Anne, Lucas's assistant at the shop, was also a regular caller. Lucas's clients were upset; sales might have been lost because Anne didn't have his expertise. And each time she came to clean a house that scarcely needed it, Mary's question was in her eyes.

Furthermore, it had by now become apparent that he'd known he might be gone for an indefinite period, regardless of his statement to her. A few days ago, it had belatedly occurred to her to wonder just how his bills were being paid. Anne had called shortly after that thought occurred to her, and Susan inquired about the shop's bills and Anne's own pay.

Anne explained that she kept the books for the shop and that Lucas had told her long ago to make out her own paycheck. Since her name was on the shop's account, this presented no problem. But she knew nothing about the household bills.

Susan had by then realized that she hadn't seen any bills in the mail, which she collected daily, since they shared a mailbox. She'd simply sorted through it and taken her own, then left his mail in his study. In her never-ending hope that the mail would contain some message from him, she'd paid no attention to the rest of it.

She had checked again and ascertained that there were no bills at all in the pile on his desk. Given the fact that he'd been gone for nearly two months, that made no sense, unless he'd made arrangements before he left. And she confirmed with that a call to Mary, who told her that Lucas had paid her in advance for the month before he left, and that she'd just received another month's pay in her mail that day. The check was a bank check from Lucas's bank, signed with an unfamiliar name, presumably a bank official.

Susan had thought about calling the bank, but quickly decided that she had even less chance of getting any information out of them than she did of persuading the attorney.

She was shown quickly into the office of Ted Rutledge, the attorney, and lost no time in getting down to business. She told him how long Lucas had been gone, despite his statement that he would be returning within a week or so. She explained that his sister was concerned, and that Anne was worried about the business, as well. Then she fixed the attorney with an unflinching stare.

"I know that you came to his house the morning he left and that he signed some sort of legal document. I assume it must have been a power of attorney and that you're now paying his bills through the bank. I understand completely the existence of attorney-client privilege, but I *must* know what's happened to him."

She hesitated for a moment, then went on in a softer tone. "I love him, Ted, and I have every reason to believe that he loves me. You *have* to help me. I'm really afraid that something has happened to him."

She felt strange confessing her feelings to a near stranger, but she hoped it would make her case stronger. And although she hadn't let her voice show it, she felt a twinge of uncertainty as she told him that Lucas loved her. He hadn't said he did. She knew that he cared for her, but . . .

"Susan, I don't know what I can do to help you. I assumed he was back, and I have no idea where he would be."

She thought he was telling her the truth. "You mean that you *aren't* paying his bills?"

He shook his head, and she explained that none were coming to the house. Then she told him about Mary's paycheck from the bank.

Rutledge nodded. "He must have made arrangements there, then."

He picked up his phone and asked his secretary to bring Lucas's file. When she brought it in, he told her that he had the name of Lucas's private banker and should be able to confirm that.

Private banker? Susan wondered what that meant. But before she could ask, the attorney was calling him. The conversation was brief, and when he hung up he told her that Lucas had indeed made arrangements to have his bills forwarded there, to be paid by the banker.

"But he didn't say how long he'd be gone," Rutledge went on. "He just told him to take care of things until he called again, and he hasn't heard from him."

"What's a private banker?" Susan asked curiously, mostly as a way of avoiding what was becoming crystal-clear, that Lucas had known he might be gone for some time.

The attorney smiled. "It's a service some banks offer for their customers who have considerable assets and don't want to manage them themselves."

"Oh." Susan didn't want to think about his assets and where they might have come from. "Can you tell me what it was he signed before he left?"

Rutledge hesitated for a moment. "Well, I guess I can tell you that, although I can't divulge its contents, of course. It was a new will."

She sat there silently, absorbing that news. "When did he contact you about changing it?"

"The evening before I went to his house. He said he wanted to sign it before he left, so I had my secretary come in early to draw it up, then took it to him myself."

Susan mulled this over. Lucas must have called him just after he'd gotten home that evening, probably right after he'd talked to that man who'd left the message. And if he'd insisted upon signing it before he left...

"I thought it seemed a bit strange myself," Ted went on, interrupting her thoughts. "After all, he travels to Europe often enough. I thought maybe he'd explain, but he didn't, and I didn't ask. To tell you the truth, he seemed... distracted. Not like himself at all."

Susan wondered how both Mary and Rutledge could have seen that, while she hadn't. Was it because she'd still been basking in the afterglow of their lovemaking? Or had Lucas taken care not to show his feelings in her presence? He was certainly capable of hiding his thoughts from her; she knew that well enough.

"We could call the State Department," the attorney suggested. "But unless we have some idea where he might be, I doubt there's anything they could do."

"No," Susan said, perhaps too firmly. "I'm sure I'll hear from him soon."

She thanked him and left his office, paying scant attention to his well-intentioned assurances. Then she went home and called Teddy, pouring out all her concerns to him, even though she knew what she was going to hear.

"Susan, I told you before, get out of there. There's nothing you can do, and now you know he lied to you about when he'd be back. I don't have to remind you that he's lied before."

"Teddy, I love him, and I refuse to just walk away without knowing what's happened. If he's never coming back, then I need to know that."

Teddy was silent for a moment, then said quickly, "I guess I already knew how you felt about him, but I didn't want to think about it, since I'm the one who got you into this mess."

"No, you didn't. I walked into it with my eyes wide open, Teddy. You said that Greg has an FBI contact. Do you think he could help?"

"I'm not sure that's a good idea," Teddy replied doubtfully.

"I frankly don't care if it's a good idea or not," she stated angrily. "If he's a criminal and they know it, then I need to know it, too. Do you think Greg can find out?"

"Maybe," Teddy admitted reluctantly. "It's some guy Greg went to school with. I don't know what his position is, but I know he's pretty high up on the totem pole."

"Then I want to talk to Greg."

Teddy finally agreed to ask Greg, and less than half an hour later, Greg himself called. Teddy had filled him in, but she added some more details.

"I *have* to know, Greg. I can't go on like this. Do you think your friend can help?"

"I can't promise, but I'll try. He and I are pretty tight, and if he can help, I know he will. But are you sure you want to hear the truth about him?"

"Yes, I'm sure."

GREG CALLED HER the following evening. Susan jumped every time the phone rang these days, and this time was no exception. Her hands were trembling as she picked up the phone.

"What it comes down to, Susan, is that I don't have any definite information for you. I didn't give my friend your name, but I still wouldn't rule out the possibility that someone might come to see you."

"What are you talking about?" she asked, her voice thin with anxiety.

"Oh, I don't mean that you're in any danger from my call, but you could be in for some questioning if they think you might know where he is. What my friend said is that he had no information he could give me."

"Then what makes you think—?"

"It's the way he worded it, Susan. Like I said, we've known each other for a long time. If he hadn't turned up anything on Andrews or that company, he would have said that. But what he said was that he had no information he could give me. That's different. He was saying that he *did* turn up something, but someone's clamped a lid on it."

Icy fear crawled along her spine. "And you think that just because you made an inquiry someone could be coming up here to ask me questions?"

"It's possible. I don't know. I think Teddy's right—you should get out of there."

She thanked him and hung up. She probably should leave, but she'd made a promise to Lucas, and she was going to honor it as long as she could. But the dark mystery that had always hovered along the edges of her mind was growing so fast that she feared for that promise.

Chapter Ten

As much as Susan tried to fight her depression, she became more sure, with each passing day, that Lucas would never return. Only work offered some comfort. Her ideas for the new program *did* meet with some resistance from the more traditionally minded psychologist from the state mental health agency, but Susan's impassioned defense and enthusiasm carried the day. When the man left after finally giving his grudging approval, Susan did a little dance around the room, then had to resist the temptation to call her former professors and gloat. That pleasure, she decided, could wait until she could prove that it worked.

Still, she could not help smiling to herself. How many times had they tried to fit her into the traditional mold, even suggesting at one point that perhaps she should reconsider her desire to become a psychologist?

However, when the pleasure faded, she was once again engulfed in sadness that the one person with whom she most wanted to share her success wasn't there. With the sadness came uncertainty, as well. Would he understand? Would he ever know how deeply personal this program had become to her as a result of her understanding of his own childhood? There were times when she thought she had never really known him at all—not just the mystery of his past, but also the man himself. But there were other times when she was certain that they were so closely attuned to each other that they instinctively understood everything.

September came, and after initially resisting the idea, Susan decided to fly home with Teddy to spend the Labor Day weekend with their parents. She had worried that Lucas might return in her absence and believe that she had broken her promise to be there when he got back. After leaving him a lengthy romantic note, she flew home to Indiana.

Her parents fortunately saw nothing amiss with their daughter, since Susan was able to talk with genuine enthusiasm about her work. But, even so, she felt for the first time almost a stranger to her own family, except for Teddy, of course, who knew her pain and shared it, since he continued to blame himself for it.

On the long trip back from the airport in heavy traffic, Susan let herself hope that she would find Lucas there. It was a foolish hope, of course, since she'd left her parents' phone number and knew he would have called if he'd returned. So by the time the uncomfortable van that masqueraded as a limousine pulled into the driveway she had succeeded in reducing her hopes to a letter or a phone message. She'd checked her own machine by remote from her parents' home several times, but hadn't brought the code for Lucas's machine.

But the mail yielded nothing, and there were no messages at all on his machine. She stood there in the quiet, empty house, unconsciously comparing it with the liveliness of her family's home. Then she walked through all the rooms, her gaze roaming over all the beautiful antiques he had collected for his pleasure. The place had begun to feel like a museum.

She stopped at the French doors that led to the terrace and stared out at his garden. She'd maintained it with great care. It was yielding a bountiful harvest. Life was proceeding without him. The realization came to her slowly that she was grieving, grieving for a man she was sure she had lost forever, and for a love that had never really had a chance.

Susan understood the complex procedure by which people let go of those they loved. There was disbelief and anger, and then, finally, acceptance. Certainly she'd felt the first two. And now, as she stood there staring at the garden and the pool, she knew she was edging closer to the last. Lucas was gone.

THE CELL WAS SMALL, with dank stone walls and no furnishings other than a slab of wood bolted to the wall and covered with a thin, foul-smelling mattress. There was a high window, set in a deep well, that admitted a little light. The only other light was a bare ceiling fixture in the narrow hallway, a few feet away from the strongly barred window. In the silence of the basement cell, Lucas would drift off into dreams of Susan that spun out over many hours.

They were swimming naked in the pool, dark shadows in the soft night, backlit by the shimmering underwater lights. Slick bodies performed an erotic dance as their lips met and her softness flowed against his hardness.

Then they would climb out of the pool, the sound of her low laughter filling the night as they fell together onto the grass. She was always worried about the neighbors, but her protests were slightly breathless.

He always took his time, his lips and fingers playing her body like a fine instrument created for him alone. She would arch and writhe beneath him with soft exclamations, just inhibited enough to make the challenge all the more sensual.

When she finally let go of those inhibitions, she would lavish an erotic attention to his body, tracing its harsh planes with her soft lips and pleasingly sharp fingernails. At first, her touch was delicate as a butterfly's, but then it became greedy and demanding.

They were joined in a frantic wildness, then lay sated amid soft murmurings and gentle touches and the pleasure of knowing that it would happen again and again.

And it was that certainty that kept him sane and alive as the weeks dragged past, marked only by daylight fading to darkness and the changing reports on the BBC.

SUSAN STILL SLEPT in his bed, even though it now seemed more hers than his. She kept the door to his closet firmly closed, where before she had often stood in there, touching his things and imagining that the smell of him still clung to them.

She regretted that she had no pictures of him. His face was still clear in her mind, but she sensed that it would soon begin to fade. Carolyn offered to send her some snapshots taken a year ago, when Lucas had visited her, but Susan asked her to wait. For now, she still wanted only her own memories.

The two women spoke regularly, but their mutual attempts to bolster their spirits had begun to sound flat and forced. Carolyn admitted that over the years she'd always expected it to end this way, that he would simply disappear into some world she couldn't begin to imagine.

One night, Susan was propped up in his bed, reading. She had only one chapter left in the mystery novel, and she knew that when she finished it she wouldn't be ready to go to sleep, especially since she knew that sleep would bring either impossible dreams or dark nightmares.

Seeking something to occupy her mind, she idly picked up one of the foreign affairs journals that lay on the nightstand. She scanned the table of contents without much interest until the title of one article caught her attention. With a prickling uneasiness, she began to read it.

The article itself wasn't long, but the impression it made was very powerful. The subject was contract agents: the men governments used to carry out various political missions for which they dared not use anyone who could be traced back to them.

Contract agents operated totally on their own, picking and choosing assignments and negotiating very high fees. Some worked exclusively for their own country, while others apparently worked for anyone who could meet their money demands. Some governments provided cover of a sort, setting up dummy corporations whose true ownership was well-hidden.

Contract agents could be anything from information gatherers to assassins, and if they had one distinguishing feature, it was that they were men who could blend in well wherever they went. They were risk-takers, danger junkies and loners.

The article went on to say that while all governments denied the existence of such agents, it was becoming increasingly apparent that some of them had played pivotal roles in the struggles of Eastern European countries against the Soviet Union and toward democracy.

Susan sat there transfixed, nearly unable to breath. And then she knew that the answer to the mystery of Lucas Andrews had been there all the time, lying beside the bed in which she'd spent so many tormented nights trying to understand how the man she had come to love could possibly be a criminal.

Or was he still a criminal—but one of a very different nature? She fell asleep still wrestling with the question of whether engaging in illegal acts—or even murder—could be justified, as the article had seemed to suggest it could.

But by the next day, she was less certain of her theory, telling herself sternly that she could be reaching too far in her attempts to justify both him and her love for him.

After a few more days and several more readings of the article, she decided that it scarcely mattered. He was gone—and *that* was all that mattered now.

LUCAS SHIFTED the scene of his fantasies. Shortly after buying his house, he'd been roaming about the nearby woods when he'd come across a spot that seemed almost enchanted. It was a small, unexpected clearing in the dense forest, a bed of moss and pine needles surrounded by tall pines and hemlocks with heavy boughs that dropped almost to the ground. The air was filled with their aromatic scent and the deeper, richer aroma of damp earth.

Following his discovery, he'd gone there often, at first to try to come to terms with the new life he'd chosen, and then, later, to read. In high school and college, he'd largely ignored the classics, but in that secluded bower he'd found peace with them. He regretted that he hadn't taken Susan there, and now he rectified that as best he could, by going there with her in his mind. . . .

It was late afternoon, with the sun riding low in the sky and casting long shadows in the woods and touching individual branches with gold. They stopped in the middle of the clearing, and a sunbeam fell on her brown curls, setting them aglow as she turned to him with wonder in her eyes.

For a time, they just sat there, saying things that were unimportant because the only truly important thing was that they were there . . . together.

They held each other and kissed, and that seemed to be enough. The need for more came upon them slowly, as slowly as they removed each other's clothes, as slowly as soft caresses turned to feverish mutual need. And then

heir cries mingled with bird songs and the susurrous sound
of the breeze in the pines.

The scent of pine and damp earth was the last image to
fade when Lucas opened his eyes to the reality of his life
now. One of the guards was at the door; it was time for his
daily exercise. He got to his feet slowly and wiped his
mouth. He could almost feel the imprint of her lips.

The guards found his exercise routine amusing, and
counted in their language as he did his push-ups. They
never really abused him, because they were unclear about
his status. Clearly he was a prisoner, but he was also an
American. He'd told them that after his capture, and had
even given them his real name. There had been no reason
not to. If he ever got out of here, he wouldn't be back, and
it was possible that his name and situation might reach
those who could help. He had friends in this country, although he had no idea whether any were in a position to
help him, with their land fracturing and fracturing again.

He jogged around the walled courtyard, feeling the
lightness in his body. And in his mind's eye he was jog-
ging along winding roads lined with big trees and widely
spaced homes and old stone fences where chipmunks and
squirrels scampered. And Susan was with him.

THE EVENINGS had become too cool for swimming most
of the time, and the first frost had nipped the garden, although there were still vegetables to be gathered. Like most
first-time gardeners, Lucas had gone overboard with zucchini, and Susan had distributed them to everyone she
knew. Teddy told her she was welcome to visit, but requested that she leave the zucchini at home. Instead, she
brought him one big enough to be registered as a lethal
weapon.

Her work continued to be her only source of pleasure.
The program was going well, and there was already a

waiting list. She began to work on proposals for addi
tional funding.

She was invited to parties by new friends and some
times went, but she declined dates without regret. Neigh
bors began to inquire about Lucas, but given the fact tha
the homes were both widely spaced and set back from th
road, she was able to put them off with vague stories abou
constant travel on business and more time spent in the city

A few times, she forced herself to look at apartments
But she soon gave up, telling herself that she wasn't ye
ready to take that step. She knew she'd have to at som
point, of course, because his house would be sold, but fo
now she made it her home, almost totally neglecting th
apartment.

One glorious fall Saturday, she set out to explore th
woods near the house. And that was how she found th
clearing. After that, she went there often, taking a bool
along and spending hours in the strange peace of the place
She wondered if Lucas had ever come here, and somehov
was certain that he must have, because she felt close to hin
there.

SUSAN AWOKE, disentangling herself with difficulty fron
vaguely remembered dreams. The bedside clock read 1:35
She listened for a moment to the silence of the house. Had
her dreams awakened her? It felt as though *something* had

Then she thought she heard a sound...footsteps? Af
ter one brief surge of hope, she burrowed back beneath the
covers. Over these past few months, she'd awakened many
times to think she'd heard his footsteps, only to discover
that they existed in half-waking dreams.

A light was burning at the front end of the upstairs
hallway, and as she stared at it through half-closed eyes,
she suddenly saw a shadow. Before she could quite decide

f it had been her imagination, the shadow grew more dis-
inct. And then the bedroom was flooded with light!

The sound Susan made began as a scream but ended
with his name. The bedcovers she'd clutched to her throat
fell from fingers that relaxed involuntarily. She thought
vaguely that she might still be dreaming.

Lucas dropped his hand from the wall light switch. For
a moment, he, too, thought he might be hallucinating. On
the long journey home, he had forced himself to face the
very real probability that she wouldn't be here, that what
he'd feared before would now have come true: She would
have vanished from his life.

The Susan of his fantasies, whose vision had kept him
sane during these past months, might be no more than a
chimera of his own creation, while the real woman had
gone off to make her own life without him. He'd told
himself that was what he deserved, that he certainly didn't
deserve the love of a woman he'd deceived from the beginning.

So now he just stood there motionless in the doorway
and stared at her until he could convince himself that the
apparition in his bed with the sleep-tousled hair and the
firm, naked breasts was indeed real.

As her shock dissipated, Susan began to see the ravages
of the past three months. His suit hung loosely on his
frame, and his shoulders seemed to sag beneath their own
weight. There were deep lines in his face and dark shadows beneath his eyes. His hair had been inexpertly cut, and
even his mustache lacked its usual neatness.

The man she saw now was not the same man who had
left three months ago. But Lucas Andrews had come home
at last!

He walked slowly across the room and sat down heavily
on the bed, then reached out to trace the outline of her face
with one finger.

"I wouldn't let myself believe you'd still be here."

She seized his hand and brought it to her lips. "I'm here, I promised."

She wasn't even conscious of the fact that she was crying until the tears slid down her cheeks and dripped onto the hand that she still held. And through her own tears she saw his.

She lowered their clasped hands to her lap and felt the heavy weight of his as it lay there unmoving. This was a man on the very brink of both physical and mental exhaustion. He seemed incapable of further movement or speech, although his shadowed dark eyes never left her face and burned with an intensity of which the rest of him was clearly incapable. She got out of bed, unconscious of her own nakedness, and began to undress him. Her fingers fumbled at the unaccustomed task, but he merely sat there, content to be helped, barely moving on his own except to raise his face to hers as she slid his suit jacket from his shoulders.

She took his face in her hands and kissed him softly and felt him actually tremble slightly in response. Then she continued to undress him. When she had finally gotten his clothes off, she could see clearly that he had lost considerable weight.

She managed to get the bedcovers out from under him as he fell back with a groan, his eyes already closed. But as she drew the covers over him again, he suddenly reached out blindly to take her hand.

"I love you," he said in a thick voice, then fell asleep.

She carried his suit to the closet and hung it up, then gathered up the rest of his clothes and put them in the bathroom hamper. When she returned to the bedroom, he was snoring lightly. Not wanting to disturb him, she pulled a chair close to the bed and sat there, staring at him.

"I love you, too," she said softly, knowing he couldn't hear her.

She had turned out the ceiling light and switched on the low bedside lamp instead, and in that softer light and the relaxation of sleep his features seemed less harsh. But she also saw now that he'd acquired some gray hairs along his temples.

She didn't want to think about where he'd been or what he'd been doing. She wanted only to bask in the pure, sweet pleasure of his return and his declaration of love. But the questions hovered there anyway, casting that same dark shadow.

After a while, she got up and went downstairs. His bag and his attaché case sat in the foyer. Something about them nagged at her for a moment, and then she realized what it was. There were no airline luggage tags attached to them. She frowned, her head turning unconsciously toward the stairs again as she thought about his exhaustion. Why, in his state, would he have taken the trouble to remove them—unless he intended that she should know nothing about where he'd been?

A brief surge of anger shot through her, almost obliterating her happiness. His declaration of love, and her own, returned to taunt her. Love... but not trust.

She went to the kitchen and fixed herself a cup of soothing herbal tea. She called Carolyn, knowing she would be asleep, and knowing, too, that she wouldn't mind being awakened. The two women shared tears and joy, and neither of them said anything about where he might have been or what he might have been doing. It was enough, for now, that he was home.

Then she went back upstairs and stood for an uncertain few minutes beside the bed as she tried to decide whether she should crawl into it with him or use a guest room. Finally she crept as quietly as possible into the big bed,

wanting to curl up against him, but not wishing to disturb
him. As she edged cautiously closer to him, he solved the
problem for her by shifting to his side and reaching out to
wrap a sleep-heavy arm about her.

LUCAS AWOKE SLOWLY, swimming up out of a deep sleep
only to fall back again into the oblivion that had been so
welcome for so many months. But something kept urging
him to wakefulness, and he finally opened his eyes.

For a moment, when he saw the familiar room and felt
the big, firm mattress beneath him, he was sure he must be
dreaming. But his mind did a fast-forward through those
months, then stopped at the moment when he'd entered
this room last night to find Susan here.

And still he wasn't sure. He knew he'd come home at
last, but had she really been here, or was he only imagining that part of it? He lifted his head slightly and stared at
the empty pillow beside him. It bore the imprint of a head,
and when he drew it to him and buried his nose in it he
caught a faint whiff of perfume. Immediately he recalled
his plan to stop in Paris and bring her a perfume especially created for her. He'd forgotten all about it, and in
any event hadn't stopped in Paris.

Still not completely awake, he let his mind drift a
bit, seeing the two of them together in the city of light
and thinking about all he could show her there and in
other places—Florence, Venice, Rome, Vienna—beautiful places, far from the horrors he'd witnessed these past
few months. He was glad that she'd never been there, glad
that he would be the one to show her all the splendors of
the Old World.

He was fully awake by now, and his mind settled once
again on last night. He had only the vaguest recollection
of what had happened after he'd come into the bedroom
to find her sleeping in his bed. She'd undressed him and

gotten him into bed, and he thought he might have told her he loved her before he fell asleep, but he wasn't sure. It didn't matter; he would tell her again and again for the rest of their lives.

He finally glanced at the clock and saw that it was nearly two in the afternoon. He must have slept about twelve hours, but he still felt tired. He dragged himself out of bed and went into the bathroom, where he stared at his haggard, whisker-stubbled face in the mirror. He recalled thinking about staying in the city last night and now wondered if he should have done that after all. He barely recognized the face that stared back at him, and he wondered what she must have thought.

Then he turned and surveyed himself in the full-length mirror on the back of the door, muttering a soft curse when he saw what the months of imprisonment had done to him. No wonder his suit had hung on him like a sack. He must have lost at least thirty pounds, and he hadn't carried much spare flesh before that.

He rubbed his scratchy face and thought about shaving, then remembered that his bag was still downstairs. So he walked into the shower stall instead and stood there long enough to feel the water begin to run cool.

Lucas knew he was delaying the moment when he would confront her, and he kept expecting her to show up at any moment. She would certainly have heard the shower running. Or maybe she wasn't here. It belatedly occurred to him that he wasn't sure what day it was. She might have gone to work. Would she do that? Just go off and leave him on his first day home?

No, he thought, she wouldn't do that, not unless she was angry with him. But she had very good reason to be mad, didn't she? She'd certainly been happy to see him, and her very presence in his bed indicated that she hadn't written him off. But by now she might well be rethinking all that.

He went back to the bedroom, wrapping a towel around his waist, then picked up his watch and saw that it was indeed Saturday. He could remember resetting it to the time here on the flight home. He walked over to the windows and pushed the drapes aside...and there she was. The months fell away as he looked down at his garden and saw her moving about in it, plucking the last of the tomatoes off vines that were already withered by frost.

Lucas felt himself a captive of time, caught between that moment months ago when he'd come home before to find her there—impossibly there—and this moment, when she bent to the dying plants in the bright fall sunshine.

She straightened up and turned to look back toward the house, and he instinctively shrank back from the windows, as though he had no right to be staring at her or to be feeling what he felt.

On the long flight home, when he'd finally accepted that he was free, he'd thought long and hard about what he would tell her. At first, in his exhaustion and his eagerness to return to her, only the truth had seemed right.

But by the time the plane was circling JFK, fear had overwhelmed the desire to be honest. He needed her too much to risk losing her by telling her the truth. Later, perhaps, when he was sure of her and her love, when they were bound too tightly together for it to make a difference, he could tell her.

He'd thought carefully about the few times she'd expressed any political views, and he remained convinced that she'd never accept what he'd been and done. Susan was no Machiavellian; the end, however good, would never justify whatever means it took to accomplish them. She was an idealist, untainted by the ugly realities he knew so well.

He tried telling himself that he wanted only to protect her from that, but he knew that what he really wanted was to protect himself from a loss he couldn't bear. He moved cautiously to the window again. The garden was empty now, and without her in it it looked dead.

SUSAN RINSED the tomatoes and the bell peppers, the last of the summer's harvest. Then she began to dice them. She would make omelets for them when he awoke, which would surely be soon. She'd crept into the bedroom several times to check on him, perhaps still not quite accepting the reality of his return.

She was carefully holding her anger at bay. She would give him a chance to explain himself. He *had* to be honest with her; there could be no glossing over a three-month absence. But beyond demanding the truth from him, her thoughts were uncertain, and she let them stay that way for now. After all, she'd been living with uncertainty for a long time, and she could manage it for a little longer.

Since returning to the house, she'd heard no sounds, but she suddenly became aware of *something,* a sort of prickling along her spine. She whirled around and saw him standing in the kitchen doorway, his hair curling damply and his face unshaven. He stared at her with an intensity that made her breath catch in her throat.

Neither of them moved and neither of them said anything for a long moment. Then his mouth curved into a smile, and he gestured at the knife she still held in her hand.

"Do I look that dangerous?"

She looked down at her hand and saw that she was clutching the knife tightly, with the blade pointed in his direction. She drew in a shaky breath and set it on the counter.

"No, but you look as though you could use a good meal—several of them, in fact."

Her voice sounded falsely bright, taking its cue from the sound of his. For just a moment, she was back to the time when he'd found her here, pretending to be his housekeeper. Could they be back to that? Would they have to start over, despite his declaration of love last night?

He began to move toward her, but very slowly. She simply stood there uncertainly until he stopped in front of her. Then she put out a rather shaky hand and touched his unshaven face tentatively.

"I love you, Lucas. You fell asleep before I could tell you that."

He grasped her hand and pressed it to his lips. "You kept me alive," he said, surprising himself with the admission.

It really was their intention to let their bodies rediscover each other slowly as they groped their way back to their interrupted love, but if their minds knew that there were matters unresolved between them, their bodies ignored that completely.

That first tentative contact unleashed a firestorm of passion that rocked them both. Lucas lifted her into his arms and started down the hallway toward the stairs. But then he stopped, and carried her instead into his study, where he lowered her onto the leather sofa.

They devoured each other feverishly with their eyes, burning with a need unfulfilled for months. Lucas tore off his robe impatiently and paused only long enough to strip off her panties, ignoring the skirt that had ridden up on her thighs. With a shaky groan, he slid into her moist, enveloping warmth, and a wildness was unleashed in them both.

Their fiery coupling turned fantasy into reality. It sent them both quickly over the edge into a mindless ecstasy that left them gasping for breath and stunned into wordless awe at their own pounding need. Susan lay there breathing raggedly. The gaps in her own breathing were punctuated by his gulps of air as he propped himself shakily above her. They stared at each other, bemused and perhaps a little frightened.

After a time, Lucas moved and settled himself at the far end of the long sofa. Then he drew her onto his lap and made an attempt to smooth her rumpled skirt around her hips. The gesture had a peculiar tenderness to it, all the more obvious for the lack of gentleness that had gone before.

He took her left hand and stared at it as he slid his fingers along either side of her bare ring finger. Without intending to do so, she tensed. He looked up at her, then let go of her hand.

"I'm sorry for what I must have put you through."

She merely nodded. Angry questions were buzzing about in her head, growing increasingly more insistent.

He kissed her lightly. "I really *am* hungry. Will you fix me something while I explain what happened?"

They returned to the kitchen, but Susan did so with reluctance. She knew, without knowing *how* she knew, that she was going to hear a carefully crafted lie. There was no gentle afterglow this time, no long, slow slide back from the soaring ecstasy of joined bodies, and it made a mockery of what had happened between them.

She made omelets and salads while he told his lie.

His old company had called him back because of his contacts in Eastern Europe. He'd gone there many times in the past, even when it was still under communist rule. There had been strict rules against converting goods to dollars, but everyone did it anyway, every chance they got. Often, he said, people sold their antiques to pay bribes to border guards and to help them get resettled in the West.

"Now," he went on, "with the economic chaos there, people are even more desperate to sell anything they can. Not to get out, but just to buy food and other necessities.

"What should have taken a week or two took three months because I was thrown into jail. It happened because of a clash between two different factions. The people who put me in jail are strong nationalists who said I was stealing their heritage. They were right, in a way, but I was paying fair prices. And you can't feed your family on a heritage.

"Anyway, the company didn't know exactly where I was, and it took them a couple of months to find out and then get the State Department to intervene. In the meantime, I wasn't allowed to write and I couldn't get near a phone."

While he told her the story, Susan worked automatically, mixing things, chopping things, beating the eggs. Her mind was at war with itself, engaged in a battle that kept her silent.

Everything he said made perfect sense. She'd begun to pay more attention to the foreign news after his departure, and she knew how torn and troubled that region was, both politically and economically. And she knew, too, about the resurgence of a virulent nationalism in the area. But none of that lessened her certainty that he was lying about his reasons for being there.

She brought the food to the table as he finished his tale, and took a seat across from him. When her eyes met his, what she saw in them was a plea for understanding, for acceptance of his lie. A defining moment was at hand, and Susan knew it. She could either accept what he'd told her or challenge him with her knowledge that his "company" no longer existed and try to force the truth from him.

If she accepted his lie, she would have his love, and they could go on from there, and perhaps one day he would tell her the truth. If she challenged him, she could lose him. She reached out to touch his hand.

"You must have suffered in jail. You've lost so much weight."

Lucas nodded. He was sure she didn't believe him, although he wasn't quite sure why. He'd thought she'd buy the story because it was close enough to the truth to make it convincing and even to salve his conscience a bit about the part that was a lie.

"It wasn't too bad," he said, in answer to her implied question. "Most of the time they were decent enough to me. And they didn't eat any better than I did, frankly. The worst of it was not knowing how long it would be before I got out, and knowing you'd be worrying."

He then went on to ask about Carolyn, Anne, and his business, eager to put the rest of it behind them. But the lie tasted bitter in his mouth, and the bitterness remained there as he later repeated it to both of them. It didn't help at all that other people would accept it easily.

He felt tired after the obligatory phone calls and told her he was going to nap for a while, complaining about jet lag. But it wasn't the long flight that made him tired; it was the burden of his lie to her. He couldn't sleep. Instead, his mind drifted to his special place in the woods, and to his need for Susan, his love for her, and trying to justify his lies on that basis. He even tried promising himself that he would tell her the truth on their first anniversary, when surely their love would keep them together.

WHEN LUCAS WOKE, he suggested they take a walk, to a very special place he knew of in the woods. The moss-covered clearing she'd found sprang into Susan's mind, and she was sure that was what he meant, but she merely nodded and let him lead her out of the house, across the terrace. They paused for a moment at his garden, and she told him about the overabundant zucchinis and they both laughed. He promised to cut back next year, and each of them wondered if there'd be a next year for them and held the other's hand even more tightly.

They left the yard and walked into the woods, maneuvering past the grasping blackberry bushes and pausing a moment to stare at a brilliant scarlet maple, made even more fiery by the lowering sun. And then they reached the clearing.

"I knew this was what you meant," she confessed. "I found it myself while you were…gone. I was sure you must have come here."

They sat down on the moss and pine needles and he told her how he'd found this place and come here often shortly after he'd bought the house.

"It's a peaceful place," he said, tilting his head back to stare up at the crimson-streaked sky visible through the dark branches of the evergreens.

"I really needed that then. I wasn't at all sure that I'd made the right decision." He heaved a noticeably shaky sigh, then turned to give her an equally uncertain smile.

"While I was in jail, I dreamed about making love to you here."

She returned his smile, but made no move toward him. Somehow she knew that lovemaking wasn't on his mind now.

He turned his face away from her. "I lied to you, Susan. I've been lying to you all along."

His words hung there, suspended in the fragrant air, echoing in the silence. She took a deep breath.

"I know."

He turned sharply toward her, his eyes searching her face questioningly. Then he shook his head slowly.

"No, you don't know," he said firmly.

"You were a contract agent."

He stared at her, so obviously astonished that she had to stifle a laugh. She wasn't sure, however, whether the bubble of laughter she held inside her was amusement at his shock or merely relief that, finally, the deception was over. Certainly it wasn't because of what he'd done.

"You couldn't have *known*," he insisted. "But how did you guess?"

So she told him what she'd found out about his "company," and about the article she'd read in his magazine.

He ran a shaky hand through his hair, then began to search her face again. "I figured you thought I was probably a reformed criminal of some sort, or maybe you think I am anyway."

"I'm not sure what I think about it," she admitted honestly. "Tell me how it happened, Lucas. I need to know."

He told her how he'd been recruited during his senior year in college, and how he'd known even then that they didn't want him to travel the world buying and selling antiques. But he'd worked for them for two years doing just that and nothing else. And then, over coffee and pastries in a Viennese café, his superior had opened the door to another world.

"By that time, I was sure that they were a front for espionage activities, and I was ready to agree to anything they wanted me to do. Part of it was the money," he admitted. "They were already paying me more than the job warranted, and I liked the life-style. But mostly it was the excitement, the risk-taking. I know it would sound better to say I did it out of patriotism—and that *was* part of it, too—but mostly it was that need to prove that I could do it.

"Still, I wouldn't have betrayed my country by working for its enemies. Some do, you know. They sell their services to the highest bidders and claim that they're apolitical. Despite my addiction to danger and money, I never took an assignment that wasn't in the best interests of the

U.S. and the other country involved. And I never killed anyone—except in self-defense.''

"Why did you decide to quit?'' she asked. Then, after a moment's hesitation, she went on. "You *have* quit, haven't you?''

"Yes, I've quit. They know that. And, in any event, my services won't really be needed in the future. My expertise is in Eastern Europe, and despite what's going on there now, those countries have become more open.

"I quit because I'd damned near gotten myself killed too many times, and it finally forced me to reassess my reasons for doing what I was doing. I no longer needed the money, and I discovered that I no longer needed to prove anything to myself, either.

"When I came back, I read a lot about children who grow up the way I did, and I understood why I'd done what I did. And I knew I didn't have to do it anymore.''

He reached out to take her hand. "Even so, I still missed the excitement—until *you* walked into my life. I need you, Susan—more than I should, more than I want to. I *was* in jail, by the way, not because I was buying antiques, but because I was caught with the wrong people. I had plenty of time to think and to face up to the fact that for the first time I truly *needed* someone. That's why I was afraid to tell you the truth. I was afraid I'd lose you.''

She lifted her free hand to trace the outline of his face. "You aren't going to lose me, Lucas. I love you.''

They made love then—not wildly and greedily, as they had earlier, but slowly and tenderly and with a sense of wonder, exploring each other thoroughly and reverently, treating their bodies as gifts they had bestowed upon each other.

It was nearly dark by the time urgency overwhelmed their desire to simply touch and caress each other, and a

ool breeze whispered through the forest as they were
united in body and soul, with no lies left between them.

Reluctantly they found their scattered clothes and left
the woods. It was full dark by now, but they were guided
back to the house by the outside lights, which had come on
automatically.

Susan was thinking about all the lies between them and
how they'd both feared that the truth would drive them
apart. It all seemed so foolish and unimportant now, but
she thought that very few people had ever had their love so
severely tested. It gave them, she decided, a far deeper
certainty about their future together.

Arms wrapped around each other's waists, they started
across the yard. But Lucas brought them to a stop when
they reached the garden.

"I remember thinking the first time I saw you in my
garden that you were right where you belonged, even if I
couldn't figure out how you'd gotten there. And after that
I spent a lot of time worrying that you would just disappear."

She smiled and hugged him tightly. "Well, I guess I can
understand that. After all, Susan Todd appeared and disappeared, and so did Sherri Thomas, not to mention a
middle-aged tourist."

"I'm glad you seem to like changing your name," he
stated dryly.

"Is that a proposal I hear?"

"It is."

"Then do it properly, Lucas Andrews. After all, a man
who earns his living dealing in antiques should be a tradi-
tionalist."

"You mean on bended knee and all that?"

"That's exactly what I mean."

He sighed and did as ordered. "Will all of you marr
me, even the middle-aged tourist?"

"We will," she said.

Where do you find hot Texas nights, smooth Texas charm and dangerously sexy cowboys?

COWBOYS AND CABERNET

Raise a glass—Texas style!

Tyler McKinney is out to prove a Texas ranch is the perfect place for a vineyard. Vintner Ruth Holden thinks Tyler is too stubborn, too impatient, too…Texas. And far too difficult to resist!

CRYSTAL CREEK reverberates with the exciting rhythm of Texas. Each story features the rugged individuals who live and love in the Lone Star State. And each one ends with the same invitation…

Y'ALL COME BACK…REAL SOON!

Don't miss *COWBOYS AND CABERNET* by Margot Dalton. Available in April wherever Harlequin books are sold.

HARLEQUIN SUPERROMANCE®

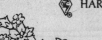

HARLEQUIN ROMANCE®

**Harlequin Romance
knows that lasting love
is something special . . .**

And so is
next month's
title in

THE BRIDAL COLLECTION

TEMPORARY ARRANGEMENT
by Shannon Waverly

THE BRIDE was an unwelcome guest.
THE GROOM was a reluctant host.
The arrangement was *supposed*
to be temporary but—
THE WEDDING made it for keeps!

Available this month in
The Bridal Collection
RESCUED BY LOVE
by Anne Marie Duquette #3253

Wherever Harlequin books are sold.

Legendary lovers come to life once more in Judith Arnold's newest Harlequin American Romance title . . .

Just Like Romeo and Juliet

Touching the statue of Juliet in Verona, Italy, was supposed to bring luck in love. But Gillian Chappell didn't feel very lucky when the sexy stranger whose kisses set her soul on fire turned out to be her father's most hated adversary.

Enemies and lovers . . . Could even Juliet save this star-crossed pair?

Relive all the romance and the passion that made Romeo and Juliet the ultimate love story. Don't miss Judith Arnold's #482 JUST LIKE ROMEO AND JULIET, coming to you next month.

ROMEO

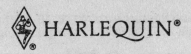 **HARLEQUIN®**

THE TAGGARTS OF TEXAS!

Harlequin's Ruth Jean Dale brings you
THE TAGGARTS OF TEXAS!

Those Taggart men—strong, sexy and hard to resist...

You've met Jesse James Taggart in FIREWORKS!
Harlequin Romance #3205 (July 1992)

And Trey Smith—he's THE RED-BLOODED YANKEE!
Harlequin Temptation #413 (October 1992)

And the unforgettable Daniel Boone Taggart in SHOWDOWN!
Harlequin Romance #3242 (January 1993)

Now meet Boone Smith and the Taggarts who started it all—
in LEGEND!
Harlequin Historical #168 (April 1993)

Read all the Taggart romances!
Meet all the Taggart men!

Available wherever Harlequin Books are sold.